F

LIE

BOOKS BY JAKE CROSS

The Choice

THE
FAMILY
LIE

JAKE CROSS

Bookouture

Published by Bookouture in 2019

An imprint of StoryFire Ltd.

Carmelite House
50 Victoria Embankment
London EC4Y 0DZ

www.bookouture.com

ISBN: 978-1-78681-441-8
eBook ISBN: 978-1-78681-440-1

Jennifer. Just for being there. At all the right times.

PROLOGUE

3.03 a.m.

She wakes from a dream of drowning into a nightmare far more terrifying.

The dream ends abruptly, in the usual way: eyes snapping open, heart thudding, skin leaking sweat. The nightmare introduces itself slowly, though, and it starts with white noise.

It oozes from a baby monitor. The little lady in slumber in the other room is five, not a baby, but she's got sleep apnoea and paranoid parents. Often, they've woken to terrifying sounds of choking. But now the monitor is emitting a crackly pattering sound. It's closer to her husband's side of the bed, and he's a light sleeper, so clearly he's already heard it, because on his side of the bed there's nothing but a humanoid depression in the mattress, as if a heavy ghost sleeps there.

But seconds pass, sixty or more, and the white noise continues. And her husband doesn't return.

One elbow in the ghost's chest, she leans across to pick up the monitor, because this is obviously a fault with the machine, or a tuning issue, and that's when she becomes aware of another noise. Her eyes, still adjusting to the darkness, latch onto the window, where the glass is soaked. Her waking brain makes the connection: the white noise isn't interference at all but rain.

It's July after all, the nights hot even when wet. At some point her husband has got up, felt the heat, figured it would make their daughter's breathing worse, and gone into her bedroom to open the window. That's why the noise of the rain is reaching her through the monitor.

But where is he? She rises, and grabs her mobile to check the time, and throws on a nightgown.

And takes her first step into the nightmare.

Around the corner of the hallway she hears the murmur of the TV beneath the throb of rain from beyond Josie's door. It's Nick's go-to device for whacking the energy out of Josie when the little lady cannot sleep. But the living room can wait a moment.

In Josie's room, the monitor's receiver is on the floor, knocked there somehow, but thankfully out of range of the rain that lashes through the wide-open window. The sill, the undersheet at the foot of the bed, part of the floor, all sodden. Anna sticks her arm into the stinging downpour and drags the window shut. Something Nick should have done when he heard the skies rend open.

She slips as she turns to leave, both hands needed to break her fall. There is no pain, though, only rising confusion. And a seed of dread, which propels her quickly from the room. A single step into the living room is all she manages before halting so abruptly it's as if she's walked into an invisible door. She sags against the doorframe, heart thudding so hard it makes her head tremble. The sounds she heard: not the TV at all.

The room is dark, but she can see that the patio door is halfway open, rain shooting in to soak the carpet, fast and loud, and that's all she can see.

Because there's no Nick, no Josie.

But she drags her eyes away from it. She stumbles across the room and peeks behind the floor-to-ceiling room divider, but she already knew the dining room would be as black and lifeless as the rest of the house.

No Nick. No Josie.

Now she cannot avoid that patio door. She rushes outside, into the stinging rain, into the black. No Nick, no Josie. She calls their names, both of them, but of course there's no answer. The world is black, and the rain distorts everything like a sheet of frosted glass, but she can clearly see that there's…

No Nick. No Josie.

Beyond the high back hedge her eyes latch onto a fragment of street, and cars, and houses belonging to neighbours floating in tranquil dreams. She can see these things because the back gate is wide open. It's never left open, which means it's as good as a sign. Big and bright and neon and undeniable: gone.

A light is on in a house across the garden and the street beyond, and she thinks she sees someone at the bedroom window, and then the pain in her throat makes her realise she's been screaming. She turns, meaning to get back, get to her phone, get the police, but she trips on the half-moon concrete step. One bracing hand thuds onto the step with a squelch, not a splash. And when her hand comes away, her skin is greasy, and the moonlight catches it, and she knows she's looking at a palm coated in blood.

PART ONE

CHAPTER ONE

'Hello, police emergency.'

'Please, my daughter. She's been taken. My husband and my daughter.'

'Repeat that, please. Your daughter and husband, did you say? What's your name?'

'Anna Carter. It's my daughter, she's gone from the house. And my husband. They must have been taken.'

'What do you mean by taken?'

'Yes, taken. From my house. The door, the patio door, it's wide open. They're gone. They've been kidnapped or something. They must have. They wouldn't go out. There's blood on the step.'

'What makes you think your daughter and husband have been kidnapped?'

'They wouldn't go out, not this late. Nick would have woken me. There's blood.'

'Have you contacted your husband? Nick, did you say? Have you tried to call Nick?'

'Yes. There's no answer. On the mobile. It's not in the house. Look, you gotta send people.'

'Have you contacted friends to see if—'

'They wouldn't go out. They've been kidnapped.'

'Was this recent? Did you just discover this?'

'Just now. I woke up. They're not here. You've got to send someone. They wouldn't go out.'

'*How old is your daughter and what's her name?*'

'She's Josie. She's five.'

'*Okay. So you woke up to find them gone, and did you say the door is wide open?*'

'The back door, the patio door, yes. There's blood on the step. They wouldn't go out, not this late. Send people who can find them, please.'

'*Has your husband ever taken your daughter out late before?*'

'No. They didn't go out. Someone's broken in and kidnapped them. The blood.'

'*Blood? Did you say blood? I thought you said mud. How much blood is there? And this is on the step outside your back door?*'

'Yes. Please, just send someone. They wouldn't go out.'

'*Okay, I'm sending officers to your address—*'

'I live at—'

'*I've got it. Have you checked all rooms in the house? The attic? The cellar? Is the house empty?*'

'They're not here. I keep saying. They're gone.'

'*You're certain there's no one hiding in the house?*'

Then it hit her. Hiding: the operator wasn't thinking about Nick, about Josie – she feared an intruder could still be here. Anna immediately thought of the cellar.

The one place she hadn't checked.

Maybe, far in the future, if everything ended happily, she might be able to joke about the cellar angle. There was none of that horror film creeping-towards-the-door, knife in hand, slowly reaching for the handle. Nick had some exercise equipment down there, so, with an image of a late-night need to burn calories and a terrible fall down the stairs, she rushed into the kitchen and threw open the door in the back wall and slapped on the light. Lurking intruders weren't even considered. Bizarrely, she would have wept with relief if she'd discovered her family hurt and unconscious down in the cold brick room.

But: 'They're gone. There's no one in the house.'

'Officers will be there within minutes. This is what I need you to do…'

Shoving the cordless phone into her pocket, she grabbed a dirty T-shirt of Nick's from the kitchen wash basket and stepped carefully across the living room carpet, avoiding streaks of mud from footprints. She could clearly see where they led from outside the house. Trying hard not to look at the blood on the step, even though the rain should have washed it away by now, she grabbed the handle of the sliding patio door and slid it across and locked it. Then she followed the wet footprints into Josie's room, where she locked the window, too. The emptiness of that tiny bed was like a void in her own heart.

Secure the house. Lock all doors and windows but try to be careful not to touch places where the officers might be able to pick up fingerprints, especially the door handles.

It was only then that she understood why the operator had given such instructions: a fear that the abductors could return. It was an irrational worry, but that knowledge didn't stop her from turning on all the lights in the house. She stumbled into the hallway and made sure the front door was locked. She caught her reflection in the mirror beside the coat hooks. Her dressing gown was soaked down one side, where she'd landed in the rain after falling. She didn't look at the hand that had slapped into blood. But as she had rubbed her face with her other, muddied hand, her cheek was dirty. She pulled a wet wipe from a carton on the shoe cabinet and raised it to her face, but then stopped.

Do not wash yourself or change your clothing, please.

She didn't understand that instruction, but it must be important. So she left herself dirty. With nothing else to do, the weight of loneliness and despair returned. She staggered into Josie's playroom, where toys were scattered all over the floor. Usually a place of joy, of noise, but not tonight. Cold and empty, like an abandoned place, and screaming that her daughter was missing. She wanted to tidy.

Don't move anything. Leave your home the way it is, please. Don't pick up any broken glass, and do not clean the mud from the carpet. Try to stay in one room until the officers arrive.

She felt the weight of the cordless in her pocket and realised that the police weren't the only people she should have called. Her finger jabbed and held the '1' key, which speed-dialled a number.

'Annie?' a croaky voice said a few moments later. *'Is it Josie?'*

Attuned, her sister knew Anna wouldn't call at such an hour unless harm or danger had befallen that most precious of things.

'They've gone. Both gone.'

'Gone?'

Anna blurted her tale. It drew Jane's equivalent of a gasp of shock: just slow, heavy breathing, in part because she knew a show of distress would add to Anna's own. But it didn't help to calm Anna's fizzing nerves.

'My god. What are the police doing to find them?'

'They're coming round now. They say I have to stay here. I can't look for them.'

'Look, I'll get ready and come round. Father will drive us there immediately. But do as the police say, Anna. Stay there.'

'They didn't go out, Jane. They wouldn't. Why would Nick take Josie out? Why wouldn't he wake me up first?'

'I'll be there in the next few minutes, Anna, okay? Just sit and wait for me, and for the police. Don't go out to look for them. But phone people. Phone everyone you can think of.'

'Father will blame me, Jane. He'll think I left a door unlocked.'

'No. No. No one is going to blame you. Nick will have taken Josie out somewhere, that's all. Just stay. I'm coming.'

Anna desperately clutched that notion: maybe Josie had been hurt in the night, might have fallen when she went to the bathroom. Unwilling to panic Anna, Nick had taken Josie to hospital.

She heard Jane trying to shout Father awake. She wanted to stay on the phone, to remain anchored to her sister because the alternative was to drift away across a cold and silent and dark ocean. But she didn't want to hear Father's reaction. So she killed the call. The silence dropped upon her like heavy rain. But it didn't last long.

There was a knock at the door.

Two officers, one female. She was short, pretty, young, which highlighted the rugged presence of her larger, older colleague, and together they looked like a snapshot of old and new police disposition. She would be college educated, versed in people skills, designed as a romantic ideal of the community-based officer, while he seemed to hark back to the bygone image of hard cases getting things done by foot chases and booting in doors.

And they played their roles. The male ignored her and cast his eyes beyond, reading the interior of the house. The female immediately introduced both – Constables Lowth and Adams – and said, 'You're Mrs Carter? You reported your daughter and husband missing from the house, is that right?'

'Yes. They wouldn't go out. They must have been taken away.' The cordless was thrust back into her pocket, having failed again to get an answer from Nick's mobile. She looked past the officers and was dismayed to see a single police car on the dark road. 'Is it just you two? Have you got people out searching? My sister thinks we should check hospitals, just in case Josie got hurt.'

Lowth pointed at the pocket holding the cordless. 'We'll do that, don't worry. Have you tried calling their mobiles?'

The big man, Adams, stepped past her and peeked into the bathroom.

Anna said, 'Nick's got a mobile. It's just a dead line. But they wouldn't have gone out.'

'We'll try to find them, Mrs Carter. You should try to calm down. Are you certain your husband took his mobile with him?'

Anna watched Adams step up to the main bedroom and cast his appraising eyes inside.

'It's not in the house. I would have heard it ringing.'

'I'll need the number,' Lowth said.

Anna recited Nick's number, and the officer dialled on her mobile.

'So what did you say woke you?'

'The baby monitor in Josie's room. The window was open. The rain.'

'Okay,' Lowth said after a pause. 'And I've got to ask. Drugs, alcohol? Have you had any this evening?'

Anna looked like she'd been physically struck. 'Do you think I imagined this or something?'

'I didn't say that, Mrs Carter. I ask because—'

'No,' she snapped. 'Nothing like that. I can't believe…'

Lowth nodded. 'Okay. Please be calm. I had to ask. Have you called friends and family, just in case they—'

'They wouldn't go out. But I did, I called a couple.'

'Just a couple?'

'Well… nobody is up at this time. They would have called me if they knew. But Nick wouldn't have taken Josie out, not at this time of night.'

'No connection on his mobile.' Lowth hung up her mobile. 'What about your mobile, Mrs Carter? Where's that?'

Anna felt in her dressing gown pocket but found only the cordless. Had she put the mobile in her pocket? 'I don't know. I thought I picked it up. Am I allowed to go out and search for them?'

Lowth's answer: 'It's best if you stay here, Mrs Carter, in case they come back. As for friends and family, if you could get me their numbers and addresses, we can check with them. Double-check, I mean. Can we see the living room?'

Anna led quickly. Once there, she pointed at the patio door. 'That was wide open. Are others on their way?'

The big male, Adams, stepped across to peek into the dining area beyond the shelving unit room divider. Lowth pointed at the muddy footprints on the carpet. 'You're certain you didn't make these when you went outside?'

'No, I didn't. They were already there. The step outside, there's…' the word was hard to eject '…blood.'

Avoiding the wet areas of carpet, especially the sodden section just inside the doorway, Adams slipped on protective latex gloves and dragged open the patio door and splashed torchlight into the dark. Lowth nodded at the sleeping bag on the sofa.

'Was there an argument between you this evening? Might that be why your husband left the house?'

'He wouldn't go out with Josie this late. Look, I explained all this on the phone. You can see it out on the step. They might be hurt.'

'I don't see clothing around. Does he sleep dressed, Mrs Carter? Maybe he puts dirty clothing in a wash basket at the end of the night?'

Anna didn't understand her point, but before she could ask, Adams finally found his voice.

'I see footprints in the grass. If there was blood on the step, the rain's taken it.'

Lowth stepped up for a look. Adams shone his light at the lock and the handle, both sides of the door. 'No forced entry here. Lock looks fine. Only unlocks from the inside.'

'What does that mean?' Anna said. 'You think the door was left unlocked?' Was this her fault after all?

Lowth turned to face her. 'We really can't assume anything just yet. Could you get me a recent photo of them both, please? Is that your address book?' She moved past Anna and picked up a battered little booklet from the coffee table, where the base for the cordless sat.

'Yes. Most of our friends will be in there. There's a photo album in Josie's room.'

'Could we go to Josie's room, please?'

All three made the journey, following the wet tracks. In the hallway, Adams stopped and tilted his head back.

'Got a ladder for this?' He was tall enough to reach overhead and try the sliding bolt on the attic door. It wouldn't budge.

'Why do you want to look up there? It's empty. We have a garage at my father's for our stuff.'

Lowth ushered Anna onwards. Adams followed, attic forgotten. Beside the door to the kitchen was the cubbyhole at the end of the hall, a curtained alcove with a desk and desktop computer and a box where they kept all their bills and other paperwork. Adams pulled the curtain for a glance inside.

'I can get a photo of Nick,' Anna said. She ducked into the cubbyhole and quickly returned with a passport, which Lowth took with a curious look as they moved into the kitchen.

Adams spotted the cellar door and opened it. He stabbed torchlight inside. As he shut the door, he glanced at the fridge and said, 'That's a mean stare-down face. He's a big guy.'

On the fridge was a picture of Nick in just shorts. Heavily bearded, shaved head, muscled and tanned and growling at the camera, his hands clenched into raised fists. He looked like an animal. It was a picture Nick had had taken when he was cutting fat for a bodybuilding competition, and now used to put him off raiding the fridge for junk food.

Anna ignored the remark. She walked through the other door in the kitchen. 'This is Josie's room.'

As soon as Adams had had a look at the wet floor and shut window in there, he turned to head out of the room. Lowth handed him the address book and got in front of the doorway, as if to prevent Anna from following him. She asked for the photo album. It was on a little shelf above the bed. Anna handed it to the police officer. She heard a loud click and knew that Adams had returned to the trapdoor. She realised why.

'He's going into the attic. My god, do you think my husband and daughter are hiding? It locks from the outside. Why on earth—'

'We have to check the whole house, Mrs Carter. I'm sorry. We have to do that. We're not assuming anything.' Her eyes cast around. 'This is a very bare room.'

Despite the officer's claim, Anna sensed a direct assumption. But she understood why. This was a tiny place that Anna had planned for a washing machine and tumble drier, since it was a kitchen annex, but Josie had wanted it as her bedroom. Hardly five feet wide, laminate wood floor, no hallway access, and bare but smooth plaster walls. Not a single toy or poster. The cheap four-foot bed was the only indication that a child slept here. A cold room, but, again, how Josie wanted it. Visitors had made the same remark, the same *assumption*, the officer just had, and Anna gave the police officer the same answer as always.

'Josie has trouble sleeping when her mind races. She can't sleep with toys and things around. She's got a playroom. What she wants here is "Just a sleepy place". It doesn't mean we don't care.'

Lowth nodded with a reassuring smile. 'My boy's the opposite. He needs a mountain of toys on his bed or he won't sleep. Why don't you show me the photos? And talk me through the events of this evening, leading up to when you discovered your husband and daughter missing.'

Anna wanted to sit on Josie's bed but the officer told her she shouldn't. They stood side-by-side and Anna allowed the other woman to flip the pages in the album. It immortalised Josie playing with toys, and riding her bike on the driveway, and donning school uniform, and so much more. Despite the emotional assault of recounting 'events of the evening', the heavy emptiness of the room faded from Anna's heart as she watched Josie's five years from baby to little lady pass in sixty seconds. The officer paused over the most recent picture of her. Ginger hair, long and wavy, in a photo from a month ago. In that, and others, she wore a colourful beaded necklace, a gift from her grandmother that she wore constantly, even asleep, even in the bath.

'I'm going to take a thousand more when Josie comes home,' Anna said, wiping away tears running down her cheeks. She slipped the photo out of its sleeve.

But the officer took it from her. 'Do you mind if I take this?' It killed the moment, which brought it all crashing back upon Anna. 'Is your neck okay?'

Anna realised she'd been scratching at her neck. She stopped. At that moment Adams appeared in the doorway and said, 'Mrs Carter, Chief Inspector Miller would like a word, please.'

That was when she became aware of other voices in the house. More police, who she hadn't heard arrive. And a *Chief*, which meant she'd been taken seriously.

*

Detective Chief Inspector Lucy Miller, Homicide and Major Enquiry, was a trim forty-something with a creased beige skirt suit as functional as her short blonde hair and negligible make-up, and she was in Josie's playroom, standing amid the carpet of toys. She nodded a greeting and introduced herself and her colleague, Detective Sergeant Liam Bennet, an older man, very tall with an acne-scarred face, who was taking photos of the room on a tablet computer that seemed like a regular mobile in his big spade of a hand. Miller didn't move but Bennet stepped up to shake her hand, which seemed to swallow hers. His movement was ungainly, as if he was unused to being so tall.

'Have you been out searching?' Anna asked, slotting away the cordless after another failure to find Nick. She no longer expected to reach him on his mobile, but each time the call went straight to voicemail was a stab in the heart.

Miller gave her a smile, soft, slight, enough just to offer a sense of comfort. 'Ah, we're going to do what we can to bring your daughter back to you. Josie, she's called?' Her voice was scratchy, as if she had a cold or a dry throat, and the accent mild, but certainly not Yorkshire.

Anna looked at Josie's painting table. It reminded her that the last time she'd seen her laughing had been right there, just moments before she sent the little lady to bed. Josie had gone with a long face because Anna had yelled at her for drawing on a wall. Anna couldn't get that sorrowful look out of her mind. Dabbing at what seemed like an endless flow of fluid from her eyes, she said, 'Yes. My husband is Nick. Have you got people out looking?'

'Well, we have to take this slowly and gather more information, but we're taking your claim very seriously. Local policing teams across Yorkshire have been informed of a possible abduction, but we need more information before we do anything like issue public alerts. And I am trained in hostage crisis negotiation. So, please, accept we're not downplaying anything here. I know you've told this before, dear, but I need you to run through for me exactly why you think they've been kidnapped.'

She didn't like the sense of doubt she got from the woman's body language. The uniformed police officers had expressed the same emotion once they'd been in the house a minute or so. She knew kidnapping was a rare offence, but surely it wasn't alien to these people, even in urban Sheffield. 'Don't you believe me?'

Miller didn't directly answer that. 'I can list Josie as missing on the Police National Computer. And the Missing Persons Unit, they can build a profile based on data from previous cases. Those are important first steps.'

'Can? You mean you haven't done that yet? Why not?'

'Apologies. This is very confusing for you, I completely understand. I'll explain, I will. A couple of things first, though.' She waved Nick's passport, which Adams must have handed to her. 'Your man, does he have friends or family abroad?'

'No. Why?'

'Just a moment, dear. Let me ask a few things first. Number two, and I apologise in advance for this, but I do have to ask it – does he ever hurt Josie?'

'What? Of course not. What makes you think that?'

'I'm sorry. I don't think that at all, dear, but it's a question that's got to be asked. Lastly, he drives a Vauxhall Combo van, doesn't he? Usually parked out the back, I hear? Can you show me it?'

She couldn't now avoid suspecting that the police weren't taking her claims seriously, and she was starting to get impatient and angry. 'Is any of this relevant? I'd like to know what steps you're taking to find my daughter. My husband.'

'It's relevant, I promise. Please? Show me his van?'

'The van is out back, yes. Why do you need to see it?'

'I'll explain shortly. Before we go, my DS Bennet here needs the password to your computer. You can't find your phone, I understand?'

'I thought I picked it up. Maybe it's still in the bedroom. Please tell me, why do you want to see Nick's van?'

'I just want to see it. Part of the process. We'll find the phone for you, no worries. Oh, and which school does your daughter attend?'

Certain that her naïvety didn't mean the police didn't know their business, Anna gave the school's name and the computer password and then followed Miller into the living room. They exited into the slowing rain and followed the slab path that skirted around the edge of the garden and led to the gate in the high back hedge. Anna had to step carefully because she was barefoot.

Just before they exited the garden, Anna became aware that she was dirty and still in a dressing gown that showed a lot of thigh. 'Can I ask why I wasn't allowed to change?'

Miller said, 'I'm sorry about that. It's a forensic thing. But we don't need your clothing now, although do you mind waiting to change until we head back inside? Just be careful of your feet out here.'

'Forensic? What do you mean?'

Miller waved a hand. 'Technical, dear. Explain later. Show me which van belongs to your husband, please.'

They were on a cul-de-sac between the rear gardens of Anna's street and those of the neighbouring one, hedges and bungalows this side, panel fencing and two-storey semis across the way. All the semis were dark except for the light she had seen flick on, seemingly so long ago now.

Anna wanted the darkness of the street to be playing a trick, but she knew that wasn't the case.

'I don't get it. I know he drove home. I always ask if his journey was okay. He would have said if he didn't have the van.'

In the turning circle at the end, thirty metres away, she could clearly see an empty space where Nick always left his van overnight.

Miller didn't seem half as confused: 'Ah, well, we think he drove off in the van. I hate to say this, but—'

'But what? Has it been stolen by the people who took my family?'

'Not what we think, I'm afraid. People with abduction in mind, they have their own vehicles. Well, of course, we're going to get whatever CCTV covers this street, to make sure. But the evidence, which, yes, I'll run through with you, well, it tells a different story.'

'What story? What are you saying?'

Backlit by weak streetlight, the detective's face was in shadow. Nonetheless, Anna was sure she could see dismay at what the older woman was about to impart. Upright seriousness had suddenly replaced her casual demeanour and genuine smile, which Anna had begun to consider an act designed to give this interrogation a coat of calm.

'We think your husband took your daughter.'

*

She was drowning, but there was suddenly a chance to surface for air. It was a desperate attempt, and she'd realise it as such in a few moments. But until then she grabbed and held tightly to what had popped into her head, just to keep afloat.

It explained everything. Unable to find the keys to her car, Nick had taken Josie out the back, to his van, but he'd forgotten his keys and had had to re-enter the house. And he'd left the patio door open because shutting it would have involved putting Josie down on a bad ankle. How could she have not realised earlier? Josie would return soon with her foot in a cast covered in *I've-been-a-brave-girl* stickers, Nick with surprise and massive guilt.

'The hospital. That's why you didn't want to say. Is that where they are?'

They were sitting on a two-seater wooden bench that faced the house from against the back hedge, which was the last fragment of the garden to lose the setting sun. This close to Miller, she could smell a strange mix of body odour and the deodorant used to try to cover it. Side-by-side, Anna had the angle to see a portion of a breast tattoo – head and shoulders of a man wearing a medieval battle helmet – poking out of the detective's bra as the woman sat up sharply.

'Anna, no, there's no evidence of that. We really shouldn't assume anything while there's no evidence. You should stop scratching your neck.'

Anna's finger dropped from her throat. 'But... the blood... on the step.'

She touched Anna's arm. 'Mud. I'm sorry, dear, we only saw mud. Probably scraped off his feet before he re-entered the house. I'm sorry if I gave you the wrong impression.'

Anna raised the hand that she had caught her fall with. In the moonlight, no red tint to the stain on her palm. Just the brown of soil. Just a basic dirty hand. Had she imagined the blood? She had a rising dread that the detective believed in something far worse than anything Anna had considered. And then it came to her, and she found nothing but straws to clutch at.

'You think Nick abducted my daughter for some reason? That's what you mean, isn't it?'

'The evidence is telling me your man left the house with young Josie. But not why. We'll find the why. I'm sorry, I must ask again – could Nick have hurt Josie?'

'Nick wouldn't run away with Josie, and he wouldn't ever hurt her. Don't say that again. How can you possibly think that Nick just... just left like that? Don't you have a family? A child? Or a husband?' Her voice sounded convincing, but inside she was sinking fast.

Miller rubbed a thumb hard across a crease on her skirt, but her eyes held Anna's. 'This is terrible for you, I know. I'm so sorry. Evidence, though, it's always about evidence. God, I hate the awkward dollops of the job. Really. But here we go again: is it true that your relationship with your husband is failing?'

'What? What makes you say that?'

'Well, a neighbour called the police, made that call right around the same time you did. Old lass seems like the neighbourhood snoop. She said she thought there had been an argument, because she heard you in the garden. A scream. She told one of my chaps that there's rumour of divorce. She was the one who told us your man's van was missing. Her tuppence worth, well, that he might have left you.'

Anna remembered the window light she'd seen flick on. 'A neighbour? A neighbour heard a noise, and now you think Nick would run away? Steal my daughter from me? That's stupid.'

'Apologies, dear. But I've worked a number of father-child snatches and—'

Anna was shaking her head vigorously, mumbling *no, no, no.*

'Sometimes, you know, with a relationship breakdown, people blame each other for everything. Which can mean one thinking the other is a bad influence on the child. It can be about forcing a child to feel more dependent on the abducting parent. Visitation fears. Forced reconciliation. Revenge. I've come across them all, I hate to say.'

No, no, no. 'This is because of the sleeping bag, isn't it? Because you think we're splitting up? I admit we're still in a bad patch. It's a slow process. I… you're wrong. For the last week he's been climbing back into bed while I'm asleep. I don't mind. We both want to work things out. For Josie's sake. And we've been trying hard to. So no way would Nick just run off with her. Please stop talking like that. You should be out looking for them instead of… this.'

'I apologise, I so really do. But it's what the evidence is saying. No forced entry, Anna. The missing van. It seems Nick might have been dressed. And the sound of rain woke you up, so I'd say there was no fight or commotion in the house…'

The detective outlined it all, and it sounded compelling, sure. As an outsider, she would have made the same assumption. And part of her prayed it was the truth, because a scenario in which Nick absconded with Josie beat the alternative horror of strangers kidnapping both. It just wouldn't set, though.

But the *why* and *how* didn't matter in the end. 'My daughter and my husband are missing. Does all this why and how really matter? I want you to get them back for me.'

Miller gave a long pause that Anna didn't like. 'I'm sorry, dear, but here we have a snag, and I hate this part of the job most of all. The police don't really get involved in family law. Your Nick would only actually be breaking the law if he took Josie out of the country. All I could really do is issue an "All-Ports Warning", if there was a chance of that. But there isn't. He didn't take his passport. He's got no contacts overseas. The APW wouldn't be sanctioned. I'm sorry.'

It hit her like a blast of Arctic air. 'Sorry? What are you saying? You're not going to do anything?'

Miller looked genuinely sorry. 'I can put you in touch with a friend I have, a solicitor. He can help you apply to the courts. They can force your man to tell you where Josie is. A Prohibited Steps Order can stop him trying to leave the country with Josie at some point in the future, but it might be easier to ask the Passport Office to refuse to reissue a new passport. Look, I'm sorry, I know these aren't things you want to hear.'

Anna's head was starting to throb with a sense of helplessness and abandonment. 'This isn't right. I wish I could prove that Nick wouldn't ever run away. Not with my daughter. You have to search. Search for them.' She grabbed the woman's hands in both of hers. 'Please. You can't do this. You can't just say my husband ran away with my daughter and then leave. You can't.'

The older woman looked at their clasped flesh, and then met Anna's eyes again. 'I must ask you one last time. Has Nick ever hurt Josie?'

Anna let go of Miller's hands as if they were white hot. Fatigue now, rolling over her, making her next words barely a whisper, and five-parts exasperation to one-part honest question: 'Why do you keep saying that?'

'The police have a duty of care, dear.'

Anna took ragged breaths as understanding set in. Duty of care. She was being thrown a lifeline. She couldn't meet the other woman's eyes as she said, 'Yes. Nick might hurt Josie.'

She felt a stroking hand upon her shoulder. 'Then I can't ignore this. I will put Josie on the PNC as missing. And Nick, too. But he'll have to be listed as *wanted*. You understand? He'll be arrested.'

That kicked a cold trickle down Anna's spine. In that moment she realised there was doubt that intruders had taken her family. But she quickly refocussed on the fact that *why* and *how* didn't matter, only getting Nick and Josie home safely. And now that would happen because the police were going to find them.

Miller's cruising agony aunt tone was gone, as if it had been an act all along. She spoke rapidly. 'Now I need you to talk to me. Tell me about your friends, and Nick's. I need to know about all those places you both like to visit, like pubs you've enjoyed, country parks you routinely go to. I need to know if Nick plays snooker for a team on certain days. Does he buy a daily newspaper from the same shop every morning? Does he have a loyalty card to a certain hotel chain? Nick might not want to upset little Josie's routines, so, is there a party coming up that Josie is looking forward to? Does she have swimming lessons? A doctor's appointment? Just talk and don't stop, dear. I want to know your family better than anyone outside it.'

Anna rubbed her face with both hands, hard enough to hurt, and prepared to unload her life for this captivating woman who, act or not, desperately wanted to play saviour. But before Anna could say a thing, the quiet black air was sliced by the cordless phone ringing in her pocket.

'Not out here.'

Her arm was grabbed, Miller's grip surprisingly strong. As Anna was virtually marched towards the house, she pictured Miller as a young uniform, escorting hardened criminals with the same vice-like clamp, if only to avoid thinking about what she might learn from the phone call.

Once inside, the behemoth DS Bennet, who was waiting for them as if he'd heard the phone, dragged the curtains across to bar the night. Anna caught this peripherally because her eyes were locked on the phone in her hands, which displayed the words *No Caller ID*.

'If it's your man, ask to speak to Josie,' Miller said. 'We need to know the little one is okay. And let Nick speak first.'

Anna slammed the phone to her ear hard enough to hurt. She hadn't registered Miller's order, but she found that words wouldn't come.

'Anna? Nicolas? It's June. Are you—'

She killed the call and dropped the phone. Realising a false alarm, Miller picked up the device and said, 'I'm sorry, dear. I'll get DS Bennet on to screening calls to make sure no more neighbours get through. But we'll have to expect return calls from friends and family you called. We'll try to keep this quiet. Nosiness. Hard to combat. Sorry.'

Anna's shoulders slumped. She knew that Miller had wanted her to let the caller speak first so that Anna didn't give the game away to the wrong person. 'But how did she…'

'I've got an abrasive young piece of testosterone with the lady who called the police. She must have slipped away from him and got to a phone. Busybodies. I'm sorry about that. Truly. I'll have him hunting stolen cats by tomorrow.'

Just then there was a loud rapping at the front door. DS Bennet nearly broke his own neck turning his head so fast, and even the unflappable DCI jumped at the noise. But Anna didn't even look up from the phone in the policewoman's hands.

'It's not Josie and Nick,' she said.

*

It was barely past 4 a.m. but, as was his way, her father had taken time to dress for the occasion in a suit under a long black coat. There was haste in his expression, though. And anger. But she didn't need emotion on his face to know he wouldn't be overflowing with sympathy for her, lost daughter or not.

Jane Middleton was tall and slim, similar enough to her sister that cast-off clothing from one often went to the other. Nobody had ever remarked that they looked the same, but the sisters assumed enough of a resemblance that they maintained different coloured hair. A long-ago agreement meant that when Anna decided she wanted to go blonde, Jane would have to darken. Under a denim jacket she wore a Lycra jogging outfit, since she liked to use the treadmill last thing at night and the garment had probably been crumpled by her bed when Anna called.

Already she looked not just wide awake but wired. Her eyes flickered here and there, settling on nothing, like those of someone high on drugs. Not the case, of course, because Jane had been blind since the age of three. The disorder had never dented her good nature and quest to always have fun, but right now she looked terrified. Anna hated the fact that she'd swept up her sister and dumped her into a nightmare.

Despite her father and sister knowing there was trouble in the air, Anna had taken a moment at the mirror behind the front door to flick loose hair from her ragged ponytail away from her cheeks, although that further exposed the dirt she'd smeared across her skin. On the shoe cabinet was a box of wet wipes for washing Josie's face before she left for school, and she'd grabbed one. She'd been instructed not to clean herself, but it made no sense and she hurriedly wiped away grime before opening the door.

Jane stepped forward first, and pecked Anna's cheek. Her lips touched dried mud that Anna had missed, which Jane then wiped away from both their faces. Her fingers ran over Anna's mouth, perhaps seeking a smile or a frown, and then the back of her fingers settled on Anna's forehead.

'It'll be fine,' Jane said, a response to feeling the hot skin on her fingers. Anna's temperature had always exposed her mood, at least to her sister. Jane's other hand brushed against the cordless clutched hard in Anna's hands.

'I tried him, too. Voicemail.'

'Thank you,' Anna said.

Jane lifted a finger and dragged it softly down Anna's nose. To the uninitiated, it might have looked like something insulting. But Anna wasn't the uninitiated.

'I have. I will. Don't worry,' she whispered.

Jane stepped aside for Father. He looked tired. She expected him to immediately launch into an attack on Nick, but he had something more pressing on his mind.

'Just the one police car? Is there any news?'

'Detectives as well,' she said. That seemed to settle him a little and he grabbed her in a hug, although it was weak. He'd never been a man known for his shows of attention. 'I've been told to tell you not to make any calls to people about this. Any ideas you have, give them to the police.'

'Are you okay?'

She nodded against his chest. There was genuine concern there, but the beat of his heart and rasp of his breath hinted at more.

'Is there any news?'

Asked with a little more conviction, which made her realise she'd forgotten to answer that question the first time. She shook her head. 'No news. They're working on it.'

'I want to talk to them.' He kissed her forehead and walked into the house. She knew he didn't trust her to give him an accurate story. Because hers wouldn't condemn her husband.

As a man who'd run a restaurant chain for as long as his daughters had had beating hearts, Father was alien to not

manning the helm. By the time Jane and Anna had entered the
house, they could already hear his raised voice in the living room
as he tried to tell the police how to do their jobs. They heard
him complain that they were sitting around using their laptops
instead of kicking in doors to find his granddaughter. And they
heard him mention his nickname for Nick – Lotus Eater. Jane
grabbed Anna's hand.

'Let's leave him to rant a bit,' she said as she led her sister into
the bedroom. Anna was happy to go because she didn't want to
hear her father further insult Nick. As they moved across the
room, Jane caught her thigh on the bedroom dressing table. A
quiet giggle slipped from Anna's lips, but only because she needed
an injection of levity to relieve building pressure.

'We moved the dressing table a couple of days ago. Nick did
mention that it might catch you out.'

Jane sat on the bed and removed her denim jacket. The Lycra
top was sleeveless and exposed arms thin and muscled because
of her exercise obsession, and bruised because of her eyes. 'That
reminds me of the time Nick said there were a couple of spiders
dangling from the ceiling. Remember that? I felt trapped. Any
other booby traps I should know about?'

'Did I mention the sinkhole in the kitchen?'

Both women laughed. It seemed like becoming a mellow
moment, as Jane intended, but Anna quickly crested the peak and
descended again, fast as a runaway train. In the five seconds it took
her to move to the dressing table and sit, she blurted everything
Miller had told her.

There was a thoughtful pause before Jane responded: 'Have
they told you what they're doing to find them?'

Anna stared into the mirror and lifted a cotton pad to scrape
away the remaining dirt from her arms and face. But before the
pad even touched her face, she dropped it to pull out the cordless

and call Nick again. When she hung up, she saw Jane's reflection behind hers.

'Turning stones, that was the term they used. I guess it means they're doing their thing, whatever they do. But they're searching my house for clues.'

In the mirror, Jane's left hand spun the large ring on the thumb of her right. She was hardwired for movement and couldn't remain motionless – it was part of the reason exercise was an obsession. But here, instead, Anna read a nervous tic, and she didn't like it. She knew something fresh was worrying her sister.

'What's wrong?' Anna asked, staring at her sister's reflection. Impossible to read the dead eyes, but Anna had studied her sister's body language all their lives. She didn't like what she felt from the one person she expected to be wholeheartedly on her side:

Doubt.

'Jane?'

'There was that missing girl in Bradford a couple of days ago,' Jane said. 'She was thirteen. Mother kicked up a stink when she didn't return from school, and friends and family went out searching. The police searched the house, though, and they found a drawing of Nemesis – you know, that ride at Alton Towers?'

Jane stepped forward and grabbed Anna's hand. 'Stop that. I can hear it.' She felt Anna's neck. 'Get some cream.'

Anna's hand had been scraping at her throat again. The mirror showed her red blotches, raspy skin. She hadn't suffered a stress rash for years.

'Turned out the family had been planning to go to Alton Towers,' Jane said, her story continuing. 'But it fell through. The police went there and found her sleeping rough outside the entrance. She'd run off to go ride Nemesis. Unreal. The police wouldn't have known if they hadn't searched the house.'

Anna's heart sank. 'Why are you telling me that story? You agree with them, don't you? That Nick ran off with Josie?'

'No, I'm not saying that, Annie. I don't believe that any more than I believe people broke into the house and took a grown man. That's not what I meant. But Nick… he must have gone out.'

Anna said nothing. She got up to grab jeans and one of Nick's T-shirts from the wardrobe.

'He *must* have, Annie. Think about it.'

'Oh, are you about to quote evidence at me, like they did?'

As Anna tossed her muddy nightgown aside, Jane turned her head away, even though blind. Anna started to dress.

'If I have to, Annie. Think about it. You said the back door wasn't forced open. There was no noise. And his van? It must be something Nick had to do, and he took Josie with him.'

'Like what, Jane? At three in the morning, without telling me, and leaving the door wide open. Like what?'

'I don't know, but let's say the police are right. Nick abducted Josie. That's horrible, but isn't it also the best answer?'

'I would love it if that was the answer, Jane. If Josie is with her dad, then they're both fine, aren't they? Even if they decide never to come back, I know they're not in danger. Nick would never allow Josie to get hurt. They'll live a long and happy life. I would love that to be the case rather than what I'm thinking. But I just know it's not true.'

'Can you really believe that someone broke in and… what is it?'

Anna had frozen, and Jane had sensed this change in her sister's demeanour.

'Annie?'

'His side of the wardrobe is full,' Anna said, a little breathless. And a little scrambled because she added, 'Look. None of his clothing's gone.'

'What do you mean? Nick's clothes?'

Jane had approached and Anna grabbed her arm. 'He hasn't packed. They think he planned to run away, but he didn't take any clothing.' She ran Jane's hand along the clothing hanging in the wardrobe. But before her sister could make a response, a hard knock on the door was followed by the appearance of the gangly sergeant, Bennet.

'Nick didn't take any clothes,' Anna blurted at him.

'We need to find your mobile, Mrs Carter. Immediately.'

His was a manner thus far mild and professional, so the urgency in his tone knocked all thoughts of clothing from Anna's mind. Instinctively, she looked at the nightgown cast on the floor, then remembered she'd been using the cordless and had no idea where the mobile was. She rushed to her bedside table, but it wasn't there, either.

'I don't know. Why? What's going on?'

'Follow me, please.'

Anna wanted her sister by her side for this, so kept hold of her hand as she was led to the cubbyhole. Miller was waiting. She indicated the computer screen.

Someone had opened *MyPhone*, an app that kept track of calls and text messages. *Nick's* calls and messages.

'Your man made a mobile-to-mobile call,' Miller said. 'Look here. USA mobile code, that. Washington, DC. America, Anna. Your Nick called America, dear. Look at the time stamp.'

'He doesn't know anyone in America,' Anna said, but her mind was so scrambled she wasn't sure if that was true. Behind, she heard her father appear and ask what was going on. Lowth, the female uniformed responder, asked him to stay back. He started to demand an answer, so Jane and then Bennet joined the party. Soon many voices were arguing, but Anna didn't take her eyes from the screen.

Nick's call to America: 2.35 a.m. – just twenty minutes before she discovered her husband and daughter missing.

By her side, Miller jabbed another line. 'Texts sent by your Nick.'

Shocked, Anna saw that her own number had been sent a text. At 03.11.

Which was only a few minutes *after* she'd discovered Josie and Nick missing.

*

DS Bennet threw the duvet off the bed after checking both bedside cabinets, and he looked under the bed. But he shook his head.

'I picked it up,' Anna said. 'I know I did. Maybe I put it down in the living room.'

They moved into the living room, and then the playroom, and then the kitchen, but in each there were just too many places for a small item to be hidden. A thorough search couldn't be spared the time.

'Cards on the table,' Miller said. 'Any chance you've seen that text, and maybe hid the phone so us guys wouldn't?'

'No,' Anna answered, shocked. 'I must have put it down somewhere.'

'You were muddy,' Bennet said. 'Did you drop it when you slipped over outside?' He was already heading for the patio door but stopped when Anna made a noise.

'Josie's room! I slipped.'

She got a head start, so that she was on her knees on Josie's wet laminate floor by the time Bennet and Miller arrived. With no memory of the device either in her hands or flying out of them, she was doubtful. But there, under the bed, she saw it. She reached for it with such urgency she cracked her forehead on the bedframe.

As she picked it up and withdrew, the screen came alive, and sure enough a text message was waiting. From Nick.

'But he didn't take any clothing,' she murmured, and then the phone slipped away and crashed to Josie's floor for a second time.

Well, I tossed a coin and you lost. Hope you've got good pictures of Josie in your head. You'll need them. All good things come to an end, I suppose. Loved you once. XXX.

CHAPTER TWO

'I said I needed a minute.'

'We both know that's not the reason, dear,' Miller said as she got into the passenger seat. 'I used to hide from my dad when he got my school results. Same reason.'

'What's he saying?'

'I imagine exactly what you feared, seeing as you came out here to get away.'

Unable to face the oncoming explosion, Anna had left the house. She'd sat in her car on the driveway, in silence, watching the dark street and trying not to imagine how her father would be reacting to the threat sent from Nick's mobile.

'He really thinks Nick sent it, doesn't he? You all do.'

'That would be bias. I don't do such a thing. The scales are always balanced until evidence knocks them one way or the other.'

'What about Father's promise? I suspect he'll have told you all about that.'

Miller lowered the sun visor to check a little scar above her chin. 'Immediately. If you married Nick, he would cut you out of all financial help. Harsh. How's that been working out?'

'He's stuck to it. I mean, he helped with the wedding and bought our bungalow, but I don't know how much of that was Mother's influence on him because she wanted me back home. Nick suspects Father only bought us a house because he didn't trust me to survive without him, after I quit my London job. But since then he's seen us fall into debt that he could wipe out at the stroke of a pen. But no. So, maybe Nick decided he needed another way of getting Father to part with some money. That's what you're all thinking. I know it.'

'Not my cup of tea, this bias thing. And that's a pretty wild theory. Your Nick didn't ask for any money in that text.'

'So what do you think is going on? I know you believe it was Nick. But why do you think he would send a text like that?'

'My only concern is finding him, dear. The rest, it'll all fall into place afterwards. It's best not to assume this or that until we know better. I've got a couple of people coming that I need you to speak with. There will also be others from my team coming and going. Now, so you know, I'll be your contact here, okay? I'll need to bring the crime scene people in, with their little brushes and sprays and such, you know, but I'll insulate you from all these new faces. You won't see a crowd and you'll just deal with me. That'll make it easier. And I'll make sure my people use the back door and move quietly so none of the busybody neighbours see. Okay? Apologies, though, but I also need to run through some things with you in terms of negotiating with the kidnapper.'

'The kidnapper? But you all think my husband is behind this. Why would I need to be told how to talk to him?'

Miller tried to scrape the tiny chin scab away with a short fingernail. 'Thing is, dear, your man might not be the next person to contact you. And you must know that because you don't believe he sent that text. It's also a protocol thing. As is bringing in a Family Liaison Officer.'

'I don't know about this. I don't need someone's pity. I'd rather this liaison person talked to my sister. It must be hard for Jane. She loves Josie, and she never likes to see me in trouble. Or Nick. She's worrying for three. I should get back inside to her.'

'Truth be, there's a chance this thing could take a while. My people might soon have to fly the nest so we can do our jobs properly. The FLO will be your bridge between us. And she can take care of any arrangements you need. My boss has already picked a lady called Gwen. She'll be in the house if you want her for anything. A tech chap will be popping by, too.'

Anna glared at her. 'Arrangements? You mean Josie's funeral?'

Miller forgot her scar and touched Anna's arm. 'Not what I meant, and not going to happen. We'll both be bones by that day.'

'Don't make promises.'

'I don't do this to lock up the bad guy, Anna. That would make this just a job. I do this to give a family member good news. Painkillers. I need to see that happy look on your face when you hug your daughter again. I need it, dear. Some scumbag is going to leave me high and dry? Not going to happen.'

Anna shook her head and repeated: 'Don't make promises.'

Miller didn't respond to that. There was a moment of silence and Anna said, 'You didn't answer earlier when I asked you about a husband and children. You don't have a family, do you? This job is your life, isn't it?'

The scar needed attention again, this time without the mirror. 'No, dear. No. No marriage partner and no little ones. Complicated. I guess I'm a career woman. But it doesn't mean I don't understand what you're going through, sweetie.'

Exactly what she'd been thinking. She didn't want promises from this woman because a broken one would plummet her like a stone, and she believed the detective didn't realise that. But she gave herself a mental reprimand, because she'd been like the detective once. Long ago, back in London. Striving for a career, no thought to a family. And then everything changed. Something maternal broke anchor and surfaced. Maybe this woman's dedication was about more than just doing a good job. Maybe there was a maternal instinct that, shy of a child all its own, strove to look after everyone else.

As if reading her thoughts, Miller said, 'I do promise, Anna. I do promise to get your little one back to you.'

Before Anna could rebuke her, Miller's mobile rang. She apologised and answered it, but only listened for a few seconds and then hung up.

'I'm sorry, dear. Another awkward moment coming. You mentioned Nick was at work yesterday afternoon, right? He called you from Sheffield city centre at lunchtime. Is that right?'

'What? Yes. He was on a job. They're building a wall at a nursing home. He called me about one o'clock, on his break. He mentioned coming to my darts night on Friday. That's not someone planning to run away, is it?'

'We put his van's reg number in the Automatic Number Plate Recognition system. We got a hit. His van was logged at 1.21 yesterday afternoon. So, twenty minutes after he called you from, he said, Sheffield city centre.'

Puzzled, Anna said nothing.

Miller looked at her. 'I really do apologise. The van was in Sunderland.'

Sunderland? They were saying that Nick was in Sunderland when he claimed to be lunching in Sheffield? 'That must be wrong. Must be.'

Miller reached down to unclasp Anna's seatbelt. She hadn't realised she'd put it on. 'If you don't mind, now we're alone and getting used to the awkward dollops, I need to do another. I need proof that you're Josie's mother.'

Her head snapped round. Miller had pulled a plastic packet from her pocket. Anna knew she was looking at a swab kit. 'You want my DNA?'

Miller opened the packet and said, 'That's right, dear. Not that we don't believe you, of course. Dotted Is and crossed Ts. We have to officially make sure you're her mother. You want to do it, or I can?'

'It's the other way round, isn't it? You need to make sure she's my daughter, don't you? In case you only find a body.'

*

Hope you've got good pictures of Josie in your head. You'll need them.

For a time the sheer absurdity and fantasy of that text message had kept it anchored far below the surface of her mind, but now it floated into the open.

The first thing she had heard when she returned to the house was Father continuing to interrogate the police, so she slipped into the bedroom. Jane had appeared moments later. Lying side-by-side on the bed, they had talked about anything and everything not involving the kidnap, or Josie, or Nick. It had helped Anna shed nerves to the point where she felt dozy. It had put Jane to sleep.

Her poor sister, pushed headlong into this nightmare. But at least she looked at peace now. Because she'd been sightless since the age of three, her dreams were always set on a beach burned impossibly bright by the sun, like a washed-out TV image. Jane theorised that her dreams were always burning white because there was too much black in the rest of her world. Anna had noted the irony of her sister's situation: the world was meant to turn from black to white when the eyes closed, but for Jane it was the opposite. Anna hoped the beach was in her head now and not a nightmare about Josie.

As she lay, she watched the clock turn forty minutes. Within that time, people arrived at her house, just as promised. She didn't hear a single knock at the front door, suggesting they'd sneaked in the back way, like burglars, to avoid stoking the neighbours' curiosity. But she heard new voices out there and imagined her house filling up as the machinery of a major police investigation whirred into life. Just the visible part of the iceberg, of course: those running the show, veteran detectives directing from the top. Beneath the surface would be the greater mass: those making calls, knocking doors, hitting keyboards. Dozens, maybe, all hoping to find a lost little girl. All hunting Nick.

The Family Liaison Officer, a skinny lady with big eyes, poked her head in to say hello. She would be around for a chat if Anna needed a friendly ear or had any questions. Anna told her that would be great, thanks, maybe later. The woman didn't insist, and maybe that was part of her skill set, and maybe Miller had pre-warned her that Anna, though confused and dejected, was level-headed and knew what she needed.

Miller leaned in to offer a cup of tea and to show her a collection of cards about the size of electronic tablets, with large printed text. The detective explained what they were and looked somewhat apologetic doing so. The tea Anna accepted; the cards she tried not to look at. Miller didn't push it, clearly sensing Anna's contempt. She praised Anna's strength, told her to try to memorise the information on the cards, even if it seemed silly, and then left when a colleague called for her.

Anna drank and nervously feared a visit by her father, whose accusations and that well-practised look of disappointment she wasn't ready for. But he didn't show himself. She couldn't fully convince herself he was busy trying to shoehorn himself into the thick of the investigation.

Hope you've got good pictures of Josie in your head. You'll need them.

She lay and listened to myriad muted voices, and mobiles ringing, and the thud of many feet, and tried to evict that terrible text message threat from her head. Nothing worked until she heard someone knock on the front door. She jumped up so fast her tea spilled, but the urgency was gone half a second later: Nick wouldn't just knock.

Someone appeared outside the ajar bedroom door. Anna approached and peered through the gap. Miller stood outside, giving a long yawn. She smoothed her hair, shrugged to get her suit jacket comfortable, and rubbed her eyes.

Ready, Miller headed for the front door. Anna heard the detective's raspy tones and the heavy Scottish accent of yet another new player. Miller led this person past the bedroom door and into the living room. He wore a long coat over a suit, very sophisticated, like her father, but a tuft of hair poking up on the side of his head suggested he'd rushed to dress after waking. Whoever he was, Miller had felt the need to avoid looking worn out.

She approached the living room door but didn't enter. She heard the new arrival introduce himself to the party as Chief Superintendent Allenberg, District Commander for Sheffield. The big boss, then. He sounded proud to announce that the chief constable, woken from slumber, had authorised the use of surveillance devices for this investigation. Surveillance? On who? Did they have a suspect?

Pressed against the wall like an intruder in her own house, she listened as Miller outlined the call she had received about the possible kidnap and events since. Anna was surprised to hear that there had been a whole platoon of police officers on standby, ready to head out into fields and outhouses and lakes, the usual routine when a youngster went missing, but that Miller had ordered this approach scaled back in respect of evidence for a father-daughter abduction by Nicolas Carter. A *media blackout* was mentioned.

Then, a rundown on the Carters. Nick: thirty-seven, landscape gardener, menial labour worker his whole life, no known mental illness, only brush with the law: a fine and a one-year driving ban for drink-driving when he was twenty.

Anna: thirty-five, once-upon-a-time employee of Conservative Party member Marc Eastman – yes, that chap who just got made Secretary of State for Education – and now a stay-at-home mother. No psychological ailments and no dealings with the law bar one occasion in September of 2011 when her car was analysed amongst hundreds of others as part of a hit-and-run fatality enquiry in London.

Here Anna decided she'd heard enough and was about to return to the bedroom when she heard voices ahead. Yet more new voices.

Someone was in the cubbyhole at the end of the hall. Now she could hear shuffling paperwork. The little alcove was where Anna sat to stare out of the small porthole window at the neighbour's trees and work on her poetry. She hated the idea of detectives reading her work and yanked the curtain.

Two detectives she'd never seen before were sitting at the small table inside and dragging their fingers through her box of personal paperwork. Only one acknowledged her: a pregnant young woman, who she'd later learn was Detective Constable Ella Hicks, turned in guilty surprise. The male, a young Pakistani DC called Zesh Nabi, didn't even look up from what he was doing. She was annoyed to see her stack of poetry jotters had been knocked over, one having slid to the floor.

'What are you looking for?'

Hicks got to her feet. 'I'm sorry about the intrusion. We're just looking for anything that can help us.'

'You're behind with a lot of payments, aren't you?' That from Nabi, who continued to sit, and spoken without even a look around. His abrupt tone, so alien to what she'd encountered thus far, stayed her tongue for a few seconds. And made her nervous.

'A holiday we had,' she finally managed. 'We'll get back on track. It's nothing.'

Still giving her the back of his head, Nabi held up a sheet of paper. She recognised it as an old printout of a house for sale in Baltimore, USA. 'There's another connection to America here. We planning a move out there?'

Again she had the urge to quickly explain. 'No. That's from years ago. Nick had this silly idea about buying one of those stupidly cheap houses the government had. To sell on. I talked him out of it.'

'But this shows an interest in making quick money, right?'

His tone was unmistakable: suspicion. Did they suspect her of hiding something? But what, possibly? Something about money?

Strangely, the notion didn't further unsettle her – it angered her. 'Are you accusing me of something?'

Hicks told her colleague to give Anna room to think. He apologised, although he still gave her his back, and that offered a chance to slow her breathing. But then Hicks, too, held up a sheet of paper. Anna recognised this, also. Hicks read from it.

'"Notice is hereby given that by a Deed Poll dated 17th October 2011 and enrolled in the Supreme Court of England and Wales on 20th December 2011, ANNA SENIOR… abandoned the forename of Janice and the surname of Middleton and assumed the forename of Anna and the surname of Senior…"'

'I just wondered why you changed your name? I thought you became a Carter after Middleton through marriage.'

Now Nabi turned his head, so they were both watching her. For a reaction.

'I wasn't married at that point. Do you know who I used to work for when I lived in London? Marc Eastman, the MP.'

'Were you his girlfriend, too? One of the Witches of Eastman?' Nabi said. And it was a serious question.

'No. I was his caseworker.'

'I thought that was his wife.'

'His wife is his political aide. I was his caseworker, so I dealt with the public.'

Anna explained that Marc Eastman had employed her in 2010–2011, when he was just a backbencher in the newly elected Liberal-Conservative government. In July of 2011, he got backlash for a remark made about a government document concerning the Bovine TB problem. He got death threats from anonymous members of the public.

'I opened a lot of those letters. I felt threatened, too. When I quit the job, I didn't want to be looking over my shoulder. I wanted a fresh start. I moved out of the city to start a family somewhere quiet and I changed my name so nobody would know me. My parents bought us this bungalow as a wedding present, but we didn't get married until we'd settled here. Is that so wrong? I don't like your attitude, coming into my house like this. My daughter and husband are missing, and this is how you speak to me? Like I've done something wrong. I'm going to tell your superior.'

It was pleasant to see a little concern on their part now. Hicks smiled and shook her head.

'We didn't mean anything by it. Sorry if it sounded like that. We're just trying to get a feel.'

Anna shut the curtain. She felt guilty at her abruptness, but there was enough residual anger that her resolve was strengthened. She decided to take advantage and confront someone she'd been avoiding.

*

She found her father in Josie's room. On the bed, staring at the window. Strangely, she had feared coming in here, because the empty bed would spotlight what she'd had ripped away, and her father's presence doubly made her want to flee. But she didn't. He'd entered the house in frustration, but she could clearly sense that he was now feeling the impact of Josie's disappearance. She wanted to console him but didn't know how to.

He didn't register her presence until she sat on the edge of the bed. He gave her a quick glance and returned his gaze to the black window, now clear because the rain had virtually stopped. She felt the numbing power of the room. All of a sudden she wanted to sleep. She knew he was avoiding her only because he didn't like anyone knowing that even the great entrepreneur, Larry Middleton, was a slave to emotions.

He scratched his left cheek, trying to hide the fact that he was wiping tears. 'Why didn't you sense that something was in the air?'

Her heart sank. She had hoped this might be a rare moment, given their shared grief, where he actually treated her like blood.

But his own father had pushed him to achieve greatness, and it had worked, so sympathy wasn't his forte. He hadn't changed his tune in ten years, so why would he do so now?

'Why run from you, Anna? He loves you.'

From anyone else, that would have been real puzzlement about why a loving dad would suddenly flee the family home. But she knew her father was building to an accusation. She didn't want to hear it. Besides, being wound so tight for so long had sapped all her energy, leaving none to fight with.

But people did not deny Father, and he would have his say. 'Did you know he was doing this? Did he convince you to go along with this?'

'"Go along with this"?' she repeated, totally bemused.

Now he turned to her. 'Anna, is this about my money?'

Remembering the puzzling attitude of the cubbyhole detectives, she let out a gasp as all kinds of understanding hit her. 'Money? You think Nick wants money? That's why those two detectives out there were talking about money. You put that idea in their heads, didn't you? My god, do you… all of you… do you think Nick and I set this up? Do you think this is some kind of fake kidnapping? A ransom thing? That Nick and I came up with a stupid plan to get your money because you're so tight with it.'

She instantly regretted the insult, but he didn't look injured by it. If anything, her words seemed to confirm things in his mind. Her obvious anger at his reluctance to offer financial aid triggered a focussed gaze and another allegation.

'He managed to make you quit a good job and leave London, Anna. Maybe you don't even know what kind of control he exerts over you.'

She wanted to hit him, but there was no energy for that, either.

'You can't talk to me like one of your overworked staff, Dad. What is it with you? My daughter is missing, for God's sake, and you accuse me of being involved? Of this being a set-up with

Josie used as some kind of… bargaining chip? Don't you have a damn soul?'

That attack found a chink in the armour. He turned away again and got up. She heard his bad knee pop.

'I can't go to your mother's without Josie.'

'I want my daughter back right now, Dad. Not in four days' time. Right now, and I'd give anything for that.'

There was no face to see, but a slumping of the shoulders said he'd acknowledged his mistake. But all he said was, 'You should have Josie's bed in your room from now on, and I'll get you a bedroom door you can lock,' and then he scuttled from the room, gone before she could think of a response.

Guilt wrapped powerful limbs around her. This was a time of great stress for her father, too, and if attacking her, if a wild accusation, was to be his way of pressure release, so be it. A lifetime of blame had immunised her to his disrespect. She would gladly take his pain, and Jane's, into her own, because they would barely dilute it. She also knew that he partly blamed himself. Her father, the great entrepreneur, business-maker, couldn't tolerate mistakes and, for the very reason he'd interrogated the police, abhorred having any aspect of his life beyond his control. Blaming himself after the unavoidable death of Anna's mother had cemented his inability to deal with failure. Scrambled emotions explained his errant tongue.

But his accusations had left an acidic residue in the air, which she couldn't avoid breathing deep into her mind. Nick. She recalled a claim both of them had uttered in anger at one point: *I hope one day I'll come home to find you've just left for ever.*

Mixed with the evidence that said he'd taken Josie, it looked bad. But not to someone who really knew Nick. Not to her. If Nick ever had the idea to leave with Josie, he would have given it a voice, if only to make a threat. No way would he just run with her, and certainly not in the middle of the night. The only concept more ridiculous was that he'd snatch her in order to extort money. But Father and the police seemed willing to jump all over that one.

She got on her knees and reached under the bed. She returned with a present in wrapping paper, which she quickly tore open. She'd spotted the item when searching for her lost phone. Then, it hadn't mattered, but now it did. She needed it to beat back all that confusing evidence against Nick and remind her that he was a good man.

The card said…

To My Darling Wife, Happy Writing

It was attached to a bow-wrapped box containing a writing pad, pen, mini voice recorder, and CD of ambient music, which she couldn't write poetry without.

'Excuse me?'

She looked round to see a brand new uniformed police officer, an overweight female in heavy boots and latex gloves. Lettering on the breast of her jacket said SENIOR CSI. A Crime Scene Investigator, Anna realised, with shock. Someone else who had sneaked in while she was in the bedroom. Someone whose job was to find fingerprints and DNA and… blood. The horror took all words from her.

The CSI said, 'I haven't worked the girl's room yet. Heard you in here, didn't want to intrude. All done?'

'Yes. I'm sorry. But my daughter, her name is—'

She stopped as the phone rang.

*

Express concern for the individual-in-crisis and ask for proof of life, phrased in such a way that only the kidnapper can answer.

She was led into the living room like a condemned woman, Miller's hands on her arm, that scratchy voice close to her ear. So many people in her house, so many more than she'd expected. Miller had promised to insulate her from them, but the ringing phone had drawn them out, and all were watching her.

The coffee table had been dragged into the centre of the living room and her mobile was there, connected to a laptop. Everyone stared at it like a ticking bomb. Around the laptop were the cards Miller had given her earlier. She noticed Bennet holding her father's arm, but unlike her he wasn't being led to the phone. He was being kept away from it. Jane was by a wall, cracking her fingers nervously, and Anna suddenly felt for her: the sisters had always been able to rise up, superhero-like, to help each other with a problem, but this was a shared one. And this one was beyond anything they'd ever had to cope with.

'It'll be fine, Jane,' she said as she was virtually shoved towards the phone.

'Unknown number,' Miller said. 'Compose yourself for a moment, then answer. Everybody else, please, move back.'

Not Nick's mobile number. She stood over the phone, staring down at it. Such a simple item, tiny and immobile, yet it terrified her.

Retain a helpful attitude while making no firm yes or no to demands or monetary figures asked for.

'How long… to stay on?' Anna said. She clutched Miller's arm like a saviour. She tried to tell herself this was silly behaviour, because Nick was going to be on the other end of that phone. It didn't work.

Leave silent gaps, including before answering the call, so that the police can determine background noises.

'The trace takes moments,' Miller said. She started to tap each of the cards. 'Keep staring right at these as you talk, dear. Cycle through them. Please, stay calm.'

Her mind was caught in a whirlwind and nothing much made sense or seemed real – it felt like a film scene – and the words on the cards wouldn't click. But she remembered it all.

Start with 'Hello', just in case the unknown number belongs to an inquisitive neighbour.

It didn't seem like much help from people with experience in these matters, but it wouldn't have mattered if she'd had a week's worth of training – this was her daughter, and her husband, and the rulebook could take a flying leap.

She snatched up the phone and said, 'Nick, is that you? What's going on? Where are you? Is our little lady okay? I'm so scared.'

That all-important silent gap was provided by the caller. She had expected those surrounding her to panic at her instant decapitation of the rules, but they just watched. Silent, unmoving, just another day at the office. Suddenly she couldn't hear the laptop's fan whirring, or the little carriage clock on the fireplace ticking; even the rain had ceased lashing the world, as if Mother Nature herself had become entranced by this sliver of the universe. Two, three, four seconds ticked by. And then:

'I believe I told you not to involve the police.'

A deep male voice, and suddenly the horror was undeniably real, no longer a simple misunderstanding but a true waking nightmare. Not Nick, so another. Someone who didn't care about Josie. Her throat closed up.

Miller shook her head, which Anna understood: don't admit it. They didn't look shocked that the caller wasn't Nick, after all their suspicions.

'I didn't,' she said. Her fear spiked. A lie, and it could kill Josie and Nick.

'Involving the police was betrayal. I should take a finger off your girl for that.'

She was about to scream an apology when Miller stepped forward, silent as a ghost, and grabbed her shoulder. Their eyes met and right there Anna realised the other woman also knew the caller wasn't Nick. She mouthed, *Don't admit.*

'I didn't,' Anna repeated, and it felt like pulling the trigger of a gun aimed at Josie's head.

'If any police know the next time I call, you're no longer a parent. I'll call soon to let you know how your man's dues can be paid.'

She was supposed to talk about Josie: what she liked to play with, cartoons she enjoyed – and her milk allergy, she was supposed to mention that. But the fear wobbled logic. 'Please, let me talk to her. I need to know—'

Click.

CHAPTER THREE

Like a zombie, she staggered for the door. People in her way got elbowed aside, even her father as he attempted a rare moment of concern during this whole ordeal. But Jane, aware of her presence, fumbled for an arm, locked on to it, and guided Anna towards the bedroom. Various voices tried to ask questions – Was that Nick? Did you recognise the voice? – and it was sweet music to hear Miller order her to be given a few minutes alone.

'Your girl,' Jane said, a moment before Anna's legs gave way and she collapsed, a dead weight, on to the bed. Jane was almost dragged over with her, such was her sister's grip on Anna's flesh. 'He said *your girl*. That wasn't Nick.'

Jane had a slight smile, as if she thought this was good news. But Anna just stared at her and shook her head.

'And he said, *if the police know next time*. If they *know*. Not if *they're still there*. I don't think he knew you'd called the police, Annie. Don't you think?'

'You're right, but don't you see?' Anna said. Jane didn't, given her puzzled look. Anna could hardly bring herself to pop the bubble. 'It's not Nick, so some stranger has Josie. Someone who might hurt her. And Nick's in danger, too.'

Jane sat on the bed and shook her head. 'But the police said...'

That word: as Anna had stumbled from the room, she'd heard it uttered loud and clear, the very same word Jane was thinking: accomplice. 'I wish that were true. But it's not, Jane. It's just not. The police think it's Nick but it's not. We know him and they don't. You know he wouldn't do this. It's not Nick and that means both of them are in danger.'

Jane's long pause cut all the flesh off her claim: 'We don't know that.'

'What did Nick do to prevent this?' The impromptu question surprised Anna almost as much as it did Jane.

'You mean what they said about him paying his dues?'

She had wondered that, but it wasn't what she'd meant. 'He was right there, Jane, when they took Josie. What did he do to stop it?'

Her sister's shock immediately yielded to something else. 'You need to kill that train of thought right now.'

But that thought was a rolling boulder, gathering power over time, and might already be unstoppable. Nick had been up, awake, but there had been no sound of a fight, no yelling – had he frozen in fear, like a little child himself, while strange men took everything that mattered to him?

She heard the front door slam, which cut through everything. Then the clack of high heels on her path, and her father saying something about needing petrol. He and a female police officer, heading out to his home in Loxley. His garage was where she and Nick kept all their old belongings, mostly duplicated items left over when they moved in together and two homes became one. Someone had told her they needed to search it for information about Nick's old life: people and places that could shed clues as to his whereabouts. So, while she'd been thinking *weak*, the police had continued to think *guilty*.

'Father's worried that he can't take Josie to Mother's,' she said. Something else impromptu.

'They'll be going, don't worry. It's days away and Josie is coming back to us today. Isn't she?'

It was a forceful prompt. She wasn't sure she believed it, but she desperately didn't want Jane to worry about her sister as well as her niece. 'Yes, she's coming back today.'

It was a weekly routine: Sundays, after dinner, Father would take Josie to see her grandmother's grave, because she had constantly asked where "Grandy" was since that day she just wasn't awaiting her at the front door. Anna tried to picture two people at opposite ends of the age spectrum sitting together on grass – but the calming image eroded as Jane jumped to her feet.

'Nick?'

'What's wrong?' Anna rose, too, shaky.

'Didn't you hear that? Someone said Nick's just been arrested.'

CHAPTER FOUR

'You can't leave.'

The young pregnant DC, Hicks, had her hand raised, palm out, a clear and universal gesture. Anna wanted to return with an equally recognisable obscene one. But instead she said: 'That's my husband and my daughter.'

'I understand, but the kidnappers might call. You have to—'

'Got it,' Anna said, holding up her mobile. 'And now I'm going.'

The dark was beginning to diffuse from the sky and a couple of lights were on in houses across the way. To her right, a bedroom curtain moved. She didn't care and ran down the path, heart thudding. At Miller's car, Bennet had one long leg into the passenger side when he spotted her, and he showed her he was as versed as his DC in hand signals.

But she barely got a word into her assertion that they would not be leaving her here: she heard Miller, already in the car, say it was okay, and he jerked a thumb at the back seat. She climbed inside and once the car was on the move, before she could ask the question she'd been desperate to, Bennet said, 'A couple reported a drunk man acting suspicious on a road near Meadowhall—'

'Nick?' she cut in. He liked to have a little drink each night, which she constantly complained about, but he hadn't been drunk for a long time. 'He wouldn't get drunk. Not… he's working tomorrow.'

Bennet continued as if she hadn't even spoken. 'Two officers arrived and arrested him for breaking into a lock-up garage. He's at the Sheffield Custody Suite, about three miles east of here. They ran his name and discovered he was wanted. He was found staggering around, dirty, incoherent—'

'What do you mean, incoherent? There's no way he would be drunk. He never drinks that much. And not with Josie. It can't be him. No. It's not Nick.' Her elevating hopes that her loved ones had been rescued began to sink.

She looked at the rear-view mirror, seeking help from Miller, who met her glass gaze and offered it. But not the kind she wanted. 'Your man's fingerprints are on file because of a drink-driving offence. It's him, dear. No mistake. And, look, we're sorry for trying to do this without you.'

Bennet said, 'It was the 999 call that said he was drunk. The arresting officers think he's under the influence of drugs.'

That hit her like a hammer. Nick, as far as she knew, had never taken drugs. It made no sense, like just about everything else on this unforgettable night. But it didn't matter. Nick and Josie had been found.

That got him a sharp glance from his boss, who said, 'But he's okay, Anna. And now we can get his story and find out about Josie.'

'Find out? What are you saying? Where's Josie?'

This time Miller turned her whole head, avoiding the impersonal mirror. 'He's not making much sense, I'm sorry. But Josie wasn't with him.'

*

The Custody Suite, a £14 million new construction, was a futuristic-looking beast three miles away, and just half a mile south of the £250 million shopping centre called Meadowhall. As Miller's £11,000 Mondeo turned into the car park, Anna's mind was thrown back to the day she had met Nick, both at a police station in Hackney to record witness statements. Anna had been there to give a statement on behalf of her friend, whose brother had broken into her car, and Nick was describing a figure he'd spied fleeing the scene of a mugging. That event had started so much; how would today's shape the future?

She tried to be first out, almost before the wheels had stopped turning, but the door wouldn't open. The DS had to do it. 'Lawbreaker locks,' he said, a joke about the child locks.

Miller was more serious: 'I'm sorry, but although you're here, for the moment we have to chuck you in a room, okay? Until after we've seen Nick. I can't let you just barge on in there. Are you okay with that?'

Arguing wouldn't help and she'd never get past all the locked doors and police inside, so she nodded. All three briskly entered the building through a back entrance and followed a corridor. She had expected the zoo-like thud and roar of caged beasts, but the place was unnervingly quiet. They cut into a second corridor and then Bennet strode ahead towards double doors at the end, but Miller turned to stop her. Anna noticed a small kitchen to her left. Suddenly, she didn't want to be chucked in a room.

She shook her head. 'I want to see him.'

'I'd be a muppet not to know that, dear. But it's not a good idea until after—'

'You'll have him in a cell. He's here and I want to see him. He's innocent. He might not tell you where Josie is, but he'll tell me. I want my little lady.'

'I know. A massively delicate moment here, though, and you can't turn it upside down. I'll have you carried away if you insist. I'm sorry. Really.'

Anna believed that last statement, but it meant nothing. 'No, I have to see him. I have to know he's okay.'

'And I don't know yet if he is.'

That was the reason? Anna grabbed Miller's arms in both of hers. 'I expected to see him dead, do you understand? Anything is better than that. I don't care how messed up he is. He's alive. You need to see my happy face, don't you?'

'As a child, I bet you got your way all the time.' Miller turned and walked away. Anna took it as permission and followed. They passed through the double doors, into a reception area where four or five officers hung about behind a counter and a thug in a shell suit was being asked officially if he was likely to harm himself while here. Bennet must have already explained why they were here because one of the officers led them onwards without a word. A door later they entered what looked a little like a corridor of lockers, although a sign above the entrance had said 'Cells 01–14'. They stopped at a door with another officer outside and Anna pushed ahead of Miller to peek through the big square vision panel.

The bed Nick sat on was nothing but a blue mat, like something from a school gym, on a low shelf along one wall. He wore plain blue tracksuit bottoms and a white T-shirt bearing a picture of Peppa Pig under a speech balloon that said 'GREATEST DADDY'. His feet were bare. His hair, much shorter than in the picture on the fridge, was matted with blood that also stained the left side of his hairless face and one arm of the T-shirt, and his arms were grimy with dirt. He was swaying side-to-side, eyes closed. Under the influence of drugs, they'd said. She thought he looked like the survivor of a natural disaster.

But he was moving, and breathing, and because of it he looked beautiful, perfect. She put her head against the door and closed her eyes.

'He didn't take any clothing. They're his pyjamas.'

But the happy moment was gone the next instant, because Josie was still missing. She tried to open the heavy door, but all four police officers grabbed her. Three had forceful words, but Miller's soothing tone cut through it all. Before Nick was ripped from her view, she saw his face turn to the door. One eye opened and seemed to stare at her. The other was welded shut by dried blood.

'Who the hell are you?' he shouted. The effort seemed to drain him, and he fell back against the wall.

'Let me in there,' Anna screamed, fighting against six hands holding her. Adrenaline strength got her close enough to the viewing panel to see him again. 'Nick! Where's Josie? What happened?'

In the second she managed to remain at the door, he stared right at her and again shouted: 'Use a towel for that, I told you. Who the hell are you?'

There was a bench against the wall and she shrugged free of the hands clamped to her flesh and sat down, hard. More like a collapse. Everyone was breathing hard, bar the unflappable DCI, who sat next to her. But the older woman didn't get chance to say a word.

The officer watching through the viewing panel gave a shout. As Anna jerked her head round, the officer rushed to open the door. Both women leaped up at the same time. Anna got to the door just in time to see all three police officers bending over Nick, pinning his arms and legs.

'Nick!'

He was on his front, thrashing like an epileptic, and there was vomit under his head, his face rubbing back and forth in the mess. Screaming his name again, she tried to move forward, but Miller grabbed her arms.

'Don't go in. Anna, stop!'

'Look at him! Do something.'

She pushed Anna aside and rushed to Nick. Anna tried to copy, but the behemoth Bennet stepped up to block her way, and snatched an elbow in his bear-trap hand as she tried to slip by. Stranded, Anna watched as Miller lifted Nick's head by his hair and jammed her fingers into his mouth, seeking a swallowed tongue.

'What's happening? Is he having a fit?'

Miller twisted Nick's head, leaned hers close, and pinched a portion of neck flesh between two fingers covered in his saliva. Anna saw a red welt and, even at this distance, a small hole.

'Get a damn ambulance, you muppets,' Miller yelled.

It was that moment, a rare burst of anger from the ever-calm detective, that made Anna's thighs lose power.

'He's just drunk,' one of the PCs mumbled, shaking his head as if Miller had requested something stupid. Still on her knees, she actually kicked out at his ankle to get him moving. And then she looked straight at Anna, who was being kept upright by Bennet.

'He's been drugged.'

Middleton's home was three miles northwest of the Carters', just past Loxley. It was on the edge of a road overlooking fields, but the three-storey stone house was denied the view by a high hedge atop a grey stone wall running the length of the road. You had to enter the grounds to determine where his land gave way to the neighbours', which was achieved through a stone archway barely wide enough for his car. Detective Constable Ella Hicks was instantly jealous because she lived in an end terrace with walls so thin she could hear her neighbour's microwave oven beep. And those fools swore by ready meals.

The old stone garage had a single sliding door, made of serious metal, that curved around the inside wall when open, but when this modern safety feature was installed, an old wooden door in the side got overlooked. The floor was linoleum, the walls tiled, ceiling painted, as if it had once been a kitchen. Now it was just a room for junk. Big boxes lined one side wall and the back, and a long bookcase of smaller boxes filled the other side wall. In the centre were two long standing racks of clothing in polythene to create aisles. It was all pretty neat and clean. Ella walked between the racks, skimming a hand across clothing that rustled. Middleton sat on an ornate stool she hadn't noticed in one corner.

'Don't pull things out, please. Point and ask and I'll clarify.'

She didn't point, though. She opened each of the big boxes and peered in. To reach the bottom, items had to be removed and stacked on the floor. There was more clothing, and there were items she imagined were useless because they were doubled up: when two households became one, nobody needed a second teapot or an extra toilet brush, and there was such a thing as too much cutlery. Most of it was stuff that should have been thrown away, but on the drive over Middleton had already pointed out that Anna's mother, swept from the world by bowel cancer three years ago, had been a bit of a hoarder, loath to discard anything because you never knew when something might have a use once again. None of it gave a clue as to Nick Carter's character or where he might run if he snatched his kid.

Another big box had three trophies lying atop a mass of items, each depicting what looked like two people wrestling. She didn't pull them out. 'Are these Anna's or Nick's?'

'Jane's. She was the best female of her weight in South Yorkshire until her elbow played up. It was the only sport she could really do.'

'I'm impressed. But why are the trophies in here?'

'I taught my girls to look to the future, not dwell on the past. Hell, tried to, anyway. Look, there's nothing in that box belonging to Nick.'

Planning to check it if the remainder yielded nothing, she moved on. In the next box she found paperwork and trinkets, and here the couple got laid out. She held up an empty milk bottle.

Middleton explained: 'That's Nick's. Lucky charm, he reckons. Silly if you ask me. He came out of a shop, realised he'd forgotten milk, and went back in. While he was in there a car skidded and hit his motorbike. He reckoned he would have been just sitting on it at that time. Like I say, silly. But he keeps it for luck.'

'I have a lucky rabbit's foot hanging in my car. I haven't crashed yet. You're a non-believer?'

'You make your own luck. Anna had one, too. It was a five-yen coin her mother gave her when she left school, for luck in life. My wife believed in it and Anna promised to pass it on to Josie when she was older. It was supposed to go down the generations, but she lost it just before she moved out of London. Did that work?'

He might have meant the irony of losing a so-called lucky coin, or the events that had even made this conversation possible. Both were impossible to argue against.

A photo of Nick and some mates on a street backdropped by chip shops and a beach. She recognised the North Promenade of Cleethorpes. Four of them on motorbikes, clad in jeans and black T-shirts that said ANGELS. An Asian-looking boy at the front seemed to be the leader, given how the others were arranged behind him.

'Nick as a teenager. He used to hang out with some ruffians. I think they saw *Easy Rider* and wanted some of that. Kids being silly.'

Sounded about right. Wannabe Hell's Angels. 'Know any of their names?'

'No. That guy in the middle, I think he was from the Philippines. You think one of his old cronies could be involved?'

'We're soaking up information, that's all.'

He shook his head.

She took a photo of the photo with her phone and dispatched it to Sergeant Bennet. Next, a picture of Anna with a girlfriend in a café.

'Jubilee Café. She would sometimes work there, waiting for her boss.'

'Marc Eastman? The man who's now Secretary of State for Education? She mentioned him. Back when she lived in London?'

'Back when she had promise,' he sneered.

'Promise?'

He got off the stool, clearly agitated, and peered out the door, his back to her. 'It was a good job. She had prospects. She met the prime minister. She got to travel. The money was good. She did half the work that Eastman's wife did.'

'Iliana Eastman? I've heard about her. Supposedly controls him like a puppet. Seemed to forgive him when the newspapers ran that Witches of Eastman exposé last week. But your daughter did a lot of the work Eastman's wife probably got credit for?'

'And she did it without seeking praise or reward.'

'And then she gave it up. Why did they leave London? Anna told me about some kind of animal cull scandal and threats against her boss?'

He loosed a frustrated laugh, which told her this was a touchy subject. 'I wish that were the reason.'

'Something worse?'

'To me, yes. I was aware that Eastman came under fire for statements made during the Bovine Tuberculosis crisis. Anna might have been weighed down at times during that period, but I believe she's fooling herself, or she tried to fool you, if she claimed that was the entirety of her reason for throwing away the good things she had. She went to King's College to study International Relations. That was set to cost me £25,000, although she quit after the first year because she met Marc Eastman. At a nightclub, strangely. Anna and Marc started talking, got on quite well, and then he offered her a job as his personal assistant, right there on that night. When the Conservatives won a few years later, she was overjoyed. Anna was smart and Eastman often asked her advice about matters. He even appeared in public a few times with her, in part because his wife kept to the shadows. In effect Anna was making a difference. She was working for the country, working to better it. Being important.'

He seemed to want her to ask for more about this 'important' work, but she was more intrigued by another aspect of his tale. 'Offered a job at a nightclub? Were they sexually connected?'

He groaned. 'You mean was she one of his Witches? Just because an anti-Conservative journalist is trying to sell newspapers and undermine Eastman's recent promotion by exposing his fondness for extramarital affairs, it doesn't mean he slept with every woman he came across. And certainly not Anna. She was very good at her job.' His face grew grim. 'And then she quit.'

'I'm not sure I heard an answer to my question there.'

'The Lotus Eater, Detective. That was the reason.'

'You mean she quit to get married and start a family? Why do you call him that? I heard you say it before. And right in front of your daughter.'

'In Greek mythology, the lotus eaters—'

'Please,' she cut in. 'I know it means a waster. I called my own brother that once. I didn't ask the meaning. I asked why you call Nick that name.'

'I have no idea what she saw in him. I don't even know how they met. She moved in powerful circles, mixing with people who shaped the country, and he worked as a personal trainer at a dingy gym. How do those worlds cross?'

That annoyed her. 'You make it sound like Nazi Germany. Should people like Nick wear armbands so the elegant like yourselves can avoid them in the street?'

'She had a good job. She could have made something of herself. London was the place for her, the hub of the country. She had a home, a good house I rented for her. I was making plans for starting a business down there. Even Jane was thinking about a move south to help run it. The Conservatives had just won and her boss was riding high. And then the Lotus Eater came along and started sleeping there more often and ruined—'

'She gave up a good career to get married and have a baby, that's your problem? And she *did* make something. A little girl, who will be a woman, who might just cure cancer. Some of those genes are from Nick, by the way. But you got your daughter and granddaughter back close to you. You bought the house for them. You'll note I'm pregnant, right?'

He turned and glanced at her belly. His eyes quickly went back to his kingdom. 'It was her mother's idea. She never wanted Anna to leave South Yorkshire. And we both wanted to make sure any grandchildren were nearby.'

She said, 'And Nick was part of the deal, of course.'

His response was a shrug.

'My partner wants me to give up work. He doesn't want me running around after criminals in my condition. He doesn't want his little daughter worrying each night that Mummy will be hurt. I plan to do just that – quit work. And my job is important, just like Anna's was. How do you feel about that? Will I be wastefully throwing my important life away to bring up a child?'

He said nothing.

'My partner runs a little computer shop. He fixes them. Our worlds crossed because he was hired as a strip-o-gram for me. That might be your answer.' She tried to hide a cheeky grin. 'Girls love a fit man. If Nick was a personal trainer, he might have been ripped and hot. Got any photos of him topless from back then?'

He turned again, probably just to show the disgust on his face. It only made her laugh. But she got serious. 'At least you're not one of those men who thinks a woman's place is in the kitchen, making the home sweet for the breadwinner. There is that. And consider this. If your daughter hadn't made that decision, there would be no Josie, would there? No granddaughter. Look at the magnificent gift she gave you. Why do you still treat her like a failure after so many years?'

He was facing away again, his head lowered and his voice was quiet. 'I don't even know.'

But there was no time for drama or family guidance. 'Please, Mr Middleton, let's get a move on. Come and talk me through these things.'

They didn't get a chance. Her phone rang. Bennet. After the call, she picked up the photo of Nick and his friends. 'Not Hell's Angels.' Reminded of that famous outlaw biker gang, she had misread the word on the T-shirts.

'I don't understand,' Middleton said. He stopped and bent close for a serious look at the photo. 'Angeles, not Angels. Like Los Angeles?'

'Like the Spanish name.' She tapped the Filipino's grinning face. 'This man is called Angeles.'

'So it was his gang, maybe. A play on the Hell's Angels? What does it prove?'

'Maybe nothing. But my boss just found out who owns the phone number Nick Carter called before Josie was taken: Fitch Alicante Angeles.'

'Ketamine overdose, most likely. But he's going to be okay, dear.'

Anna stared at Miller. 'What is that? I've heard of it. He'll definitely be okay?'

'They gave him benzodiazepines, and he responded awesomely. And they got the bubblegum out with mayonnaise. Someone stuck bubblegum in his hair, right on the laceration on his head. Some kind of joke. But he's doing well. But they want to keep him for a bit. Not too long. Precautions.'

'It can cause a coma, though, that ketamine stuff,' a uniformed officer standing at the door said. 'And he'll be addled for a bit. My brother's mate, he once—'

'Go check the car park for pickpockets,' Miller said.

When the foul man was gone, Miller apologised and told her Nick would be moving from A&E to a private room in the hospital shortly. And that the uniformed idiot was right about one thing.

'Your man might be a bit confused for a bit. So we might not get many good answers from him. But he's agreed to talk to us.

We'll go up shortly. You really should stop clawing at your flesh like that, dear.'

Again, almost of its own accord, her hand had crept to her neck rash, fingers grinding back and forth. She wiped and saw a faint smear of blood on her palm. Or, like before, was it just dirt?

'Nick told me to scratch through a towel. He had eczema as a boy and that's what he did.'

Miller's jaw muscles tightened. Anna realised she was stifling a yawn. 'We can get a nurse to look at it.'

'Do you think they tried to kill him?' The abrupt shift of subject didn't even make Miller flinch, as if she'd been awaiting the question. Her answer backed this up.

'It'll be money, just money they want. That line about your Nick paying his dues, well, perhaps they were simply referring to paying a ransom.'

There it was again, that reference to money. But at least Miller hadn't accused Nick of complicity. Anna still wasn't convinced this was someone's get-rich-quick scheme, and the detective hadn't really answered her question. And had no plans to: claiming she was going to oversee Nick's move upstairs, Miller left the small staff kitchen, where Anna had been placed because she wasn't allowed by Nick's bedside while the doctors tended to him. When another uniform arrived to man the entrance, as if Anna needed observation like a patient, she shut the door on him. She ran water to splash her face and burning neck. She tidied the worktop where someone had spilled sugar and coffee granules. But no mundane activity would shift her mind from Josie, the terrible danger she must be in and her own helplessness, and the possibility that the kidnappers might have tried to kill Nick by overdose, so after that she sat to wait. She pulled out her phone and typed a name into Google.

The uniform knocked fifteen minutes later and let in DS Bennet, who said he would escort her to see Nick. Like Miller, he warned her that her husband might not have many answers for her. He also gave the same answer she'd sought a dozen times since leaving the police station: *no news about Josie, but we're following leads.*

As she expected of patients in Intensive Care, Nick was connected to plastic and rubber and electricity, but she was buoyed to see him awake and sitting up in bed all by himself. And cleaned. A big laceration above his eye had already been stitched. She sat by his bed, with four police officers in the room and more uniforms outside. And an emergency medicine consultant, who she'd been told had refused to leave the police alone with Nick.

He was groggy still, but his eyes recognised her. Earlier he hadn't seemed to – *Who the hell are you?* – but apparently he'd been screaming that line to all and sundry before and after his arrest. But not because he recognised no one, as she would soon learn.

She was dying to ask him about their daughter, but was terrified he wouldn't know anything, or wouldn't remember because of his cloudy brain. Until she got that terrible news, she could believe she was moments from discovering where Josie was.

So she stayed silent and he went first. As soon as he saw her, he moaned, 'Oh… Josie… where…' But his head seemed to spin and he looked ready to throw up. That word pinned her soul: *where*. He didn't know where Josie was. She slammed the lid on a wail and put her hand on his hot forehead. Strangely, everything else got swept aside for a second as she realised it was their first intentional flesh-on-flesh touch in over a week.

But only a second: 'Do you know where she is?' she pleaded. 'What happened, Nick? Where is Josie? Please.'

He looked at the police officers standing nearby and shook his head. She knew then that she'd only been allowed access to Nick because their own efforts to get him to talk had failed. She was their next hope, now gone.

His eyes closed and he lay back. But they snapped open a moment later when the door flew open. It was Bennet, who must have slipped out while she was distracted.

'Mrs Carter, with me, quick.' He mouthed something at Miller.

Anna turned back to Nick, whose eyes looked clear, but scared. 'What's… Anna, what's going on?'

Before she could react, Miller had her arm. 'Quickly.'

Anna was marched out of the room and down a corridor on legs that wanted to fail. She knew something bad was afoot but couldn't find the voice to ask what. But when she saw a uniformed officer standing in a doorway ahead, clearly awaiting her, she knew, just knew.

'It's him, isn't it?'

She was jerked into the room, hands on her back, and pushed into a seat before a desk loaded with paperwork and two computers. And a phone that was ringing. Her mind was spinning.

'We've asked for the call to be lobbed up here from reception,' Miller said, her grip on Anna's arm now soft, like a friend's.

A call for her. Her fears had been correct. 'It's him, isn't it?'

Miller slapped her hand on to the ringing phone, but didn't pick it up.

'The call will be on speakerphone. You can do this, dear. You're strong. Ask to speak to Josie this time. Use silences so we can determine background noises.' There was more, the usual stuff she'd been told before. Now it was undeniable.

Somehow, the kidnapper knew she was here and had called the hospital, not the mobile in her pocket, to speak to her.

*

'Right now, in rooms close to you, are people with renal failure. It's £17,000 for a kidney transplant and £5,000 a year for immunosuppression treatment.'

The faces in the room mirrored her own puzzlement. 'Where is my daughter? Please. Her name is—'

'Transplant survival is about ten years. That's £67,000 for ten years of life. You can buy your kid a much longer and happier life for just £50,000. That's what we want. Good old-fashioned cash. All in £20 notes. And you'll get it by ten this morning, won't you?'

So, it was about money after all. Just as everyone had claimed. 'I'll try my best,' she said, just as coached. A line that avoided rejection but promised nothing. Her teeth were gritted. 'I want to speak with my little lady.'

The clenched jaw wasn't a symptom of fear. There was no fear, surprisingly. Worry for Josie's safety had momentarily been subdued by anger. This man had taken her everything, and just for money. How she wanted to burn him alive.

'Been watching too many films, have we? That's not how this is going to happen.'

'I want to talk to my daughter. I want proof she's alive and unhurt.'

'Alive and unhurt? You could have just said unhurt, since that would also mean she's alive. We're going to call your house at ten and tell you where to take the cash. Have it sealed in a freezer bag and inside a typical shoebox. Not Nike, I hate Nike. You better get your arse right out the door when the call comes, okay? On the dot. With the cash. Freezer bag and shoebox. I know you got the cops listening. Tell them to try nothing—'

'I want proof of life, you…' She stopped herself just in time. But it didn't matter:

'Arse-licking tosspot freak bastard, is that what you were about to call me?'

'No.' The fear hurtled back, exploding inside her like a bomb blast. One of Miller's cards had covered 'Barbs' – aggravating points of discussion. Boiled down: *never refer to the Hostage Taker's moral make-up. Never say that his actions were cowardly or insane or unfair. Never insult him.* 'Look, please, I'm sorry. I don't want my daughter to be hurt. She's only five. She has breathing problems. Please don't hurt—'

But he interrupted her with laughter. It was a sound that cut, but it was also good to hear. Laughter meant he wasn't offended.

'You mess this up and I'll send you proof of death instead, how about that? Your kid's head wrapped in a copy of today's newspaper. You want that?'

'No. Please. I just want her unhurt. You can have what you want. I just want her back. She'll be hungry. But she needs soy milk, because she can't—'

Again, laughter.

'You know, this humanising your kid bit only works against people who aren't raving psychopaths. So stop it. Get my money. Mess this up, I'll charge you 25p for the newspaper I buy.'

Click.

*

Angry, but unsure why, she ran out of the room, ordering those who wanted to restrain her to give her a minute. She headed around the nearby corner, where there was a bench in a windowed alcove. She knelt on it and stared out at a small illuminated garden enclosed by four walls. The mobile was in her hands, already ringing Father's number. He answered quickly, clear hope in his voice, and she cut it down immediately.

'They want money. £50,000. I'm sorry.'

She hung up and turned off the phone, loath to take a return call. She had promised to contact him if they got word about Josie, and obviously he'd assumed her call was good news. But it so wasn't. She tried not to think about Father refusing to pay.

She stared at the window, but no longer saw the garden beyond. Instead, playing there as if upon a screen: images of Josie tied up in a dark room and crying.

The movie ended when she heard footsteps closing, and a voice say, 'Answer, you dick.' It was the foul male detective constable, Nabi. He stopped a few feet away, just around the corner, and she listened to him moaning about the person he was calling not picking up the phone. Another voice, even his, made it easier to dispel those vile images from her skull.

She was beginning to calm down, but then she overheard Nabi say, 'Ah, hello. I called a few minutes ago. Someone said you'd have an ETA on a cadaver dog. Detective Constable Zesh Nabi, down here in—'

'Cadaver dogs?' Anna hissed.

He jumped and turned to see her standing just feet from him, as if having appeared out of thin air.

'Dogs trained to find dead people, is that right? You people think my daughter is dead?'

Phone to his ear, Nabi just stared at her, clearly unsure of what to say next. She wanted to hit him but knew he didn't deserve to be the object she vented her anger on. Instead, she punched the wall, once, twice, and would have landed a third blow, but Nabi grabbed her arms, calling out for assistance. She sank to her knees.

CHAPTER FIVE

2.45 a.m.

He's awake before the alarm dings, probably because he spent the previous evening terrified that it would also wake his wife. Fifteen minutes to go. He dresses, and takes his mobile phone from the bedside table, and exits the bedroom. He's nervous as hell about the phone call. He will do it in the living room, because this is not a call his wife can overhear. If she wakes and wonders why he's up, he'll jokingly blame the Devil's Hour, the infiltration of something paranormal into his mind. She might doubt his sanity, but that's better than her knowing the truth…

*

'And who did you call?'

Upon waking, the panic had instantly closed around him like a fog. A small woman had tried to hold him down, but he'd fought like any caged animal fearing pain, desperate to rip away the tubes filling his blood with poison, and it had taken the additional input of a large man to finally subdue him. He had been aware of his voice, somewhat disconnected from his brain, screaming, *Who the hell are you?*

'A friend called Fitch Angeles. For a job.'

'A job? Explain, please,' the woman called Detective Chief Inspector Lucy Miller said.

The small woman had been trying to soothe him with soft words, long sentences, but nothing had worked until the large man had yelled one little word right into his ear from an inch away: 'HOSPITAL'.

'I lost my job a couple of weeks ago.' He indicated Anna. 'We had an argument and I was stomping about at work. I nearly dropped heavy piping on to a guy's head. I got let go. I was calling a mate who owns a limo company for a job.'

As if the man's breath had pulsed through his brain like wind and swept away the fog, clarity descended in an instant. Not some madman's laboratory, and not tubing pumping poison. A hospital. His jigsaw memory pieces knit together fast, and as the whole solidified, his body relaxed.

'And you didn't know he'd lost his job?' the male, Detective Sergeant Liam Bennet, asked Anna.

She shook her head, looking horrified.

'You were scared of telling me?' she asked Nick.

He gave a childlike slow nod with his eyes looking anywhere but at her. 'I wanted to get another job before I told you. So you wouldn't worry.'

'You should have told me. It would have been fine. I wouldn't have been angry. So you were going out every day, pretending to work?'

'In America?' the detective cut in. 'You wanted a job in America?'

'The job isn't in America. It's in Nottingham. A bit of a drive, but it would have been a stopgap.'

'That's why your van isn't there,' Anna said, somewhat gleeful about this. She gave the detectives an accusing stare, which confused Nick.

'Yeah, they took it back,' he said. 'Since I always parked it around on the back street, I figured you wouldn't know it wasn't there.'

Bendall Lane lock-up garages, Sheffield Custody Suite, Northern General Hospital – they told it all, filling in the gaps in his memories while he hugged his wife and the hospital staff made sure he was okay. The fog of confusion had been replaced by a storm of anger and depression and regret, but also embarrassment. He wanted to sleep, and he wanted to talk alone with his wife. He wanted to be back home, and he wanted to be out there hunting for Josie. He wanted to curl into an inert ball, and he wanted to pound the world into splinters. But those surrounding him wanted black spots in their own knowledge erased, starting with events seemingly aeons ago, way back in the dead hours…

'Please, Nick, let's go back to the part about America,' Miller said.

'That's where Fitch is at the minute. A business meeting. He was my old pal from school, part of our crew—'

'A biker gang, right?' the DS said.

Nick wasn't sure how they already knew that, but didn't enquire. 'Yeah. I hadn't seen Fitch for years, but I knew he ran a company. Found him on Facebook and messaged him. Said I was after a job. He messaged back and said we should have a chat about it. I didn't want to wait until he got back, and I said I'd call him in America the next day about nine in the evening, when his meetings were over. But 9 p.m. in Washington is about three in the morning over here.'

Anna touched his hand and smiled at him. Right then he understood why she seemed so happy. His addled brain hadn't clicked on, but now he knew: the police had had a theory that he was involved. They weren't just seeking his help here, they were trying to find anomalies that would prove his guilt. But Anna had refused to believe it and his story upheld her claims. She had defended him, despite their rocky times over the last half-year. He squeezed her hand right back and returned her smile.

The detectives were unimpressed by the magical moment between husband and wife. The DS said, 'We confirmed the job loss with your landscaping boss. But we'll be chatting to Fitch

Angeles soon to get his story. So, after your phone call, then what happened?'

2.58 a.m.

He opens the patio door, lights a cigarette, and steps out, and spots movement. Shifting black shapes that paranoia paints as intruders in his garden and then logic tells him that cannot be, surely. In the next millisecond his brain picks a side and he's shouting, 'Who the hell are you?' before he really even realises it.

Except he doesn't. No words come, locked in by shock. But he manages to toss the cigarette at a figure as it rushes towards him. It bounces off the attacker in a mini firework display. He sees the clear shapes of three men in black, one holding what he thinks is a crowbar. The one standing by Josie's bedroom window.

Nick's phone is still in his hand, fresh from his good news call to a pal, and he lifts it, ready to call the police. But the approaching shape hasn't ceased moving.

He doesn't remember the blow, but a strike certainly occurred because in the next moment he's on the wet ground and his head is throbbing. He's staring up at the patio door, at rain pelting towards him. At a black figure standing over him, towering high, seemingly deep into the black sky.

Josie.

The figure bends, something in its hand, aiming at his face. He turns his head away, wanting to save his eyes, and feels the sharp jab in his neck. A knife for sure. The black of the world deepens, but just before it becomes absolute his eyes see another figure. At Josie's window, seemingly just waiting there.

The window opens from the inside, a black-clad arm attached to the handle.

*

'Did you recognise any of the men?'

'Masked. They were masked. Balaclavas maybe.' He put his face in his hands, made a moan as his tense fingers gouged into his stitched head wound, and then slapped the bed. 'Early bloody Christmas for them. I opened the door. Let them just walk right in.'

No sympathy in the faces watching him. From the DS: 'The man at Josie's window. Are you saying they passed Josie out through her window, even though the patio door was open?'

Nick's head still swam. He said nothing.

The DCI said, 'Nick, my friend, any chance one of those men was actually a woman?'

Anna looked at her, puzzled.

He wanted to ask why, but the line *Who the hell are you?* continued to bounce around in his brain. But neither was what found its way out of his mouth.

'This is down to her dad.'

The detectives glanced at Anna. She was at the back of the room and he looked at her and wanted to apologise for what he'd just said. But that didn't come out of his mouth, either.

'I checked up my arse earlier and I don't have a stash of money up there.'

He grabbed and squeezed his chin, as if punishing his errant mouth. The drug he'd been injected with, that was the cause, and they'd know that, right? Anna would know that. Despite the way she hung her head, clearly hurt by seeing him this way, or by the accusation he'd just laid down about her father, she'd know he wasn't in control of what his brain wanted to say. Right?

'What do you mean?' the DS said. 'How did you know this was about money? And why do you think this is about Anna's father?'

He saw that everyone was giving him a suspicious look, as if he'd done something wrong. But he couldn't work out what. 'What else would it be about? I'm not the prime minister, I can't be blackmailed into starting a war.'

That got puzzled looks. The consultant stepped in here, announcing that he didn't think this interview should continue just yet. His patient was still suffering the effects of—

'Of course it's about him,' Nick snapped, one hand raised to warn the doctor to keep away. And this time he wasn't appalled by the words that slipped out unbidden. This time what he'd said made sense. 'He's always promoting his businesses on Facebook. He put his page from a companies' index website on there, didn't he? With his account finances, just to show off how much he's got. Trying to make people jealous. All he did was make people want some. Now they're going to get it, aren't they? And he'll pay. He won't buy us a new dryer, will he? But he'll pay this for Josie, I tell you now. I tell you now.'

He saw Anna scuttle towards the door and he called her name, loaded with a pleading tone. She stopped. But she didn't look at him. And then she was eclipsed by the tall detective sergeant, Bennet, who stepped into Nick's line of sight.

'You're right, Nick. These people do want money. Your wife called her dad to tell him. He's just called me because her phone was off. He's already agreed to pay the money. They've asked for fifty thousand. My question to you is, do you think Josie was taken in order to force Mr Middleton to pay up?'

'Who the hell are you?'

That got him disappointed looks and another plea by the consultant. But this time the DCI held up a hand to stop the guy.

'Just a moment, please. Nick, what made you say that about Anna's father? Has he received any threats? In recent days? Have you?'

'Anna, can I see you? Can you come here?'

'Just a moment, dear,' she said to Anna. 'Nick, please. Do you know of anyone who's shown interest in your father-in-law's finances?'

'Anna!'

But he saw the door open and beyond the big detective saw her slip out. The DS turned to watch, then put his attention right back on Nick.

'Give her a moment. She's got a lot to process tonight. So, from your garden to a lock-up garage in the city centre…'

*

Black with them closed, and black when he opened his eyes again. The pain in his head told him he wasn't dreaming. Cold all along his left side, which ceased when he rolled over. Now, he saw light in a thin strip and crawled towards it. A metal door, which rumbled when he hit it head first. His head was still swimming, and he failed to stand. But there was nothing wrong with the power in his muscles. His fingers scraped along the floor, dug into a gap between it and the sharp bottom of the door, and lifted. A roller shutter, which ground its way up slowly. Light crawled in and he crawled out.

He found himself on gravel beside a road. A lock-up garage. Similar garages ran away left and right, and ahead, far side of the road, was a tall hedge before a wide and tall brick building. High up on that building was a sign that said, NEXT. Clothing store, he realised. But he had no idea where he was.

'Who the hell are you?' he said. His eyes flicked left and right, as if seeking the source of his brain's cry, as if part of him had registered a danger the rest wasn't aware of. No one around, though.

Three men flickered into existence and the concrete beneath him changed to grass. But a moment later men and grass were gone. He got to his feet and it happened again. Like a subliminal image in a film reel, grass instantly sprouted under his feet and black-clad men materialised. Just for a flash of a second. He remembered them, he realised.

'Who the hell are you?' he shouted. But the men had gone.

He started to stagger. The open street once again turned into his back garden and three men in black appeared to block his way. They rushed him, but this time they winked out of existence just as one was swinging something at his head. Still, he jerked back, one arm up to defend himself.

Then he remembered Josie. Poor Josie. Her window, opened by one of the men. Poor Josie, gone. They had taken her. He dropped to his knees on the gravel and stinging pain knocked the cobwebs away.

A scraping noise turned his head. Other side of the road, by the hedge, a man and a woman were quickly walking by. They seemed not to have noticed him. He opened his mouth to yell for help—

'Who the hell are you?' he shouted instead. Their pace quickened, and they didn't look at him. He tried to approach, but his legs gave way and he tumbled.

'Who the hell are you?'

The man and woman scuttled past and away. Before he went out again, he heard one of them, probably on a phone, asking for the police.

*

'And that's the last thing you remember?' a voice said. He turned, seeking the source, but saw nothing. 'Until the police found you stumbling along?'

It took him a moment to realise his mind had mixed some kind of present/past cocktail. The tall detective sergeant was standing close, looking very much like a guy awaiting an answer. Nick just nodded.

'Nothing in between? All black from the moment you were knocked unconscious and drugged, until the point where you woke up in the garage?'

Nick knew his pause aroused suspicion. When he shook his head, eyes averted, he expected someone to challenge his memory. But nobody got the chance because the door bashed open.

Anna was in the doorway, red-faced from tears. He felt awful knowing that she'd been crying out there somewhere, doubtless about his attack on her father, while he recounted his hazy tale. He wanted to apologise, but kept his mouth clamped shut because it couldn't be trusted while remnants of that damn horse drug still rampaged through his veins.

'I want a moment alone with my husband,' she said.

Nick expected refusal, but the DCI ordered her people out of the room. The doctor wasn't her employee and Anna had to ask him. Twice. When they were alone, she sat close by him and the distress on her face made him realise something that had eluded his cloudy head: he hadn't considered what had happened to her. They'd told him the basic facts of the night, but not what she'd been through; how she'd learned he and Josie were missing, or what turmoil she felt. Her night had probably been just as bad as his and they'd both suffered alone. He took her hand and knew he had to risk words.

But she didn't answer his question of what had happened. Instead, she said, 'About my dad…'

He squeezed her hand harder. 'I'm sorry about saying your dad was to blame. I'm just… messed up.'

'Maybe not.'

'What do you mean?'

'Father has already said he'll put up the money. Maybe that was the plan.'

Now he understood why she'd fled the room. His claim had struck a nerve. Understandably, because they didn't have anything close to £50,000 and her father did. So his claim didn't provoke any ideas other people hadn't already had. But he tried to backtrack:

'Maybe it was our house. It's a nice bungalow. Maybe someone came along and saw Josie playing in the garden and figured we had money. They wouldn't know the house was a gift. Josie might not have been taken because of your dad. Just a random thing.'

Because she saw the empty conviction in his eyes? Whatever, she was shaking her head. 'She was taken from her bedroom. This was planned. And you're right, we don't have money. Father does. But I don't get it. Why not take me or take Jane? Why a little girl from her bedroom? Anyone could have got to me out on the street. Much easier.'

Because subterfuge was unnecessary now, he felt all the anger coming back. 'Big, fully grown adults? Harder to control, more likely to escape or remember faces. Josie is five and they can manipulate her more. And she's smaller, so there's not such a big hole to dig to bury—'

She yanked her hand away from his with force and tense fingers, so that her nails clawed him. 'Don't say that! Josie is coming home to me today. Understand?'

He rubbed his uncontrollable head and nodded. But he still wanted to rage. He wanted to smash something. He'd never had a child kidnapped before, so maybe this was a natural reaction. Maybe it was just the drug. Maybe he felt impotent, unable to help his daughter from this hospital bed. Maybe this was all a damn nightmare and he'd wake the night before he nearly killed a pal with a stone pipe.

He closed his eyes to lock in tears he felt trying to escape. He would rest his brain, settle his mind, hope that both would reorient soon. He expected Anna to get off the bed and leave, but she remained there. And her hand found his again. That was the woman he loved, he remembered: she of bottomless compassion, who despite being absolutely overwhelmed with grief for Josie, had still found room to think about tending to her husband.

He squeezed back hard, and decided he would unleash building rage and hate no more. He would save and store every ounce that knit inside him, and gift wrap it for the man who had Josie.

*

When the door opened and Miller walked in, Anna realised she'd lost track of time while gripped by terrible thoughts. A glance at the clock showed only seven or eight minutes had passed. Nick was asleep.

'Anna, dear, it's time to leave. The consultant, though, he wants your man to agree to see an addiction psychiatrist before we leave.'

Addiction psychiatrist? Anna realised Miller must have spun a lie to the A&E staff, or just refused to explain how Nick had overdosed and why he had such a big and official entourage. She wasn't sure how she felt about that.

'He's okay to leave? They said that?' She looked at him. He seemed at peace and she hoped the sleep would clear his head. 'He won't have a... a relapse or whatever?'

'They said he can leave,' was the ambiguous response. 'The psychiatrist will have a quick word, then we're heading out the back way. Police presence here – big gossip. Nobody knows about the kidnap and we kept schtum about what actually happened to your man. The consultant is sworn to secrecy. I need you to do the same if you're asked. We can't have word leaking out. We don't know if any of the kidnappers might be in the building. His overdose of ketamine was accidental, okay?'

'They might be here?' Anna said, shocked. 'Have you looked at cars outside?' She stood up, suddenly buoyed by the notion that Josie could be nearby. Nick had a death grip that Anna needed her other hand to break. It woke him up.

'Oh, dear, don't think like that. Just a precaution, that's all. I've got people out there, just in case, but please don't think it's likely. We should get you back to your home, okay?'

Moments earlier the idea of going home hadn't appealed. The hospital crowd somehow helped with the pain and the house had seemed like a big old reminder of tragedy, like footprints at a cliff edge. But now she was suddenly eager to get home. It was Josie's home and being away emphasised their separation. She wanted to see Josie's toys, her photographs, touch the lock of hair they kept in a vase and to stand in her room and inhale her smell.

But Anna remembered something she'd overheard Bennet saying to another detective earlier. 'You want to move us to a hotel, I understand. To avoid the neighbours.'

Miller shook her head. 'No, no, no. That was my superintendent's idea, but I said no. He was worried about growing public interest. I said we can keep a lid on that, dear. You and your family, well, you need a comfortable place. You need to be at home.'

'And the people who have my daughter will be calling there. They expect us there. We can't give them surprises.'

Miller nodded slowly and gave Anna a comforting smile.

'I dreamed Josie got kidnapped,' Nick said. Both women stared at him. He looked from one to the other, and then around the room, as if he'd never seen it before. Anna's stomach lurched as an old memory surfaced: her grandmother, riddled with dementia, asking where her beloved dog was and having to be reminded, almost weekly, that the animal had died months before. She was horrified at the prospect of having to inform Nick all over again that his daughter had been kidnapped. Sensing this, Miller put a hand on her shoulder.

But he rubbed his left eye and added: 'And the kidnappers would only release her if I got on all the newspaper front pages for a crime the next morning.'

Anna took his hand again in relief. Miller turned for the door.

'I'll bring the psychiatrist in. And I'll get Nick's clothing. And then we'll get you guys home.'

Half an hour later, Nick was dressed in fresh clothing someone had found and had a handful of drug-help leaflets. They took a locked staff staircase down and into a section of the hospital patients never saw, and through a keycard door leading to a fenced car park. Anna felt like a hated criminal being protected from an angry public as she was escorted to trial.

*

'You asked if one of them could be a woman. Why?'

After all that had happened, and after being parted from Nick in such circumstances, the last thing she wanted was to be split from him again. But the police needed Anna back home in case the kidnappers called, and they needed Nick at the police station to officially be told 'No Further Action' and released. So off he went with Bennet in a panda, while she rode with Miller. In the back seat, because she wanted at least to be able to pretend to be alone so she could think. But she only managed a few minutes before something ethereal that had been niggling at her grew flesh.

Miller didn't look round, but said, 'We're just trying to cover all angles, dear.'

'So this isn't something from your Recogniser days?'

Now Miller turned in her seat, the question in the furrow of her eyebrows.

'I googled you while I waited to see Nick. You knew Nick wasn't the caller as soon as you heard the voice. But did you recognise it?'

Internet research on the captivating woman leading the hunt for her daughter had intrigued Anna. Forty-four, never married, no children, a career woman as long as she'd been of an age to watch any classification of movie. Gloucester Constabulary at eighteen, Ministry of Defence Police Marine Unit at twenty-two. At thirty, she transferred back to Gloucester Constabulary and into detective status, rising to chief inspector. Then, in 2016, she was headhunted by Scotland Yard's Super Recogniser Unit, a new and groundbreaking and unique team composed of officers with an uncanny ability to recognise faces based on part-obscured or grainy images. Eight months there before a desire to return to major crime investigation propelled her into a DCI role with South Yorkshire Police, on whose website Anna had found this information. In her time with Scotland Yard, she showed an ability to recognise voices, not just faces.

'I'd already heard Nick's voice. An old voicemail message on your landline. But I've not heard the other voice before,' she answered. 'But I know it was a woman doing a very good impression of a man.'

'A woman?' Perhaps the biggest shock of all. She didn't know how to feel about that. At first, there was a sliver of relief, because surely a woman would be less likely to harm Josie. But she quickly lost that hope. 'Why would she pretend to be a man?'

Miller said, 'Apologies on that one. Unsure. But I know accents, you see. She tried to hide it, but I got a weeny hint of a place.' She paused before adding, 'Sunderland.'

Of course, she'd heard Nick's terrible tale of multiple attackers, but hearing it from someone clear-headed and wise added irrefutable weight. Somehow, things had just taken a turn for the worse. 'I don't know anyone from Sunderland. I don't think Nick does. What does it mean? I can't…'

'Oh, don't you worry, we're looking into it and I'll get the recording checked out by a specialist. But it might come to nothing, dear, so, please, don't think anything of it unless I tell you otherwise. I wouldn't have said if you hadn't asked. Okay with that?'

She wasn't. 'But what if you're wrong? Do you know what city for sure? What if it's not this place you think and you look there and end up missing them? If you're wrong, Josie won't…' She couldn't say it. But she forced herself to be optimistic. Miller had been headhunted for her linguistic skill, and she'd said Sunderland.

Sunderland. Where Nick's van, driven by another, had been clocked by ANPR yesterday.

*

They used the dead-end back street where Nick had parked his van, but they didn't avoid all eyes. Anna spotted neighbours at windows, including at number 18, where the woman who'd called the police lived. Just before they'd left the hospital, Miller had told her that the home phone had received three calls from the six friends Anna had called. Jane had spun these people a story based on her own initial theory: Josie had hurt her leg falling out of bed and Nick had taken her to the hospital, but both were okay and on their way home. They'd tried Anna's phone first, but she'd been instructed not to answer because she would fail to keep stress out of her voice. Miller had had to post a plain-clothes man on their street with the sole task of having a quiet word with any neighbours who tried to approach the house. So far, so good, but even this tactic had to remain shadowy and, alas, Anna might need to answer the door with a lie of her own if word continued to diffuse. But she wasn't thinking that far ahead.

Miller shut off the engine and stretched.

'You should sleep,' Anna said. 'I heard Mr Bennet say your team was working all night on a case. Delegate tasks or something and use my bed.'

Miller gave her a smile in the rear-view, below groggy eyes. 'True, but we're on-call this week and we sleep when we can. Like cats. The team got to go home and kip in the afternoon.'

Anna got out. She noticed a small van parked outside her back fence that said, K9 WONDERS, with a picture of a dog in mid-run. A guy in blue coveralls with the same name on the back was leaning against his ride and smoking a thin cigar. Any other day, it would have appeared to be a company that groomed dogs for their posh owners. Not today. Someone had told her that South Yorkshire Police had only a handful of Victim Recovery Dogs and if none were available they used private companies. But in the hospital, the foul detective, Nabi, had used another term.

'Cadaver dogs,' she said as Miller exited the vehicle.

Noting Anna's interest in the van, she quickly suggested they moved to avoid the neighbours. At her back gate, Anna stopped. Her eyes were on the garden, portions of which had been taped off using sticks driven into the soil, like little plots for planting bulbs. She hadn't noticed while it was dark, but the police had cordoned off places where they'd found footprints, and that was good. It meant they were trying to identify unknown abductors.

'Forensics think they've isolated more than one set of footprints made since the rain started. Three, at least. That goes some way to confirming your man's story,' Miller said.

That wasn't any sort of good news, because she'd never doubted Nick's innocence. But the evidence plots weren't what had caught her attention. It was the K9 guy. She looked at him again. Why was he just standing there, waiting, instead of out with his dog, searching old barns or whatever?

Miller said, 'Please, dear, let's get inside.'

Anna didn't move. Miller clearly didn't want Anna to dwell on the K9 guy, who was watching them. Then she made a connection. 'He's not here to search old barns or whatever, is he?'

'Please, Anna, we should go in.'

'He's been searching my house, hasn't he? For blood or whatever. For signs that Josie was hurt there. You still think we had something to do with hurting her. That her kidnap is a lie.'

Miller objected, but Anna tried to tune her out. A police car turned on to the street and they watched it approach. Anna was surprised to see Nick exit it. He did so slowly, still not out of his ketamine funk.

'I called the station to do the release,' Bennet said as he got out and told the driver to depart. 'No need to take Mr Carter all the way there for a signature. There were no belongings to collect.'

Anna looked at the way Miller nodded and didn't believe a word of it. Only now did it make sense why they'd said Nick needed to be processed at a police station. They had wanted to keep the couple separated during the drive home, maybe so they couldn't confer. Despite the fact that Nick had clearly been a victim, they still had suspicions.

She pushed ahead of everyone else to get inside first. While hauling the patio door open, she jumped as someone inside yanked the curtain open. It was her father, and behind him, standing by the sofa, was Jane, who had a mug of tea. From this angle she could see into the dining area, where a number of the bit players lurked and had created a NASA-like control centre with their laptops. They were all watching her, so she stepped to her left to kill their line of sight.

'Why isn't that man handcuffed?' Middleton said, staring over her shoulder in absolute shock.

'Dad, don't. I'm not in the mood.'

Middleton grunted his displeasure and turned away. 'These detectives have been questioning *me* about my past now. Who I know who could have done this. What's that all about, Anna?'

'Father, please,' Jane said from somewhere behind him. 'Until we know, we don't know anything, do we? They've asked me, too. Whoever it is and whatever their connection to us, that's hardly our fault, is it?'

Middleton moved to a wall, probably to make sure there was space between him and Nick. Anna stepped inside and was immediately grabbed in a tight hug by Jane. Nick entered with Miller and Bennet close behind and Jane somehow knew it was him. He got the same squashing hug. Middleton glared at everyone but kept silent. Jane traced a shape on Nick's cheek and over his chin with her finger.

'It means everything will be okay.'

He couldn't read Braille and he didn't know this secret language of the sisters, either. So he gave her a thumbs up and pressed it against her arm so she could feel the shape. She understood because she gave her own thumbs up.

'Except that the police still doubt it's a kidnapping,' Anna said. Everyone looked at her. 'They want to bring in a dog to search the house for signs of Josie's blood. In case the kidnapping story is a lie and really we killed her.'

Middleton and Jane voiced their shock, but were washed out by Nick as he spun on the detectives and roared, 'What?'

Miller stepped forward. 'Nick, no, that's not right. We don't—'

'That dog van outside, is that it? You want to bring a damn dog in to search for blood? Okay, I'll help you.'

Miller started to object, but Nick ran over to the living room doorway and stamped on the carpet. Everyone else watched, shocked. 'Here, the carpet gripper. Let it sniff there. Josie cut her knees crawling around three years ago.'

'Nick, calm down,' Bennet said, 'because you've got this—'

Nick approached the fireplace. 'Or did we bash her head in right here? I guess you'll soon know. And don't forget the cellar. Actually, maybe we cut her up in the bath.'

'Nick!' Anna yelled. 'Don't you dare say such things.'

Nick jerked as if he'd been slapped. He took a step towards Anna, but stopped when she dropped on to the sofa, crying. Jane sat with her.

'The superintendent sent the search dogs,' Bennet said. He looked at both Carters, back and forth, as he spoke. 'But DCI Miller objected. It's protocol, but she said no. We trust you. Normally we'd have all of you out of here and down the station so a whole team could come in and search this place. But we didn't, and we won't. The dog handler isn't being allowed inside. We know you didn't hurt your daughter.'

Nick took another step towards his wife, but she didn't look at him. 'Anna?'

Still she refused to look up. He rubbed his forehead, looked at every shocked face watching him, and then quickly strode from the room.

Miller sat on Anna's free side, but said nothing. That made it worse for Anna, who looked at her and mouthed: *I'm sorry*.

The DCI took her hand and shook her head. 'Don't you apologise. Okay? Not for anything, dear. Nothing you do while Josie is missing requires any kind of apology. I'm sorry, me, because the dog handler should have been gone. I don't know why he's still outside. You weren't supposed to see him. And you'll never see that face again.'

'Like Josie's, then,' Anna moaned.

*

Nick needed a drink. In the kitchen, he opened a high cupboard full of cereals, but he wasn't after cornflakes. From a bottle hidden behind the boxes, he poured a big dose of Jim Beam into a plastic beaker.

'Drugs and alcohol?'

Nick turned to see DS Bennet in the doorway, watching.

'The alcohol is my choice, at least.'

'Don't you need to be clear-headed for what's coming?'

'And what's coming? Viewing my daughter's body at the morgue? Watching your dog search for her body under the floorboards?' He snatched up a large knife from the counter.

'Put that down right now,' the DS ordered. His stance changed slightly, as if readying for an attack. Nick tossed the knife into the sink and the DS added: 'Protocol, remember? Imagine if a week from now you admitted Josie was under the floorboards and that we didn't even search the house. Remember also that I said we're not using the dog. And what's coming are things you need to be clear-headed for. Step away from that sink, please.'

Nick spat the alcohol into the sink. 'Gotcha. A in that police ABC mantra, eh? A: accept nothing. Your wife must find life one long party.'

He almost upended the bottle's contents down the plughole, too, but stopped himself. He put the top back on. And backed out of arm's reach of the whiskey-soaked weapon.

'It's for celebrating good news, anyway,' he said, meaning the whiskey. Meaning he still might have the chance to celebrate.

'Why was the bottle hidden? Do you have a drink problem you're hiding from your wife?'

'What are you, a detective or something?'

Bennet's phone beeped the arrival of a text message. He quickly read it and lost the device. 'Then hopefully we can all have a good news nip very soon,' he said. 'Now, can we go into your daughter's room, and you can run me through your story again?'

'Looking for holes in it?' Nick said as he slapped the bottle down on the worktop and slid it away.

'I'll understand the story better if you tell it here at the scene. Maybe it'll help your memory, too.'

'What's that supposed to mean? You think I gave you a line? Ah, wait. C: challenge everything.'

'Maybe you missed some things. Your head is clearer now.'

'Like what?'

'Only you could know that. Maybe something that happened in the long black zone in your head between when you were knocked out and woke up in a garage.'

The DS's glare confirmed it: the police knew that Nick had fudged his tale a little. He did remember something from that black zone. Unable to meet the police officer's gaze, he looked at a framed picture above the microwave oven: a quote, from author Josh Jameson, about those moments in life when one needed to turn the page rather than close the book. Nick felt this book trying to close itself.

In Josie's room, he sat against the wall facing the bed and Bennet sat on the mattress. Nick glanced down, under the bed, then away.

'Just before we do the story, Nick, let's see if your long-term memory is better. Enemies.'

'You asked me that in the car. No enemies.'

'The people who took your daughter away from you said you had to pay your dues. You. Sounds personal. Doesn't have to be someone you know. Someone you annoyed. Cut anyone up on the road recently?'

'You told me already. Look, anyone I pissed off recently, I didn't give them my name and address, okay?'

'How about your job? You do gardens. Easy to trace you through a business. Anyone unhappy with the finished product?'

'Now and then. Bit extreme, don't you think?'

'I could tell you my snowball story, which I use at times like this. Tell me about the latest unhappy garden fanatic.'

'She was about eighty years old.'

'Prison is full of vicious young thugs with eighty-year-old grandmothers they love dearly.'

'Look, Detective Bennet, I keep to myself and I'm nice and sweet on days when my daughter hasn't been kidnapped. No enemies. No one pissed off enough to do this. This is about money and they know Anna's dad has enough to spare.'

'Anyone at all you've had recent contact with, even if it didn't seem as if you got on their wrong side?'

Nick sighed. 'Couple of weeks back, a guy a street over had to brake coming out his garden because he didn't see my van. A corner shop owner in Mexborough accused me of buying alcohol for teenagers hanging around outside. Some girl the other day knocked on the door and tried to get me to buy organic pizzas. You want to chase these people? Like I said before, someone has done this because they want money and know Anna's dad has enough to spare.'

Bennet nodded. 'Okay, Nick. Seems your memory is back nice and fine. So let's run through the story again, if you don't mind.'

'Fine. But is there a point to me retelling this? After all, you guys swear by your B: believe no one.'

*

After the story was told, again, Nick found Anna in the playroom. She was at the painting table with her back to him and didn't turn when he entered. But she knew he was there.

'I hoped this time of day might be easiest. Because Josie's usually at school. So she's not normally here anyway. But for some reason it's worse.'

Nick took the seat opposite. He didn't know what to say, and it wasn't just because of the nightmare they shared. This was the first time in a long time that they'd been alone together in a place with no distractions like a TV or a road to watch or a five-year-old backing vocalist. He was still thinking about taking a bellyful of whiskey and it influenced what popped into his head:

'I hope they're feeding her.'

His line teased a sensitive nerve because the left side of Anna's face twitched. She tried to rub the feeling away. Done, her fingers crawled to her raw neck, but didn't scratch the scaly rash. 'We need a holiday when she gets back. All of us.'

'They won't know she's got a milk allergy, though.' He felt anger rising. 'They could have at least taken her damn soy milk with them.'

He reached out to trace his finger across the sun on Josie's latest drawing. Anna's hand laid atop his.

'It's July, but she misses the snow already. We could go to Iceland. Josie would love the rocket ship church, and the Blue Lagoon.'

The picture was the usual suspect: dodgy-looking line house with a spiky sun and stick family far too big for the thin garden path. Nick's form was bigger than the others, because he was Josie's giant dad, the superhero, but the perspective made it appear as if his stick representation was ahead of Anna and Josie, closer than the house. Further from it. Parted from them. As if walking away. Going to work, Josie had said, and she'd called it BUSY DAY, but that wasn't how Nick saw it now. He chose to believe Josie had painted him apart from the others because she had sensed the breakdown between her parents.

There was a beep from his pocket. He registered the single beep by his expression, but made no move to take the item out of his pocket because Anna was watching him.

She didn't miss a thing, though: 'Is that a phone?'

'Back in a minute.' He went out and slipped into the bathroom, unseen, and locked the door and pulled out the phone.

It was time to do this.

CHAPTER SIX

She managed three minutes, but by then there was more worry than curiosity. Anna stepped out into the hallway but didn't see Nick. She could hear voices from the bedroom and the living room. But not Nick's.

Nabi said, 'I think HOLMES is a bit silly. I mean the name. HOLMES, with L for large and M for major. Large major enquiry?'

'It's a major enquiry, and it's a large one,' someone replied. It sounded like the young pregnant detective, Hicks.

She noticed the bathroom door was shut.

'Murder cases are all large, and major means big. So it's like saying a large big enquiry.'

'What I mean, fool, is that it's a major enquiry, but it's the system that's large. Large system for major enquiries.'

'You just thought of that. That's not what you said.'

Anna realised they were discussing the name of the police computer database. They would have used that, of course. Fed in information, or however it worked, with a hope of finding who took Josie. She went to the bathroom door and tried it. Locked.

DC Hicks said, 'HOLMES, though, is from Sherlock Holmes. They had to cover the L and the M in the acronym. With no L it sounds like an estate agent's system.'

Nabi's reply was: 'But it's a police system, so we're hardly going to get confused. Anyway, they should have done SHERLOCK, which sounds better.'

Anna knocked on the door. 'Nick? You okay?'

No answer. Nick would have responded, so there was probably a police officer in there. She was about to make sure with a louder knock when there was a burst of laughter from the living room. A moment of mirth highlighted her utter distress and it dug right under her skin. She banged the living room door open.

Nobody in the living room, but through the room divider she saw them in their little NASA control room. As guessed: Hicks and Nabi and three others, one of whom was a new face, all sitting around her dining table like Sunday afternoon dinner guests. She stepped up to the gap at the end. Hicks had a pained face and was rubbing one side of her bloated belly. Anna opened her mouth to shout at them – if Miller had ordered her people to stay in their little sanctuary to give Anna peace, it surely included not filling the house with their mundane chatter – but the anger quickly subsided. She was tired of anger on top of pain. The moment the detectives spotted her, she spoke.

'I find it hard to picture Josie smiling in my head. Does that sound normal?'

The new face was caught halfway standing, as if to introduce himself. Everyone just stared at her.

'The last thing I said to her before she went to bed… it was something bad. I told her off because she was being naughty. I last saw my little lady with a grumpy face, and now it's the only face I can picture when I think of her. She said to me, you don't love me. But I just left the room without speaking. What if I never get another chance to tell her I love her?'

Nabi didn't seem to care, but Hicks got up and approached.

'Don't think like that,' she said, standing close. 'She's coming back to you, and very soon.'

When the detective took her into a hug, Anna couldn't stop a deluge of tears. She had sought a reaction, that was all, but hearing the words aloud drove their potency home. What if she never again got the chance to speak to her little lady? What if there was a dead spot in her mind, like a scratch on a vinyl record, and she was never again able to imagine Josie smiling?

What if... 'She thinks she's been taken from her mum and dad as punishment for being naughty?'

Before the detective could answer, they heard the front door close, and then a shout from another room, by Miller: 'Did someone just leave the house?'

No one from the living room. As if an alarm had sounded, and with more haste than anyone had moved when her five-year-old vanished, they jumped into action. By the time Anna got to the front door, five detectives were already in the garden, staring off to the right. Miller ordered them out of sight, quickly. As they retreated into the house, Anna saw her own car bolting down the road. Nick.

She remembered thinking he'd had a phone. Had he got a message, or a call, while in the bathroom? But Nick had claimed his phone was taken by the kidnappers.

*

She ran into Josie's room and Bennet appeared just as she knelt by her daughter's bed and lifted the end of a cable that ran under the frame and into a wall socket.

'Was there a phone plugged in there? Has Nick got a phone?'

'Yes. Josie's. An old one we let her have. For Tetris when she can't sleep.' And it had been there earlier, when she'd retrieved Nick's birthday present to her.

'Does it have credit, is it active? Was it here this morning?'

'I don't know. Probably. Why? Yes, it had a couple of pounds left over from a top-up ages ago.'

He cursed and rushed from the room. She heard him bellow that Nick might have made a phone call. Then he was back, wanting Josie's number so they could trace the call. Then she heard her father's voice.

'I knew it. He's gone to meet his accomplices. How did you let him out? Didn't you hear the car start? Ten police officers in this tiny house and he got out.'

Someone urged him to calm down. She heard more footsteps, and then various voices, all urgent. So much noise, adding to the pain. She ran to the door and shoved it shut with a bang.

Accomplices… couldn't be… could it? But… the Sunderland connection… No, no, Nick must be out searching for Josie. Maybe he had a clue. Maybe he had remembered something, something about the kidnappers who attacked him. Perhaps one had worn an item of clothing with a badge or a logo identifying a place of work. Yes, that was it: over the effects of the drug, Nick now had a clue and was pursuing it alone because the police didn't like vigilantes. He was doing something proactive to get back his daughter. She cursed herself for doubting him – again.

She pulled out her mobile and dialled Josie's number from memory. The call went to voicemail and she heard a fumbled message from her daughter, reading from a script that Nick had written. Hearing her little lady's voice cut her deep. But she didn't hear Nick's voice, because he didn't answer. As she hung up, Jane crashed through the door.

'Annie, you here?' Her head twitched in Anna's direction as she heard the beep of dialled numbers. 'Where's Nick going, Annie?'

This time Anna wasn't trying to reach Nick. She just wanted to hear Josie's recorded voice again.

*

Nabi was sent in pursuit, but Nick had gone east, and within ten seconds of the house by car was an X-junction. It took him ten more to pull his phone and dial a number, so within a minute, all told, Miller knew that Nick had vanished. Then she got a radio call from base: Lowth and Adams, the officers who'd responded to the 999 call that started everything, had just called in to say they'd seen the Carters' car leaving the area and were wondering if it had been authorised. *No* got bounced from base to patrol car and soon Nick had a tail. But only a tail, Miller ordered. 'Don't stop him. No arrest. Keep me updated on your location.' Her father questioned this, and it was Jane who had the answer: they wanted to see if Nick led the police to Josie. Anna leaned against a wall in the living room, far from the mass crowding Miller and her radio, and dared to hope this nightmare could be winding down.

'Junction of Meadow Street,' the responders finally announced. *'Corsa's pulled on to the kerb outside the Early Language Teaching Centre.'*

'Who does he know at that place?' Miller asked. She looked at all three family members in turn, and three heads shook.

'He's waiting outside.'

Numerous eyes bored into the radio in Miller's hand.

'IC1 male just exited. Both men in the car now. Heading northeast on Meadow again.'

Nick had just met someone? Someone he'd planned to meet, using Josie's phone? What did that mean?

Bennet was on his phone and he reported to Miller: 'You can order those responders away now. Second unit, plain clothes. Got him in sight.'

Miller told the responders to back off. 'Who's the new guy?'

Bennet told the room that an off-duty constable had been giving a lift home to a female mugging victim after his shift when he heard the radio call to base. Nearby, he swung in for a nosey, clocked the Corsa, started following. He was in contact with base by mobile.

'Get him to call me.'

Bennet relayed that order and Miller's mobile rang a minute later. She introduced herself, asked the caller's name and location. She put her phone on speaker and laid it on the coffee table.

'Just tailed the Corsa east off the roundabout, four hundred metres along the A61. He's… yeah, just taken a left.'

'The driver isn't to be stopped. And don't get spotted. Keep reporting.'

'He's at Kelham Island, approaching the Fat Cat pub.'

Bennet announced that he'd contacted another two teams of responders, now en route, moments away. Two cars, four officers.

'Stopped outside a residential block near the Fat Cat. I've pulled in a hundred metres back. No movement, though. He's just sitting there. There's a guy in the passenger seat.'

'Who does Nick know there? That area of the Kelham Island Quarter is an industrial zone. He's picked someone up and now he seems to be awaiting something. What's he doing there?'

Because of Miller's alien abrupt tone, it took Anna a moment to realise she was the target of those questions. Her answer to all: *I don't know.* But her hopes that Josie could be found very soon were rising.

'Some kind of works pick-up truck just arrived. Turning in. Yeah, it's pulled up next to the target car.'

The off-duty guy relayed the registration, and Bennet hauled his radio to get on to base for a trace. Everyone waited. A minute in:

'IC1 male exited the pick-up. And a woman's exited the residential block. McDonald's uniform. Now they're all out. Approaching her. Might be this woman… hang on.'

'Nothing outstanding on the pick-up,' Bennet announced. 'Registered to Barker Land and Gardens. Nick's old company. Waiting for info on that address.'

Someone Nick worked with? She felt her heart rate go through the roof. A friend of Nick's, which looked good. He would want people he knew to help if he—

'It's not the woman. They went past her. Inside the block of flats now. Looks like they waited for someone to open the security door.'

Anna pushed away from the wall on legs covered in goosepimples, and took a step closer, towards that phone. If Nick was involved in the kidnap, he wouldn't want Josie to be hurt, or uncomfortable, and so he would want his daughter to be in a nice place – like a flat in a residential block. And he would want to show her a known face here and there. She willed that radio to blast the air with good news.

'Could this really be the end of it?'

That question from Anna turned all heads. Jane moved towards her – 'Annie, please, you shouldn't listen to this, let me take you to the bedroom' – but her reaching hands were pushed away – 'I'm fine. It's okay.'

'Responder teams have just arrived,' Bennet said. 'Ready to go in. I've ordered radios on open.'

'Two pandas just turned in. So this is something big. I'm off-duty, remember, but I want in. Are we taking this guy, or what? Can I ask what he's done?'

Across the radio waves, both mobile and radio, came shouting and thudding footsteps. Someone asked someone if they'd seen three men. Someone shouted, *stairs*. Someone else ordered someone to *damn well get out of the way*. The tinny screech of action sliced into Anna's head like nails on a blackboard. Shouts of *there he is* and *stop* and *that door, go* made her legs feel weak. A door slammed. Someone ordered it kicked open. After that, the symphony of noise became too much to fathom beyond a wild mêlée, like a bar-room rumble. Cops tackling bad guys in a small room. She tried to tell herself that the ruckus constituted an endgame, like the final action scene in a movie, and that she would have Josie back in her arms soon. But when a fragile voice screamed, *Help*, terror overwhelmed her and she fled the room with Jane right behind her.

Anna didn't go for the bedroom, her safe haven, though: she went for the front door. Jane ordered her to stop. When Anna reached for the hook where they hung their keys and remembered that Nick had taken the car, she dropped to her knees and was unable to prevent a flood of despairing tears. Jane hugged her from behind.

'Just for a moment there, I thought… I hoped Nick had taken our Josie.'

'Don't do this to yourself, Annie. Please.'

Anna shrugged her off and got up. Angry – in part with herself for wild hope – she yanked open the door and stepped out. She could feel her neighbours staring through their windows, eager to know what was… 'Going on?' she yelled at the road. 'Do you? Well, everything's fine here. So go back to your TVs.'

'Annie, no, please, come here.'

Jane managed to drag her back inside, but caught her own head on the door and yelped. Anna immediately felt for her and forgot her own anguish. Look at the pain she was causing to those who loved her. She grabbed her sister and hugged hard, and spouted apologies.

'False alarm.'

Both sisters turned their heads at the voice, but only Anna saw the gloom on Miller's face.

'It seems Nick was just following a hunch. What you witnessed was Nick and a pair of friends breaking into the home of someone we've already questioned as a possible suspect. It's over and he's not hurt. No one is.'

If Miller expected joy, she got a shock when Anna made a wailing sound. 'Over?' she yelled. 'Was Josie there?'

Jane tried to soothe her. Miller shook her head. 'Sorry, dear, truly. Josie isn't there. The man in that flat is someone we cleared of involvement quickly. Solid alibi.'

'Then it's not over, is it?'

Strangely, she hated Nick in that moment, for giving her useless hope. For not being the man who took her daughter. Because the nightmare continued. Josie was still missing. And nobody knew where she was.

*

'Thinking? What was I *thinking*? There were nearly thirteen hundred child abductions last year, and most of those were girls for sexual abuse. So have a guess what I was *thinking*?'

Bennet had been sent to collect Nick. No explanation for the responders and the off-duty officer, who'd been left clueless after their prisoner was taken out of handcuffs, out of a police car, and whisked away in the DS's vehicle.

'You're lucky you didn't hit him. I'd feel quite bad arresting someone whose daughter got kidnapped.'

'I haven't hit anyone since I was at college. It was a scare. I just wanted to… I felt someone should talk to this guy, that's all. So I did your job for you.'

'We've already got people looking at all the registered sex offenders in the area.' Bennet watched him in the rear-view mirror. 'It was the first thing we did. This guy was cleared while you were still in the police station. How did you learn about him?'

'Someone outed him at a neighbourhood meeting for something a few months back. Everyone around our way knows about him. And if you people told us more about what you're doing, we wouldn't be out here. But how do you know he's clear?'

'You'll get information as soon as we get it, Nick. But you're waiting on positive news that moves us forward, aren't you? Not useless information like leads that went nowhere. In regard to the man back there, he has no car, no contacts, and every single one of his neighbours blanks him. He gets spat on in the street. It's why he holes himself up in a secure residence. That's the life some of these people live, once they're burned. He was the only one you knew of?'

'That's not proof. Where was he last night? How do you know he hasn't got a prepaid phone hidden?'

'He's on the sex offenders register. Every time there's a report of some child being so much as flashed, we knock on that guy's door. He's been cleared. Trust me.'

Nick scoffed. 'This quick? How many of those sick bastards live within fifty miles of me? There were nearly ten thousand sexual assaults on girls under thirteen in 2018. That's a lot of predators. You cleared them all already?'

'I didn't say that. But that guy's cleared. We're on it, okay? We've been playing at this police lark quite a while and we kind of know what we're doing.'

'How many others are there? Where are they?'

'If you really want to know, call a station about the Disclosure scheme. I'm not about to tell you where these people live so you can go strong-arm every single one of them. What you did was wrong, and you could have got in serious trouble.'

'Yes, that's my biggest worry right now.'

'Nick, all you did was sidetrack everyone for half an hour. And maybe caused some damage. Our door-knocking teams are being very secretive so word doesn't spread, and you might have ruined that if you mentioned a missing child. What did you tell those two work colleagues who helped you?'

'Don't worry. I didn't say my daughter was missing. I told them that sick bastard was spotted hanging around her school and needed to be informed what a bad idea that was.'

'Unfortunately, Nick, I was told you accused your victim of taking her. So your vigilante friends have been arrested and we'll have to keep them at the station for a good part of the day. To maintain their silence. We'll see if you're all still friends afterwards.'

'My new biggest worry, of course.'

'I don't mean to moan at you, Nick. I just want you to let us do our jobs. Now, let's go back to your house and wait for the next phone call. Your father-in-law has the money ready. And gargle some mouthwash or something before you talk to your wife.'

Nick turned his head so he wouldn't breathe more vodka fumes on the detective; he'd swigged from a bottle in the child molester's house, and wasn't even sure why – Dutch courage? He wished he had more. 'And I'm sure her dad's asked if his money will be insured. He'll make us pay it back. What's to stop these people just taking the money and killing my girl? I mean, how many kidnapped kids actually get returned? Are we supposed to just trust them?'

'At the minute, that's all we can do.'

*

When Nick came back into the house, Anna was waiting at the door. They stood awkwardly, as if not sure whether to hug.

'That was risky. Don't do something like that again. I want you here, Nick. You stay with me, okay? We stay with each other until we get Josie back.'

And then you'll kick me out of the house, he wanted to say. But chose instead: 'It's about time someone did something. The police seem to be just sitting around.'

'And attacking child molesters is the way to do things, is it?'

Both of them turned their heads at the intrusive voice. It was DC Nabi, but they couldn't see him. Then the toilet flushed, and he walked out.

'What did you say?' Nick hissed.

But the detective walked away, shaking his head.

'What's his problem?' Nick said.

'I don't know. He doesn't like us. I don't like him being here.'

Nick said he needed water and went into the kitchen. He actually wanted alcohol, but stopped dead when he saw Middleton at the kitchen table, typing something on his BlackBerry while eating a McDonald's burger. Unwilling to back away, he aimed for the sink and got a glass of water. Middleton ignored him until Nick was almost out the door.

'You need to leave this for the police to sort out.'

Not the scolding he'd expected. Reckless, but perhaps his beef with the known paedophile had shown Middleton that he cared deeply about his daughter. Or maybe Middleton sensed that he was still worked up and ready to fight. He continued his journey out of the kitchen.

Bennet was at the living room doorway, also eating a McDonald's burger. He jerked his head: *come in*. Nick entered, but Bennet left. Nobody else in the living room, but through the room divider he could see Anna and Miller sitting at the dining table. He went there. There were three McDonald's bags full of meal trash, as if someone had gone out to fetch food for the detectives.

Miller got out of her chair as he appeared and indicated he should sit. Her eyes were droopy with tiredness. 'It's time I gave you both an update. Sit, please, Nick.'

Nick sat. He suspected that Bennet had relayed Nick's frustration that not enough news was being shared.

'First, we've spoken to your former colleague at Barker Land and Gardens, the one who was driving your old van in Sunderland yesterday afternoon. He's clear, that chap. The Sunderland clue was nothing but a coincidence.'

He simply nodded. Miller stood behind the couple, leaning between them to work the laptop. He caught her body odour.

The laptop showed a map of central England, focussing on Sheffield. Then a switch of Windows displayed a photograph of a littered, pockmarked road, something left to rot, and a grass verge before lock-up garages, one of which was cordoned off by police tape. Nick recognised where the police had found him. As Miller spoke, she cycled through various photographs of the area, some wide, to give perspective, others close, including of the bare interior, and then a close-up of the grass verge out front of it, and a close-up of one side of the metal doorframe.

'Alfredon Lane, near Meadowhall, a couple of miles from here. The lock-up where you were found. Your phone, Nick, it was tracked by a cell tower near these garages not long before that text message was sent, and again not long afterwards. Now, no signal. We found tyre tracks in the grass. Not wide enough to be a van.'

'They swapped vehicles?' Nick said. 'Into a car. So where is the van?'

'We don't know. Not at the site, though.'

'So Josie might still be in the van?'

'I don't think so. These people can control their routes and locations to avoid CCTV, but not here, not around your house. It's the danger zone. The van could be compromised. It's probably why they swapped it so quickly. I expect to find that van a smouldering wreck some time soon. But here, look, we think the car scraped along the side of the garage doorframe as it left. We found green paint.'

'So, the contact and exchange principle,' Nick said. 'So you can do a solvent test to match it when you find the car.'

A child doing applied mathematics wouldn't have got such a surprised look. 'How did you know that?'

'You police like to let TV companies film your investigations. You give up all your tricks—'

'Just tell us what you know,' Anna said, visibly upset and clearly impatient.

'I'm sorry, dear, of course, yes.' She hit the keyboard, pulling up a still from a high CCTV camera covering a garage forecourt. A car barely visible on a portion of the main road at the top of the screen had been circled in electronic ink. 'A631, heading south. We reckon this is the car. There's another camera later, further into Brinsworth, but we don't see the car on that camera. It might have stopped somewhere between.'

'Josie is being held in Brinsworth?' Anna said. 'That's only a few miles away.'

'It could have turned off a side road. Or they could have swapped vehicles. They swapped from a van to this green Volkswagen Passat, so maybe they swapped again. Please, let's not assume anything until we know.'

'A Passat? So you know which kind of car. Are you tracing Passats?'

'Of course, yes. Yes. Now take a peek at these.'

Anna grabbed Miller's wrist, preventing her from working the keyboard. 'But have you searched Brinsworth for this car? There can't be many green Passats there.'

'There are none seen so far, dear. Sorry. We've driven the area. We're still looking, but it takes time. Now have a look here. Do you recognise anyone?'

Four photographs. Four police mugshots. Three men and one woman, each of whom was registered as owning a Volkswagen Passat, and a criminal record.

'You said the first caller was a woman pretending to be a man, for whatever reason,' Anna said, jabbing the mugshot of the sole female. 'Is it her? Have you arrested her?'

'They would have already said, wouldn't they?' Nick said. A little too harshly.

DCI Miller jumped in: the Driver and Vehicle Licensing Agency had provided details of current Passat owners, but these four were the only owners from South Yorkshire with criminal records. There was the whole country to check. Not all Passat owners would be in police files. Some cars might have been sold on or scrapped without paperwork being updated. These searches would take time. And although they had no such reports so far, it was likely that the target Passat was stolen, which would make all owner traces useless. No good news yet, in other words. Did they recognise any of the faces?

'No,' Nick said, and Anna agreed. 'So you've got nothing, have you?'

For the first time, the unflappable DCI gave him an annoyed look.

'So tell us what you've got,' he said by way of an apology.

'The run from the lock-up garage to here, where this photo was taken, is southeast, and if we continue that way, we hit the M1 at Junction 32.'

'So they went to the motorway?' Anna said, visibly deflating in her seat. 'So Josie could be anywhere? Anywhere in Britain? You don't know that until you've searched Brinsworth more. No, you're wrong.'

Miller rubbed Anna's shoulder and sat beside her. Anna wiped wet eyes.

'I'm sorry. Please carry on.'

A pair of cell towers about twenty miles south alongside the M1 picked up the first phone call to the house, at 5 a.m., from a new device, not Nick's now-dead mobile. The call originated on the A38 heading east off Junction 28. The signal wasn't picked up leapfrogging towers, so the kidnappers probably stopped their vehicle to make the call. The A38 ran between Sutton-in-Ashfield and Kirkby-in-Ashfield, both market towns. They were being scrutinised for, amongst other things, abandoned buildings and recently rented properties – the kind of place kidnappers might hold someone. And the kind of people who might do the holding.

The next call, to Anna at the hospital, was made from the village of Nuthall, west off Junction 26, about eight miles south of the previous call. On a photo, someone had marked the route from the lock-up garages, across the M1 and into the two Ashfield towns, and then across the motorway again to Nuthall, creating a > symbol with the M1 running down its middle.

'Brinsworth, then these other towns, then Nuthall?' Anna moaned. 'You have no idea, do you?'

Just eight miles separated the two calls, but they occurred two hours apart. Possibly knowing the police would assume an M1 run, the kidnappers were taking a series of smaller roads to reach their destination, resulting in a much slower journey, and they had passed from one side of the M1 to the other. This might be to avoid CCTV on major traffic lines, or because the motorway offered no escape routes in the miles between junctions. Alternate routes were being examined, of course. But there was no doubt whatever vehicle the kidnappers had, or whichever roads were being used, it was going south. Any clue why?

Nick held up a hand. 'Wait a minute. They called the hospital, they knew we were there, so they might have been watching.'

'Well, possibly there's a second team, see. One with your daughter, one to watch the family.'

'Wait a minute,' he said again. 'If they want money for her, she must be nearby. Close to us. Here, not in bloody Nuthall. Are you hunting the kidnappers instead of our daughter?'

'Second team?' Anna cut in. 'How many people do you think are involved in…' She tapered off and shook her head. 'No, no, she's here, I feel it. I'd know if she was far away. Josie is in a room somewhere, not in a vehicle, not driving away. She's here, she's close to me. You don't know anything yet. It's all guessing. And you're wrong. You need to search all of Brinsworth.'

She got up to leave. Nick reached for her, and she let him take her arm. But just for a moment, and then she said, 'I want to see my sister.'

When she was gone, Nick hung his head. 'There was a time when it was me she turned to. Now I'm no good for her. For anyone.'

The detective leaned past him to tap keys. 'Try not to let paranoia get you, my friend. But this is actually the main reason I wanted you in here. I didn't want your wife to see this.'

Nick sat up straight when he saw another CCTV image. But this one had a 'PLAY' symbol: it was video.

'I know you blame yourself,' she said. 'I want to prove that you shouldn't, my friend. Do you think you can watch this?'

He didn't want to see it. But he needed to.

It was CCTV covering his backyard, and he knew it was going to show Josie's kidnap.

*

It was a low-level night vision, taken from a house on their side of the road, six or seven down, found during a neighbourhood canvass that had started once the police knew that Nick hadn't absconded with his own daughter. The camera was aimed to the right in order to cover the parking area, and the Carter backyard was visible on the right side of the screen. Grainy and grey, but a portion of the image was lit by the light from the living room; although this area was so bright because of the night vision that it was washed out. Like a glowing pool of lava. The road and parking area resembled a lollipop leaning back and to the right.

A van entered stage left, slid slowly up the road and turned in the parking area. It came back and parked outside the back gate. All the lights were off. Three dark shapes exited, but one black mass remained behind the steering wheel. One climbed the high gate and unlocked it for the others. In they slinked, moving fast and careful, like ninjas.

When the black shapes entered the glowing pool, they became fuzzy and lost contours, like objects in a heat shimmer. The patio door wasn't visible at this angle, but Nick realised he must have opened it right then, because the three shapes darted aside. He saw a fourth shimmering form enter the scene, stage right. Himself. Phone call to his friend done, he had decided to step out for a cigarette. Seeing this, he realised he hadn't craved one since. Only alcohol.

Here, in his still-hazy memory, was where he froze in fear and got struck to the ground. But that wasn't what he saw now. His little dark shape floated out, into the garden and towards the three. It merged with one, then veered to the right, following a second.

The first was down on the ground. Shocked, he realised he had taken out one of the kidnappers.

'If I'd had a gun…'

But he didn't fare so well with number two. He thought he saw an arm come up, curling defensively across the figure's head, as if to protect itself from his blow. But then the other arm came up, out towards him. It didn't seem to strike him, too far away, short by a good two feet, yet down he went, as if a magic sleep spell had been cast. The black shape then moved forward, and hovered over him, bending. He thought he could see his head on the doorstep. This, he knew, would be when a syringe of ketamine got a cameo and sportsmanship left the production.

Then he saw the third figure slip out of the right side of the screen. Into the house, through the door he had opened for them. Nice and easy. Nice's little dark form didn't move.

Miller stopped the video. 'I wanted you to see that you tried to save your daughter, Nick. You did all you could.'

'If I did all I could, she'd be here with me now. I don't want to see them take her.' Nick grabbed the laptop, ready to slam it shut, shut away that video.

'But I do,' a voice said, startling them. Anna was behind, watching.

'Anna—' Nick started.

'Don't. I need to see it.' She sat next to Nick and lifted his hand from the laptop screen. 'I need to know what my daughter went through.'

*

Miller left them alone to digest what they'd seen, and to talk. But they didn't get the chance. Into the detective's void stepped Anna's father, and immediately, which meant he'd probably been waiting for her to leave. Nick audibly groaned. Middleton took the nearest seat, which might have been for ease or because it was the furthest from Nick.

She hoped there wasn't going to be an argument.

He put a glass of Coke on the table.

'I was told by DS Bennet. The kidnappers are heading south. Maybe to Nottingham, right, Nick? Or London. You know people in both places.'

The hope vanished.

'Don't start,' Nick said. 'I'm trying to have a moment with my wife. Keep out of it.'

'What are you accusing him of, Dad? Don't you know how stupid it sounds to think Nick is involved in this? That's his daughter. This video proves he's innocent, that he's a victim like Josie. Do you want to see it?'

In response, Nick slammed the laptop.

Middleton said, 'That video doesn't prove he didn't tell people about my money.'

'What are you saying?' Nick said. 'Just come out with it.'

'You should leave,' Anna hissed. 'Go, please.'

'You know exactly what, Nick. Come on, who did you tell? Maybe you told those dodgy biker friends of yours about how well off I am. You've been hurting ever since I cut you off—'

'Bullshit,' Nick cut in. 'You didn't cut *me* off from your precious money, and you know it. You cut Anna off. You think I can't see right through you? You dream that every time we're short of cash, she regrets the last ten years. When the washing machine breaks and we can't afford to fix it, you pray Anna will regret not becoming a business tycoon. She'll look at that pile of dirty washing and think how the great Larry Middleton was right all along.'

That clearly got to Middleton because he took a deep breath and a moment of careful consideration. 'I think you told your cronies there was a way to make me hand some of my so-called precious money over. And your share would be half. For unlocking a patio door.'

Nick shoved the closed laptop across the table. It struck the glass of Coke and sent it spinning away. The glass smashed on the floor as Middleton jumped to his feet, splattered with Coke.

'I'll pay it to get my granddaughter back. You win, Nick.' He started to leave, but paused to add something. 'But I'm going to pay double that to ruin you afterwards. Just watch.'

*

In the playroom again, Nick once more traced his fingers over Josie's BUSY DAY drawing. Nick's stick form, standing apart from the others. Leaving the house, leaving the family. Had Josie known about the trouble between her parents? Nick and Anna had discussed a possible split many times, over many hours, but all Josie knew was that Daddy might have to go away for a bit. Or so Nick had thought.

He was going nowhere. He had felt the pain of losing Josie, of seeing a kidnapper pass Josie, drugged into sleep, through her bedroom window and into the arms of another man, and the image, ever-replaying behind his eyes, was heart-wrenching, and he swore now he wouldn't feel that emotion again in any form. He wasn't moving out of the house. Hell, he was going to sleep in Josie's room every night when they had her back. He would soak Josie up like a camel taking on water, just to fill himself with emotion and memory because he wasn't sure he'd otherwise cope the next time Josie was away from him, even if it was for school or a day trip or when she saw her grandfather. And he would never again do anything to disrupt the family. If Josie repeated her wish that Daddy and Grandpo 'made bestier friends', well, Nick might even attempt that.

But the thought of Josie being helpless, begging for Daddy, heightened a sense of impotence borne of his inability to stop those masked kidnappers from taking his girl. He'd put up a fight, but they'd taken Josie with ease, hadn't they? Because anyone could

fight, if pushed, but not everyone had a strong fight in them. That
night had proved that Nick wasn't strong enough to look after his
girl. And Nick's stick man was thinner than the others, he noted,
as if Josie believed her father was weak, insignificant.

When Anna walked in with two cups of tea that Jane had
made, she stopped dead. Nick realised his face was wet and quickly
rubbed the tears away. 'I couldn't save her.'

'You're not invincible. We'll get her back.' Said with conviction.
She seemed to be the strong one. She was taking this better than
he was. Overcome with grief, and a sense of the end, he said,
'What if we don't?'

Her face was stony, sincere, when she said, 'We will. I promise.'

She put down the teas and sat next to him. He put his head
on her shoulder, and she put her hands on his back.

'We have to prepare ourselves for—'

'No,' she cut in. 'It will all be okay.'

Like a distraught child, he said, 'How can you know?' He held
up his phone, ready to show her some of his research into crimes
against children, but thought better of it and put the device down.

She said, 'It will. Everything will be okay.'

He knew her boldness was a mask designed to ease his distress.
If possible, she would take aboard all his grief and let the mass eat
her alive. That was Anna, always thinking of someone else first. She
deserved a stronger man. Perhaps, when this was over and Josie
was back, he should do the right thing and leave the family home.

Thinking about that made him suddenly see something else in
the drawing. Not just a weak dad. Far more than that.

Josie hadn't drawn a future she predicted, but one she desired.

CHAPTER SEVEN

9.01 a.m.

He felt his voice cracking up at the first word.

'Hello, yes. It's about Josie Carter, year two. She won't be in today.'

'Thank you. Josie Carter, year two. I'll make sure to pass the message on. Is she ill?'

He had to pull the phone away because a tickle in his dry throat instigated a coughing fit. The school receptionist was from Sunderland, just like the owner of the voice on the ransom recording he'd just listened to, and it choked him up. When able, he told the most painful lie of his life: yes, Josie was ill. She was in bed with fever. But after the lady asked if Josie would be back tomorrow, there was no need for a lie:

'I don't know. I hope so.'

That should have been it, but the receptionist told him the headmistress, Mrs McKinley, had asked to speak to him. He was put through to an extension. By then he'd already told himself not to scream at the woman if this was about some trivial naughtiness Josie had been up to.

'Mr Carter? Thank you for waiting. It's nothing to worry about. I just wanted to speak to you about the event yesterday in the music room. Did Josie's mother tell you about it?'

She had, he said. Josie had gone to the toilet, then taken a curious detour into the music room, just for a look around. Fearful of getting in trouble, she'd hidden under the piano stool when a class entered. For the entire half hour lesson, she'd remained hidden while just about every teacher combed the school. Her teacher, Miss Hood, actually had the police on the phone when the first kid from the next class into the music room spotted Josie under the piano stool.

'I must apologise again. I was off yesterday, and this is the first opportunity I've had to express my grave apologies. It's not like Josie to go missing.'

That speared like a harpoon. 'No,' was all he could muster in reply.

'You can't turn your back for a second at that age, can you? I always—'

He blurted that he had to go, sorry, and hung up. He didn't realise he'd been crying until a tear dripped off his chin and splashed on to the screen of his phone.

As he turned to leave Josie's room, he saw Anna's father just beyond the doorway, leaning sideways so he could peer inside. He said nothing and vanished. When Nick left the room, Middleton was at the kitchen sink, filling the kettle, his back to Nick. Nick quietly got out of there.

9.03 a.m.

Testing a theory, Jane collared DS Bennet alone at the dining table. She sat by him and put Anna's photo album and two mugs of tea on the table.

'Retinal cancer at twenty-nine months, just in case you're dying to ask,' she said.

'I wasn't,' Bennet said after a careful, detective-like pause.

'Oh, didn't give a hoot, eh?'

'I didn't want to intrude,' he said quickly.

Jane laughed. 'Just yanking your chain. I can't see these photos. Find me one of Josie about three years old.'

He took a sip of tea. She could sense his unease, but she heard him slide his laptop aside and pull the photo album closer. Heard pages turn. 'Here.'

She traced her fingers over it. 'I wish someone could make a Braille version. Yes, by the way, people do treat me like I'm inferior.'

Now he laughed. 'But you make up for it with mind-reading abilities.'

'I get that sort of thing, too. Do I have superhuman hearing? Do I dream with pictures? And on a Saturday night, do I correctly imagine what a man's penis looks like?'

'And I bet you've got a bunch of one-liners prepared for all that.'

'The other day I was with my friend at a greasy spoon and the fellow behind the counter asked my friend what I wanted to order. That annoyed me off so much I put my hand on his chest and then told him he needed to get to a doctor quickly.'

It took a couple of seconds for Bennet to understand. 'Oh, like he thought you had a special power to sense illness. Got you.'

'The man tried to give me burnt toast, too. It's only the first bite that's with the eye.' She tapped the photo album. 'So, describe this picture for me.'

'Erm. Well, Josie is about two, I think. She's on one of those rides at a supermarket. A fire engine. The ones you put a pound in.'

'I remember it. I was shopping with Anna. Nick got left to watch Josie because she didn't want to go down the aisles. It cost a lot to put Josie on that ride for half an hour. What's she wearing?'

'Well, she's got…'

Aware that Anna thought the police were treating this case as just another day at the office, Jane had had an idea to force one of the detectives to study Josie more closely. Now, she figured, the sergeant was infusing her niece deep into his soul, which turned Josie from an object to be investigated into a real little girl who'd miss her parents. It would hopefully put that little bit of extra

urge into him, make him go that extra mile. And it would help
her to feel like a part of this, like she was helping her family. Like
she wasn't a useless piece of furniture.

9.06 a.m.

In a panic, Anna opened her wardrobe. On the top shelf they
kept fresh sheets and rarely used clothing in vacuum bags, and
the thing she was after. It was in a small aluminium biscuit box
along with other valuables, like the necklace her dead mother had
given her at six, which she'd worn every day until she was eight
and a new physical education teacher at her school forced her to
take it off. It reminded her of the beaded necklace Josie wore, a
gift from the same woman, and which the little girl tried to avoid
taking off if possible, once even arguing with a PE teacher who
tried to insist on its removal. Strangely, she hoped it hadn't got
accidentally torn off when those foul Ogres…

The item she wanted was a 3-D glass image of Josie. It was here
for safekeeping because her daughter had dropped it once and
chipped a corner. The quality didn't beat a high-res photograph,
of course, but photographs didn't have the same impact. This small
cube was the only way she could see Josie in profile, and behind
the ears, even though it was a computer guess. If she was lost from
her, a photo wouldn't do. This wouldn't do, either, but at least she
seemed to have flesh and blood, as if she'd posed for a mould. She
wished she'd not been so cheap and bought the smallest version
available; a giant Josie's head, almost full-size, would have cost
only £400. Nothing. That seemed like nothing now.

But the box wasn't on the shelf. She saw it on the floor of the
wardrobe, all but a corner hidden by the hem of her red River
Island dress. When she scooped the clothing aside, she saw that
the lid was missing and the contents were scattered everywhere.
The photo cube was damaged. Another giant piece had come free

and there was a big chip in the front, right on Josie's face. Her heart sank.

The shelf was missing a bracket in a back corner and the wrong kind of pressure could topple it. That was what had happened. But she and Nick, and even Jane, knew that.

She found DC Nabi in the kitchen, talking on his phone. She showed him the cube. 'You broke this.'

He held up a finger because he was in mid-call. She strode over and tried to snatch the phone, but he held it away.

'Hey, what are you doing?'

'You broke this. It's irreplaceable.'

'I didn't touch it.'

'You knocked my wardrobe shelf down and it broke, you idiot.'

'I'm on the phone here. You want your kid back, or what?'

'Don't you speak to me like that. Stay out of my things, okay? All you people.'

'Get out of my face, missus.'

He got out of hers, though, by walking from the kitchen, phone to ear, a finger in the other to drown her out. She followed, demanding an apology. But he ignored her. He aimed for the front door and was quickly outside. He slammed it shut.

She turned to see Miller standing in the living room doorway. 'I'm so nosey, dear. It's what this job does to you. What did I miss?'

A polite way of asking what Anna and the DC had been arguing about. Anna was eager to tell her, because she wanted that horrible detective out of her house.

After, Miller apologised. 'Apologies. He's young and brash. Even worse, I'm afraid DC Nabi is one of *those*.' She even made floating speech marks with her fingers.

Anna looked puzzled.

'It's the university graduates, dear. All those years of study, just to be slotted on to the bottom of the ladder. You should have seen the mess when young new blood started being given senior roles. Now it's about fast-track opportunities. But CVs and interviews don't highlight a person's ego, I'm afraid. It's when these gifted youngsters are firmly rooted in the job that you learn they think they know better than those with real policing experience. Believe me, Detective Constable Nabi is a bigger pain in my behind than yours.'

Miller vanished again, just as quickly, and Anna found that her anger had gone. Had that been Miller's plan? Make Anna the listener as someone else moaned in order to calm her?

But she preferred the anger. She couldn't fabricate rage, but she could supplant fear with pain. She squeezed the photo cube hard, digging the broken top corner into her palm, hard enough to pierce the skin. And she would have squeezed and squeezed and wrung free every drop of blood, but a line of red trickle slid down the 3D image and made her gasp in shock.

Blood, all over Josie's face.

'Josie, no,' she moaned, frantically rubbing at the photo cube. When the blood smeared, becoming an image a billion times worse, she shut her eyes and used her sleeve and didn't look again until she was certain the glass glistened once more. Josie was back, and without blemish, all beautiful again.

But with her anger gone, pain dissolved, the void deep inside rapidly filled once more with despair.

9.11 a.m.

Nick walked into Josie's room, where the crime scene investigator was re-fingerprinting the window sill. He'd heard DCI Miller order her people to give Anna some space, so the Family Liaison Officer was here, too. Since Anna had turned down her help, and he'd refused to talk, the lady had just been hanging around like a ghost, barely seen, barely heard. He'd heard DCI Miller order her people to be seen and heard as little as possible.

She asked him how he was doing, but he only nodded in response. He lifted the cover of Josie's bed and found his daughter's special camouflage-print teddy, Blaze, which slept by Josie's feet to keep them warm. The teddy had been waiting for her when she was born, and she'd never slept without it. Ever.

But she wouldn't have it tonight.

'You know, last year had the highest number of child kidnappings this century, and it's on the rise.'

'Mr Carter, statistics like that don't—' She stopped as Nick pulled out a butter knife and drove it into Blaze's neck, hard and deep.

'Wow, what the hell?' the CSI yelled. The FLO jumped back and spilled her tea all over the carpet. 'Put the damn knife down. In here, quick! Knife!'

By the time both present and another officer who appeared had grabbed Nick, he'd already cut the teddy's head off. He dropped both pieces as the knife was wrestled from his hands.

Anna appeared in the doorway, alerted by the noise. 'What's going on? Nick?'

She gasped when she saw the headless toy. 'Nick, what have you done?'

'This can't end perfectly for me,' he said. He shook the detectives off, and they let him go once the CSI had secured the knife. Nick picked up Blaze's head and body. 'Josie will hate me for ever for doing this. And I'm already scared about it. I'll have to face her. That's why I know now she'll come back. Sod's Law says sod the statistics.'

9.18 a.m.

Miller took Anna out to her car and showed her its new features. A Rewire Security magnetic tracker, for one. Three microphones and three cameras, one for each front seat and one covering the back. But Anna was more interested in watching the twitching curtains along the street, and a guy who came out to pop his bonnet for unnecessary work, and a woman who felt her wheelie bin needed dragging a couple of inches back, and another guy who forwent a sham and just planted his feet on his garden path and stared. Now that it was morning proper, the street was beginning to feel the buzz of something big happening at number 44. She felt better for being wrapped in glass and metal.

'Don't worry about them,' Miller said. 'I wanted them to see you. See you're looking okay. Apologies for the trick. I'm buying the car, if anyone asks.'

'I don't want cameras,' Anna said, shivering.

'Dear, it's just a precaution. When you get where you're going, there's a chance the kidnapper might want to get in the car.'

She forgot the neighbours. 'Why would he do that?'

Miller touched Anna's hand, which lay limp on her thigh. 'It's just in case. You may be told to drive somewhere. Apologies. We just don't know, but we need to cover such things.'

'No cameras.'

'I'm afraid we have to insist. Also, you'll wear a body mic and camera.'

Anna was shocked. 'You think they'll want to take me somewhere?'

'Again, apologies, but it's possible. But we'll be protecting you. We'll have people within range.'

She didn't care about that. She just couldn't shake the feeling that something would go wrong. She'd been hoping Josie would be back with her very soon. The thought of trickery, or even just a delay, was unbearable.

'And we'll be in contact with you throughout—'

'No. No talking. Not unless it's absolutely vital. I'll need to concentrate if I'm driving. I mean it. *No damn chatter.*'

Miller gave her a long stare, clearly trying to examine this outburst. Anna saw slightly bloodshot eyes. The lady was starting to look like a zombie from lack of sleep, even though Anna had had less over the last twenty-four hours.

'Let's head on back in, dear. Give your neighbours a wave, would you. Keep them calm.'

She wasn't sure she could do this. She took deep breaths as she exited the car. Up the street, wheelie-bin woman waved. Anna knew her neighbour was hoping for a gossip breakfast. She waved back, just to keep up the pretence of *nothing going on here*.

9.21 a.m.

Nick's second phone call was worse than the first. His hand was shaking as he waited for the phone to be picked up. He fought off images of whiskey in his hand. When the call was answered, and he'd said, *Hello, it's Nick*, he got:

'Nicolas? My Lord, where are you? What is going on?'

'What do you mean?'

'Where are you? What's happened? Your mobile number didn't work, have you changed it? We haven't got a home phone for you. Your brother is worried to death…'

Two minutes later, visibly shaking, Nick stormed into the dining room, where the DS sat with Miller, working at a single laptop. Both looked round when he roared:

'I just called my mum to tell her, and she already bloody knows. You sent the police in London to her house. They knocked her up at God knows what hour and told her I'd vanished. She was worried sick. They made it sound like I'd been killed. Why the hell did you do that?'

Miller stood up, but the DS wore the sheepish face, so Nick glared at him.

His boss said, 'You did vanish, Nick, and I'm sorry about this, truly, but that's a hard and fast rule: we talk to the family. But I thought the London lads had been told that you'd been found.'

Now they were both looking at the sergeant, who offered: 'I forgot to update them. I apologise. But they shouldn't have said anything about Josie being missing.'

Nick shook his head in frustration. 'They didn't, small mercies. And I didn't tell them yet. Because she's coming back today, so they need never know, do they? But that's pissed me right off, guys. What other cock-ups have you done? Maybe write me a list of them?'

He stormed off without awaiting an answer.

9.30 a.m.

Off-duty volunteer regular officers were getting a taste of detective work by sitting in cars in plain clothes, dotted around the estate, their job to report all moving vehicles. It wasn't outlandish to think the kidnappers might have a scout floating around, watching. Anything intriguing was noted, reported, checked, and anything considered remotely relevant was added to the bloating action list. But nobody was stopped or questioned. One of the vehicles logged was reported to Miller as belonging to a fifty-two-year-old male with a conviction for assault back in the 1990s.

'That's my bank manager,' Middleton said.

Bank managers love their wealthy clients and this one had agreed to personally deliver Middleton £50,000. That amount, in tightly wrapped £20 notes, neatly fitted into an old shoebox of Nick's, but it was brought to the house in a large briefcase and Middleton met his old friend on the street to take it. The neighbours would see a businessman collecting his forgotten bag; a scout amongst them, or somehow watching from afar, would know the Carters were planning to pay the ransom.

Middleton sat on the settee and started to transfer the cash into the shoebox. Slowly, somewhat reluctantly, as if tossing money on to a fire. Most were entranced by the show, but not the Carters.

Nick wasn't there and Anna felt only frustration in with all that despair and sadness.

'How many people have died across the world, even just today, for this stuff?'

'Just remember it does some good in the world, too,' Bennet said.

'If we'd had this earlier, they wouldn't have needed to take Josie,' she said, and turned, and left the room. What she'd said made no sense, she knew, because the truth was if they'd had money aplenty, Josie might have been taken earlier, and the threat of repeat would hang over them indelibly.

Middleton watched his daughter leave, and while his eyes were still on the doorway Nick appeared.

'The magic potion, eh?'

Someone actually stepped into both men's line of sight, perhaps aware of what was coming. But he couldn't block sound.

'Fifty thousand is a lot, Nick,' Middleton said. 'With that you could rent a decent place of your own.'

'You're an idiot. I'll be around for ever.'

'Calm it down, guys,' the detective between them said.

'Fifty thousand, Nick. If you could keep it and give up Josie, which would it be?' Middleton said. His tone was sweet, like that of a guy just curious, if a little out of line. Enough so that the detectives in the room missed the underlying message.

But not Nick. He got Middleton's message loud and clear.

His response was hawked over his shoulder as he turned to leave.

'I'd burn that up and you with it if it would get my little girl back right now.'

*

Anna found him in the cellar, where there was a pull-up bar, and he was working himself hard, as he sometimes did when upset or stressed. The old hanging bulb was off, probably so he couldn't be distracted. In the light from the kitchen, he wasn't much more than a silhouette. She was still a little angry with him for the debacle with the child molester because it had injected hope now eroded, and she wanted to make him promise not to take any sort of wild action again.

He didn't notice her descend the steps. She was about to call his name when she spotted Josie's phone on the floor by a small stool. Focussed on burning his muscles, he still hadn't fathomed her presence, so she picked up the mobile, now consumed by an urge to find out exactly why he had targeted the abuser. She got something far more shocking.

There was a Wikipedia page of famous child murders. She found a page about police protocol in kidnapping cases. Child murder statistics. Reasons children were abducted. And then worse in a drop-down search history.

'UK child organ harvesting.'

'UK buying a daughter on black market.'

'UK child trafficking.'

She pulled her eyes away in disgust, and fear, and tossed the phone aside. It clacked on the concrete floor, but Nick didn't seem to hear it.

The anger that had brought her down into this cold room was history. Now all she knew was pity, and shame because she should have been by Nick's side throughout all of this, to prevent his still-addled mind from running amok. She reached out and put her hands around him from behind and her head on his back, and felt ashamed that she'd been trying to cope with her own stress while all along Nick had been most in need of help.

'We'll get her back,' she moaned against his slick skin.

He hoisted himself up one more time, dragging his weight through her tight hug, and paused until his muscles began to tremble. Then he dropped to his feet. But he didn't turn. She still had that clamp on his torso. The muscles remained tight, still hard even though he'd let himself gain some body fat over the last few months that their relationship had faltered.

'Maybe they should give her cow's milk,' he said, barely audible.

'What do you mean? She's allergic.'

'If she gets ill… if she goes into anaphylactic shock… they'll have to take her to a hospital.'

She released him and stepped back. 'Don't say that.' She didn't want to hear such a thing, because she'd thought about it herself. But in her visions, the kidnappers didn't leave Josie outside a hospital. They ignored her illness, until it was too late, and they fled from her cooling, unmoving body.

Her breathing got rapid and he turned to her, regret just visible on his face in the gloom. This time he took her into his arms.

He said, 'I'm sorry. I just…'

'It's okay,' she told him. 'This is impossible for us both. But these people, they just want money. They won't hurt her. They won't. Please believe that.'

He said nothing, which said everything, and she squeezed harder. For a few seconds they remained locked together, motion-less and silent, until what little light oozed in from the kitchen was cut down further. Their eyes ran up the stairs. Bennet was in the doorway, head slightly bent so he could fit.

'Take a look at this guy.'

Nick dragged himself from her grip before she could let go and ran up. She was half a second behind. Bennet showed them a picture on his phone. High-angle grainy black-and-white shot, suggesting CCTV, of a young man in a blue tracksuit, hair in a ponytail but shaved at the sides. The environment looked like a small reception. Nick snatched the phone for a closer look.

'Who's this guy? Another Passat owner? Is he a suspect? Where is he?'

The DS took his phone back. He reminded them about paint traces found on the doorframe of the lock-up garage where Nick had been found. 'When tracing a car through paint—'

'Yes, infrared spectrometry, or whatever it's called. Move on. Who's this guy?'

'Infrared spectroscopy. And how did you know that?'

'The cops came to look at Anna's car years back. They were tracing 05 plate blue Fiat Puntos in a hit-and-run. Paint transfer. Forget that. Tell me about this guy. Where was this photo taken? Do you think this guy has Josie?'

The DS stepped out into the kitchen and indicated the table. No one sat. Nick urged him.

'The DVLA checks gave up a name one of my DCs remembered. Beryl Jackson. He wasn't sure why he remembered that name until we ran it and it popped up as grandmother of James Jackson. My DC arrested him for car theft a while back. He's got quite the history of it. A couple of officers went to speak to the grandmother. Her husband had an 03 plate Passat and it's been sitting in her garage for five years, since he died, gathering dust, kept as a reminder of him—'

Nick threw his hands up, impatient.

'She opened the garage to show us, but it was gone. She thinks her grandson might have fixed it up and borrowed it.'

'This guy? So it is him?' Nick snatched the phone again, and used two fingers to zoom in on the man's head, although the quality took a dive.

'She must have informed him because he just called the station about the car. He's on bail for car theft so he was quite helpful. He told us a friend of his wanted him to steal a vehicle. Last night. He didn't want to, but didn't want to say no. So he pretended he nicked an old VW Passat, only what he gave up was his grandmother's car. We got a partial plate from another CCTV camera on the A61 near Brinsworth, and they match. It's the car we're after.'

That intrigued Anna enough to take the phone from Nick, who said, 'Who's the other guy, this friend? Are they both in on it? What else do you know?'

'Well, the Jackson kid has an alibi. He was at a pub lock-in last night, till about four in the morning, which we've confirmed. The "friend" who wanted the car is someone he claims he met only recently and only knows as Dom.'

'Bollocks. You believe that?'

'We're checking it out. According to Jackson, this Dom doesn't live in South Yorkshire. He's staying up here in a B&B.'

'Which one? Did this Jackson idiot say which?'

'Nick, just let him talk,' Anna cut in, a hand on his arm. Bennet gave her a look of thanks.

'He's been calling Jackson from that B&B, so we know which one and we're watching it. That's where we got that CCTV image. He stayed out last night and hasn't been back there so far today, according to the owner. But when he returns, we'll have a chat with him. Jackson's been warned not to tip Dom off if he calls again.'

'Where's the B&B?' Nick said.

'I can't tell you that.'

'Why? I want to talk to this guy. He might not talk to the cops. Let me wait there for him to return, no police presence. He'll talk to me.'

'A nice, friendly chat? Why do I doubt that, Mr Carter?'

'I don't want you going there, Nick.'

Nick said, 'It's probably a false name, being a B&B. Have you considered that I might know the guy? I need to speak to him. I'm no good with faces on photos.'

Anna remembered something: 'Your boss, she's good with faces. She might recognise him. Has she seen this photo?'

Bennet shook his head: 'She doesn't know him.'

And then the landline rang.

It was time.

*

'There's a phone on George Street, near Rotherham train station. Be there at 11. We'll phone. Make sure you answer. Just you, alone. No dawdling. Pick up the receiver and answer immediately with "Hello, my master. I am so scared". And make sure you hold it in both hands so I know one isn't pressing record on a tape machine. Then I'll tell you where to take the money. We'll have people watching. You won't like what happens if they spot police.'

Click.

Anna staggered to the sofa and fell on to it. Jane sat beside her.

'No way she's going on her own,' Nick said, shrugging free of the hands holding him. Bennet and another officer had had to physically prevent him from answering the phone. He stood by the sofa, a hand on Anna's shoulder.

'We have to do this the way the kidnappers said,' Miller announced. She had a map on her phone. 'Six-mile journey. Busy areas. The car will pass a thousand people, and it only takes one of them, my friend, to make a call and report a breach of the rules.'

'No way. Don't you see something is up here? Why her? They want someone small and frail they can overpower. They're going to try something. This sounds like bullshit. No way she's going on her own.'

'Someone has to bring the money, and, apologies, but the kidnappers and I share the same idea. We'd both prefer that someone not be a big, angry father. You're staying here, Nick.'

'No damn way.'

'Please, Nick, think about the risk—'

'And the risk to both of them if something happens? Are any of you people thinking about that?'

'Stop it, Nick,' Anna snapped. 'They're right. I'm going on my own. We're not taking any risks that could hurt Josie, okay? We're not. The police will be watching on camera. I'll be fine.'

'Cameras?' he spat. 'YouTube is full of proof that cameras don't stop people getting murdered.'

'Nicolas!' Jane yelled. It silenced the room.

Anna slipped out, with her sister hot behind.

Nick found them seated at the kitchen table. Jane told him not to come in if he planned to continue the argument.

'Just think of it like going to school to pick Josie up,' he said. It was his way of admitting submission. He sat next to Jane, across from Anna, and flicked a salt pot. It skidded across the varnished wood and she caught it.

'Believe me, I really don't want to go there on my own. But don't you see I have to?' She flicked the pot right back at him. Jane moved her chair back, as if to remove herself from a private moment.

'I do, yes,' he said, which was a total lie. 'I'm sorry. I just don't like it.'

'Neither do I. But we have to do it. And don't try to follow me. We can't do anything they might think is a trick. We do whatever they want to get Josie back home, okay?' She flicked the pot back and he caught it.

'Ace,' he said.

It made her smile. Salt tennis was a game she played with Josie, who thought every unreturned shot she made constituted an ace. But she quickly lost her smile and he knew why: she'd never played this game with Nick. Because it was always Josie. And now it was Nick because there was no Josie.

He flicked the pot, but she ignored it and it crashed to the floor. 'Stay here? Please.'

He nodded. It felt like condemning her. At that moment, Bennet appeared in the doorway, like an alarm call. She stood.

'Time to collect Josie from school.'

*

George Street was bookended by two small public car parks. The phone box was just a few feet down, virtually where the street met College Road, which led into the city centre. From the box you could see a supermarket, and the train station, and the busy A630, and the College Road roundabout. Commuters, shoppers, drivers: a whole host of faces around, any of which could be a guy ready to report cop-like behaviour to who Anna had begun to call the Ogres. They chucked out ideas.

The cars were easy, because of the roundabouts at each end of the A630: nobody was going to notice the same bland vehicle, if it passed back and forth every minute, amongst the hundreds zipping by in that timeframe. George Street ran under the A630 by tunnel, and a cop could lurk in there, about fifty metres away, only grimy clothing and a bottle of white cider needed for a homeless drunk disguise. Someone could shop at the supermarket, with its nice big glass windows. Someone could lurk outside the train station, awaiting a pal's arrival. Someone could wander past with shopping bags. There were a host of taller buildings in the background where guys could have binoculars. The openness of the area could hinder as much as aid the kidnappers. There was a council CCTV camera on a giant pole a hundred metres away and a guy was sent to the Control Centre.

She was aware that eyes watched, ears listened, and her own took in neighbours on the street, but against all of this she felt deathly alone. The route was in her head and Bennet, connected to a hidden speaker by radio, made her repeat it. She said it aloud, street for street, as if mentally flying along it like a superhero. And then she started the car.

Nick was at the bedroom window with Jane. Father was at the playroom window. All looked distraught, as if she was leaving for ever. She was reminded of the day she'd set out for university, for her new life in the London, except that Mother had been by Father's side, and they'd been waving and smiling. A lifetime ago, it felt. Another universe. Back when her father had respected her. Back when she had deserved it.

She turned the car on to the street, which was step one – the easiest part – but making that small move, which she'd done a thousand times, was like leaping off a cliff with a homemade parachute.

'Remember, do as they ask and Josie should be fine,' Bennet's crackly voice said.

Should be?

*

In the playroom was a little bubblegum-pink safe that Josie had wanted for her secret items. As Nick was bending to tap in the code, he stopped and picked up one of the *Batman* comics laid atop. He had a terrible vision of putting these comics in the bin; of taking all of Josie's clothes and toys to the charity shop. Of redecorating the room, because there would be no Josie to ever occupy it again.

Kids often thought of their dads as superheroes and Josie was always asking if Nick could beat up Batman. The answer was always yes, but it was a lie. Batman would kill him. Batman would have saved Josie from the kidnappers. Nick was far from a superhero.

It was a silly thought, so he tossed it. He put the comic back and opened the safe for what he'd come for.

He took the item into the living room. Despite their worry that he'd run out of the house again on a vigilante mission, nobody had watched him leave the room and only Miller saw him return. They were in the dining area and beyond the room divider he saw her head turn his way. The others, including Anna's father, were too captivated by the six cameras displaying Anna's journey on laptops, each split screen. Cameras #1 and #2 covered the view behind and ahead of the Corsa, #3 and #4 displayed the back seats, and the remaining two showed the empty passenger seat and Anna behind the wheel. At any time, if something worthy happened, a specific camera could be cast to full screen on all three computers. He stepped up to the room divider, staring past a goldfish bowl full of coins and at the image of his wife. Anna was driving as she had ever since the day of that horrible event that had propelled her to leave London: both hands tight on the wheel, leaning forward slightly, wide-eyed and deep in concentration, as if she was a learner on a lesson. And alone. Since that day so many years ago, she had always driven alone, except for when taking Josie to school. If ever he and she had gone out, he had always had to drive. And never at night, because night was when that horrible thing had happened.

'It's her birthday, by the way. Happy birthday, eh?' he announced to the detectives. He waved a wrapped present. Nobody said anything, but Miller turned to smile at him.

He tore off the wrapping as he crossed to the TV stand. The gift was a CD. On the cover was Josie, standing in her room with a plastic microphone. It said: JOSIE CARTER LIVE AT THE APOLLO. He put the disk in the Xbox under the TV and fired up both devices.

*

'Thank you, thank you. It's good to be here.'

Every car behind her, every bike that pulled alongside, every van that raced past drew her eyes from the road ahead, so much so that she was surprised she hadn't crashed. Now, hearing that voice, and a background of applause, she stared at the radio, which Miller's 'tech chap' had wired his own speaker into. Her breath caught: was that?... couldn't be...

'Doctor, doctor, I get heartburning every time I eat birthday cake. Well, take the candles off.'

But it was. The realisation hit like a jolt of electricity and the car rocked as she accidentally stamped the accelerator. Josie. Josie's voice. At first she didn't understand.

'When is birthday cake like a footballs?'

'Golf ball,' Nick whispered.

'I know, I know. When is birthday cake like golfs ball? When it's been sliced.'

She welled up instantly, realising she was listening to a recording being played from her home. Birthday jokes: a CD Josie and Nick must have made for her.

But the rush of pleasant shock rose and fell as quick as a heartbeat on an electrocardiogram. She shouldn't be hearing Josie's voice like this. Not here, and not now. Josie should have brought the CD into her room in the morning, but she hadn't been able to. Josie should have watched her unwrap it, but she was gone. They should have listened to it together, but the worst of God's creations had snatched her little lady away.

*

Nick had to get away.

He should have loved hearing his daughter's voice, but it didn't work that way. All he felt was despair. If Josie never came back, her birthday stand-up act would be the last thing she ever committed to eternity, and Nick would never forget this moment, when he played it for his wife and foolishly still believed his daughter would return. But onscreen he could see Anna wiping her eyes, face creased with emotion, and he couldn't bring himself to stop the CD. So he quietly slipped out of the room. As he exited, he glanced back and saw Middleton watching him.

He had planned to sit in Josie's room, but stopped at the doorway. Jane was in there, making the bed. Unable to see what the cameras captured, and told by Anna not to talk to her in case of distraction, she had opted not to be present at the doorway. Nick didn't want to talk to anyone just now so sat at the kitchen table and put his head in his hands. Whiskey floated into his mind.

'Nick.'

Middleton. Nick didn't want to look up. Didn't want a fight. He gave no response.

'Thank you for that,' Middleton said. 'It will calm Anna. It was a nice touch.'

Now he looked up, but Middleton was gone.

But Jane was in the bedroom doorway. 'That's Josie's voice. What is it? A recording.'

Her enhanced hearing hadn't picked it up: Nick realised he could still hear Josie's voice. Perhaps prompted by Anna, someone must have turned up the volume. Maybe Middleton.

'What age is a caveman on his birthday? Stone age.'

Jane gave a laugh. Nick managed a smile. She held out her hand and he took it to lead her to the living room.

*

At one point, two miles out, there was a jam while a supermarket delivery truck backed out. A van in the next lane pulled alongside Anna and the passenger window came down. A plain-clothes policeman in a car three back saw it happen and told his base. Someone paused Josie's stand-up routine and Bennet asked her what was going on.

'Just a guy coming onto me,' Anna answered. 'Put Josie back on.'

A mile out from the destination, she saw a ginger girl Josie's age with her father. She was riding a toy scooter, weaving in and out of pedestrians. Anna's foot came off the accelerator. A van behind, with PHOENIX KNIFE AND SLICING BLADE SPECIALISTS and a mobile phone number on the bonnet, had to slow down. He blared his horn.

Child and father started to traverse a zebra crossing ahead. Anna hit the brake and watched them. The girl was looking the other way, so Anna jabbed the horn to get her to turn. An uncanny resemblance to Josie, combined with her daughter's voice in the car, broke Anna out in goosepimples. The father was a few metres ahead of the girl, strangers between them, and she wanted to wind down her window and scream, *Keep an eye on her, there's animals out there!*

Then they were across and the way was clear, but she didn't move. She watched girl and father walk past her, so much closer now. She even had Josie's blue eyes. She willed the girl to look at her again, but the child was too busy slaloming around shoppers' legs.

The father was typing on his phone, ignoring his kid, which she found bizarre. All these people about, any one of whom could pick the girl up in a flash. If she ever took Josie out again somewhere busy, she was going to get one of those reins she'd seen on toddlers. No way was she going to go gallivanting off ahead.

She jumped as someone rapped on her window. A man was standing there, a snarl on his face.

*

'Some guy's shouting at her.'

That was the report from an officer in the car four spots behind Anna's. Bennet ordered the CD shut off.

'Anna, what's going on? Who is that guy?'

Camera #6 showed her leaning away from the door, and the unseen man beyond it, in fear. But there was no fear in her voice when she said:

'I don't know him. Be quiet and put Josie back on.'

'Looks like a road rage thing. He wants her to get moving.'

'It was that girl,' Nick said. 'The camera showed a girl about Josie's age go over the zebra crossing. Someone tell that dickhead to piss off.'

'Can't you help her?' Jane pleaded.

'We can't, we don't know if she's being watched,' Bennet said.

Camera #6 showed Anna's door jerk open. She tried to grab it. A pointing finger stabbed into the screen. Now that the door was open, external sounds found the microphone.

'Are you bloody stupid, woman? Why are you just sitting there? Move your fat arse out the way.'

'Base, you want me to move in and stop this?'

'Negative, Car 2. Keep reporting,' Bennet said.

'No, you've got to do something,' Jane moaned. 'What if he hits her?'

Miller nudged Nick's arm and tapped the feed from camera #2. One of the detectives said, 'Are we sure this guy's for real and it's not part of some test to see if she's being followed?'

'Get moving, or I'll shift you, you silly bitch. What's your problem? Don't just sit there looking stupid.'

But onscreen, Anna was still cowering away, unable or unwilling to answer him. Now she looked terrified.

'Let's just think about this,' Bennet said. 'What are the chances this guy is part of it? Someone Google that firm.' He pointed at camera #2, rear-view from a lens above the number plate, which clearly showed the van's bonnet with the company name and mobile number.

Middleton couldn't hold his tongue: 'Someone help my daughter, please.'

'The guy's pulled out his phone. I think he just got a call.'

Heads turned as Nick said, 'Hey, Phoenix van man, that's Ronnie Kray's granddaughter you're messing with. You want your head cut off with one of your own knives? Get lost.'

'Something going on here, boss. Guy just panicked and ran back to his van. Jesus, U-turn in the road and he's out of there.'

The DS glared at Nick. 'That wasn't very clever, Mr Carter. What if that driver…'

But he stopped as Nick tossed Miller her phone back. 'Just put the CD back on for my wife.'

*

The phone box on the corner just sat there, innocent, nothing but a piece of street furniture nobody out and about gave two hoots for. But she was terrified to go near it. She fingered the tiny lump under her top.

'Try not to touch the transmitter,' Bennet said, referring to the small microphone/camera they'd ordered her to wear. *'Eleven minutes to go. Are you okay?'*

'Put Nick on.'

'I'm here,' he said.

She looked at the rear-view mirror, where one of the tiny microphones was placed. She smiled at it. At Nick, who would be watching.

'I'm okay. Don't worry about me. I'll be back with Josie very soon. Why don't you make her one of those egg salads for when we get back?'

'I will. Are you sure you're okay? I wish I was there.'

'It has to be this way. I'll have a cheeseburger.'

'I know, I know it has to be this way. I'll make us both a bacon and cheeseburger, and egg salad for Josie. Waiting on the table for you.' He paused. *'Try not to be scared. They have police scattered around, so nothing will happen to you.'*

She said nothing. If this was some kind of trick to get at her, she didn't care. It would mean Josie was gone. Next to that, her own plight meant nothing. But she nodded for the camera, for Nick, for all of them, to keep them calm.

'Ten minutes,' Bennet said. *'You should go now and wait in the phone box, just to make sure nobody else can use it.'*

She scanned her surroundings. Nobody seemed to be paying attention to the Corsa in a paint warehouse's car park, but the Ogres would surely manage that without being spotted themselves.

Bennet said: *'We can hear you once you leave the car, but you won't hear us. We'll see what's ahead of you. If there's a problem—'*

'There won't be,' she cut in.

She didn't want to think that way. She picked up the shoebox of money and got out. She took a breath and started to walk across the car park, feeling the weight of eyes upon her. Ten, fifteen, twenty or so people on George Street, walking this way and that. Dozens more passing by on the main road into the town centre. Hundreds of cars zipping by on the dual carriageway. She was boxed in by myriad eyes, and any of them could belong to a man who might already have put her girl's blood on his hands. Not knowing who was out there made her feel blind, so she ignored every piece of the whole world except the shoebox, which she carried in both hands like a tray bearing something fragile, and the phone box, which waited to pounce like a predator.

The tall security camera a hundred metres away seemed to stare right at her as she crossed George Street and approached the phone box. From this angle she could see the busy roundabout, and the train station, so close now, and the supermarket next door. Eight minutes until her world blossomed or wilted. Her legs barely carried her the final few feet to the phone box.

She hugged the shoebox to her chest to free a hand for opening the door. She wasn't looking forward to a long wait alone inside the phone box, as minutes that seemed like hours crept by; she was scared that someone would come along and insist on making a call; she was worried that she'd snap mentally, like someone trapped for years on a desert island, and the phone box would become her coffin.

But the phone rang even as the door was swinging shut behind her.

The moment she picked up the receiver in her left hand, something seemed to click in her mind. She remembered the order to answer immediately. She had already told herself they were just words, and they would help get Josie back. So there was no shame when she said:

'Hello, my master. I am so scared.'

She put her other hand on the receiver, as ordered. There was a pause. The fingers of her right hand traced along the inside of the receiver handle as the wait jangled her nerves.

'Pay careful attention to what you feel. It will help you do the right thing. Remember that any trickery and your kid doesn't see old age.'

Growing shock made her unable to speak. The same disguise to the voice. It was hard to picture a woman at the other end.

'So you understand the message I'm giving you. Good.'

She got her mind back on track and remembered the rest of her instructions: 'I will do whatever you want.'

'We don't want you to do this. We want your husband to bring the money. Go home and we'll call again.'

Click.

Anna dropped the receiver. It yanked against the end of the cable and cracked into her knee, but she barely felt it. She leaned on the phone book shelf, gripping it tightly with both hands, and laid her head against the wall. For a few seconds, she just stayed like that. Then she stood, removed one hand from the shelf and grabbed the swinging receiver again.

'Hello?' she cried into it. But of course, there was no answer. The faceless voice had gone.

She put the receiver back in its cradle, slowly and carefully, and rubbed her hands together. 'You'll be okay, Anna,' she said aloud. It was a careful sentence, designed to ease Nick's pain and not arouse suspicion if the Ogres were listening. God knows what Nick was going through. And Jane and Father. She picked up the shoebox and rushed from the phone box, eager to get back to her husband, because he would need comfort after her failure to get Josie back. The moment she flopped into the driver's seat, Nick was right there.

'It's okay, Anna, it's okay, they probably want me to do some running around, so there's no police surveillance, that's all. Please, don't be worried. Are you okay?'

'I'm fine. But are you, Nick? This wasn't what we expected, but it's not bad news. I don't want you to worry. Look, I'm coming home.'

'*Good. But stay calm, baby, please. Come on back. Everything will be fine, I promise.*'

'Let me drive, Nick. I don't want to talk just yet. Let me get out of the city centre. You know I can't drive and talk.'

'*Okay. But watch how you go. Are you sure you're okay? Drive carefully, please.*'

Drive carefully? That elicited a wild cackle that quickly transformed into uncontrollable sobbing.

PART TWO

CHAPTER EIGHT

Nick grabbed the radio, shook his head in answer to a question from DS Bennet, and strode from the room in order to speak with his wife in private. In Josie's playroom, he sat at the table, where BUSY DAY caught his eye. He put the radio down, and stared at it, and waited for her to speak. He could hear the car's engine because the channel was wide open at Anna's end. And the sound of sobbing. But he held his tongue to give her time.

'Earlier this year a woman threw a petrol bomb through a house window.' Nick looked round to see Bennet in the doorway. 'It only killed the dog because the owners weren't in. But she admitted trying to kill the family. It was retaliation for a snowball the owner's kid threw at her two months before.'

'So this is your snowball story? I get it. People can hold grudges for the slightest thing. Okay, ten years ago I spilled a guy's pint in a pub in London. Go get him.'

'The kidnappers mentioned you paying dues, Nick, and—'

'This is about her father's money,' Nick cut in. 'He flaunts it. Someone wants it. Sounds to me like this *dues* thing simply meant I should be the one delivering it, and lo and behold that's what they've now asked for. Seems straightforward and I don't know why everyone's worrying. Now, can you please leave me alone to speak to my wife?'

Bennet came closer so he could watch Nick across the table. 'Start taking this seriously, Nick. They mentioned dues and now they want you to take the money. Not, as you put it, someone *small* and *frail* they can easily overcome. Why pick you, a bodybuilder with attitude, unless these people wanted to get you in a certain place at a certain time?'

'If they wanted to hurt me, they could have done that when I was drugged up in the back of their van. They could have killed my girl in front of me, if getting to me was their plan.'

'Maybe something's different now,' Bennet said.

It was something Nick had already considered. But what mattered was that Anna was out of danger. And if there was trickery ahead, Josie had a better chance of rescue with brawn and anger playing a role.

Despite his last line, Bennet suddenly changed his mind. 'Maybe you're right. Perhaps whatever the kidnappers have planned has been delayed. Maybe they picked you just because you were drugged and they figure you're still not thinking straight.'

'That'll be it. Now I'd like five minutes alone, if you don't mind.'

Bennet didn't move. 'I need you to talk to my DCI about negotiating with—'

Nick said, 'So I can learn "pseudo-therapeutic communication strategies"?'

The DS paused. 'Someone's been on the Internet. Did you also read about Red Centre training? DCI Miller has studied for kidnap scenarios, Nick, so it would only be helpful to speak to her on this matter.'

'No, DS Bennet. Okay? No. I don't care if she knows all the tricks. No tricks are needed. Just a bag of money, which I have.'

'And ego with a dash of inferiority complex. Why are you so averse to help? Early midlife crisis?'

'You're right, Sergeant, I did go on the Internet. It seems here in South Yorkshire not a lot of kids need rescuing from kidnappers. Suicidal students, though, quite a lot of those need talking down from high windows. Look, Detective, I'm not an angry man and it's not my go-to emotion when things go wrong. But I'm all over the place because I can't help my kid. I don't know how else to act—'

'*Nick, are you there?*' Anna said.

Nick snatched up the radio and waved Bennet from the room. Thankfully, he left without a word.

'I'm here. Are you okay?'

'*I'm okay. I know everything will be fine, don't worry. And when Josie is back with us, we're going to Iceland. That rocket ship.*'

'Yes. For a whole month.'

'*And we're going to get proper security on the house.*'

He picked up a pen. 'We? Does that mean we're okay now? Me and you?'

'*Let's not talk about that just now. Are you okay with doing this? Taking the money, I mean.*'

He knew what she meant, of course. He drew a speech bubble above the stick version of himself on Josie's picture. He knew it wasn't the right time to discuss their relationship, but he wasn't being selfish. This was still all about Josie. How could he leave the family home after this? Josie would need extra protection. She would need her big, strong dad to watch her. Until paranoia dissipated, it would take two parents to watch her in shifts 24/7.

'I'm okay with it. Detective Miller just said there's probably been a delay of some kind. That's why the kidnappers want to call us later. I'm sure their wanting me to bring the money is nothing to do with me.'

He wasn't so sure, but couldn't say anything that might worry her. He needed to keep her calm. He asked her to tell him all about Iceland's famous rocket ship church. And as she spoke, he wrote inside the speech bubble:

I'm going nowhere today, Josie. Never again. Going to stay right by your side until you're big and strong enough to take care of yourself.

CHAPTER NINE

For half an hour, Nick threw his fists and tried to relieve pressure with each powerful punch. When Anna had arrived home, they hadn't let him say much more than a greeting. She needed to be debriefed while her memory was fresh. So he'd slipped down into the cold cellar to sluice away frustration on an old sofa cushion nailed to the bare brick wall. When his knuckles burned from the heavy impacts, he turned to the pull-up bar. He'd told someone to call him the moment he could have his wife back, but the first he knew of it was when her hands lay on his back as he hoisted himself up, teeth gritted, grunting with exertion and frustration. The shock made him release his grip and thud to the floor. He wanted to turn into her arms, but he didn't want her to see the rage on his face. He needed to say something.

'We have to prepare for the worst.'

Anna's voice was sharp and confident. 'No, Josie is coming home today.'

He grabbed the bar again. The effort was putting pain in his muscles and he needed that. Right now, unable to share his wife's optimism, he needed his brain to focus on something other than the hole in his heart.

'This is my fault,' he moaned. 'I was too weak. I did nothing. I couldn't stop them from taking her. What if I can't help her this time? I can't promise.'

He felt her arms encircle his chest from behind. The extra weight felt good to power against. The extra pain. He wanted the pain. He deserved the pain, for his weakness.

'Well, I *will* make you that promise,' she said. 'I'll get our little lady home.'

*

Nick pushed open the door of the playroom and found Miller on her phone, her back to him. She was at the window, absently running a toy police car back and forth along the sill.

'But I said I can't, darling,' she said, her voice cracking a little.

He stopped, realising he was listening to a personal call.

The next thing she said confirmed it: 'No, don't be like that, Liz, you've known about the Sunday rota for weeks. I…' Her head twitched and Nick knew his presence had been fathomed. 'Call you later. No, look, I—'

She looked at her phone, then put it away. Whoever it was had hung up on her. A domestic of some sort, with another woman. He felt awkward overhearing, for all of two seconds. Then more pressing matters took over.

'Bennet said you had some information for us. So let me ask you something while my wife isn't listening. And I want the truth. The NSPCC has had nearly two thousand cases of trafficked children in the last ten years. Is my little girl on her way to London or abroad even, to go work in a brothel?'

'There's nothing to suggest that, Nick.' Still with her back to him, Miller took a moment to raise a finger to one eye, which he figured was to wipe away a tear that hadn't fallen. Then she turned his way, back to business, wholly professional again. 'Where did you get that idea? Reading on the Internet? Unwise, my friend. There's been a ransom demand, remember.'

He tried to read deception in her face, but it wasn't there. If anything, she was surprised he'd made such a leap and it made him realise he had, indeed, paid too much heed to a bunch of statistics posted online. He turned to leave. 'We're in the kitchen when you're ready.'

*

She got to the kitchen twenty seconds later, carrying a laptop. Anna was seated, Jane was making tea, her fingers fast and deft within her comfortable body space, but Nick buzzed with too much energy and virtually hopped from foot to foot.

'Thank you all for meeting me,' Miller said, her voice croaky. As she lay the laptop on the table and stood behind it, Anna got up and approached the fridge. The detective was working the mousepad when Anna put a sandwich in foil and a bottle of water – Nick's packed lunch for a job he no longer had – right down on the keyboard.

'You need water,' Anna said. 'And you fed your people but I've not seen you eat.'

Miller looked ready to object, but took a sip of the water and a bite of the sandwich. Just a fragment of each, as if only to appease Anna. Then she leaned over the laptop again and started working the keyboard, doing everything upside down. Her position exposed more of her chest tattoo – the helmeted warrior had a muscled torso, but the legs of a horse: a centaur. It provoked a strange thought in Nick: *No one really knows anyone, do they?*

The map Nick and Anna had seen earlier was back. The > shape that traced the route of the hunted VW Passat from the lock-up garage now looked like an elongated Z, because another pin had been added, this time a mile east of the Nuthall mark, still in Nuthall but on the other side of the M1. The M1 was a line cutting the Z in half.

Miller waited a few seconds until Jane had put a tea before Anna and taken her seat. Nick stood behind both women, still fidgeting with excess energy.

Miller tapped the top left point of the Z: '03.11 text message from Nick's mobile. At the lock-up garage.' She dragged her finger to the top right corner: '05.02 call to your home. From the A38

near the two Ashfield market towns, east of the M1.' Bottom
left: 'The 07.13 call to the hospital. From around the town of
Nuthall, west of the M1.' And lastly the bottom right point of
the alphabet's ultimate letter: '10 a.m. call directing Anna to the
Rotherham phone box. Still in Nuthall, but barely a mile east of
the call that came nearly three hours earlier.'

'Seems to me they've reached their destination if they barely
moved in three hours. So it's Nottingham after all.' All turned to the
voice from the doorway. Middleton. He seemed to take their silence
as a point proven, and vanished just as quickly as he'd materialised.

'Ignore him, Nick,' Anna said, fiddling with a watch she'd
recently put on. 'I'll talk to him.'

Miller stared right into Nick's eyes. 'Nobody is accusing you
of anything, Nick.' She got back to business to quickly shift the
subject. 'As we've shown, they're probably avoiding major roads
like the M1 because of the cameras. The zigzagging south could
be so we can't determine a straight path to a particular place. But
the movement west between the 07.13 and 10 o'clock calls is tiny
given the three-hour gap. As Mr Middleton said, they might have
reached their destination. Nuthall. Possibly the portion west of
the M1, location of the 07.13 call.' She jabbed the bottom left
corner of the Z. 'They might have made a little journey east for
the 10 o'clock just to make sure their phones weren't captured
in the same spot. It's possible they're hanging around in Nuthall
awaiting something and will move on. Of course, it's possible they
had a delay, like a puncture or such.'

Nick said, 'Maybe they made a little journey, as you say, but
not for the ten call.' He leaned between his wife and sister-in-law
and jabbed the screen hard enough to rock the laptop. Bottom
right corner of the Z. 'This big housing estate here. Maybe they
already got where they were going, but drove a mile west for the
7 a.m. call. This B600 here, it goes right under the M1 and just
about connects the two pins. Maybe with the last call at ten they

just couldn't be bothered to move and made it right from where they've been holed up.'

Miller raised her eyebrows, clearly impressed with Nick's theory. But Anna surprised everyone by saying, 'Does it matter? They're going to give Josie back. We just have to wait for the call.'

'If there's a chance to find her, Anna…' Nick said. 'We don't know if they will give Josie back, not for sure.'

'But the police can't just storm into a housing estate and search all the places. What if they are there and they panic and run? And hurt her? I don't like that idea.'

'But if we can get her back for sure, why no—'

'No, I don't like it.' She pushed back her chair and stood. 'I don't want that risk. They just want the money. They're going to give her back.'

Nick couldn't believe what he was hearing.

Miller put her hands up. 'Hey, guys, just calm it down. Nobody is invading anywhere just yet. I'll have this area looked at, but, apologies, we don't know anything yet for sure.'

'They just want the money, and they'll give her back,' Anna said, and hurried from the kitchen.

Annoyed to see her upset, and needing someone to blame, Nick glared at the detective.

'That's all we've heard from you people so far. You don't know anything.'

*

Nick, taxi alone, join the Bongos.

This time the contact came to Anna's mobile, by text, twenty minutes before midday. She jumped off the toilet and rushed out, calling for everyone.

Google faced an inquisition. Bongos: 'nickname for members of Bongo Bingo, a bingo club on Corporation Street' – again in

Rotherham, just a few hundred metres from the George Street phone box.

Twice made for no coincidence and the detectives decided that the kidnappers had a big tie to that town. Databases got hit to cross-reference Bongo Bingo with Nuthall, then Nottingham, then Nottinghamshire. Someone offered to try to find someone with a criminal record as well as Bongo status. Someone else said they should check out the club's staff. Another said becoming a member of a gambling establishment meant filling in a form and handing it to reception – under the glare of CCTV.

But they couldn't contact the club yet, because that might alert the kidnappers, if they had a contact or a scout therein. And because there was no time: the text hadn't said when, but nobody doubted the kidnappers had meant *right now*. A taxi was called. Nick kissed Anna's cheek and told her everything would be fine.

'Don't worry about me. Good luck.'

Happy that she seemed confident, no longer a shivering wreck, he grabbed the shoebox and went out. Middleton even wished him luck.

*

Corporation Street was lined with commercial establishments on both sides, but partly open to the east with access to Minster Gardens and All Saints Church. It was also one-way. The taxi found a spot right outside the bingo club. Nick paid and got out. The shoebox was tucked under his arm with bear-hug strength. He had a horrible fear of being mugged.

Bongo Bingo's ground floor glass frontage allowed him to see inside reception. One old lady sitting behind the desk in a pink shirt with a cartoon bingo balls motif. A couple of women, and a young man in a tracksuit and baseball cap playing fruit machines against one wall. If he'd seen a unicorn inside, this day wouldn't have felt more surreal.

'Yob on the fruit machine,' he said, trying not to move his lips. He felt silly doing it. There was no reply: the transmission was one-way because an earpiece couldn't be risked.

Nick watched the young man as he entered and approached the desk. He pretended to take in the reception, turning in a circle. It was so he could sweep his tiny collar camera over the young man.

*

In the Carters' living room, Nick's crackly voice was heard asking to join the club. The female receptionist told him to fill in a blue form. He thanked her and then there was silence, presumably as she got back to work, and Nick jotted down his details. Anna listened from her place by the patio door. She opened the blinds with two fingers and peered out, her face grim.

Nick's camera had given the detectives a description of the receptionist, which was passed by Bennet down the phone to the bingo club's general manager, who'd been contacted at home on his week off.

'Negative on the receptionist,' he said a few seconds later. 'Sixty years old, wheelchair, only friend is her dog.'

Anna glanced out into the garden again, and shook her head in frustration.

On speaker, a phone rang. The room heard the receptionist say the call was for Nick. Someone asking to speak to the guy in the black T-shirt who just walked in. Whispers flowed around the room as everyone realised the kidnappers had called him at the club.

Nick's camera shuffled forward and his arm lifted the phone out of shot. The picture vibrated, but not because of a technical fault. Nick's whole body was shaking.

'Hello?' Nick said. But there was no response.

'His mic can't pick it up,' Miller said. 'Everyone, get ready to move. This is it.'

The room got tense, but Anna was looking out the window again. Unable to bear listening to the showdown, Jane had opted to sit out in the garden, in the sun, and the Family Liaison Officer, probably bored because her social skills had been sidelined, had joined her. They were out there now, chatting away, and Anna stared, and then checked her watch, and wished Jane would damn well get away from her.

*

'How are you, Nick?'

His stomach lurched. This was the man who'd taken Josie. And a man it definitely was, even though a woman had called Anna using a voice disguised as male. He'd been warned of the danger of antagonising this person, who could react excessively and destroy his world. But stress and fear had short-circuited the part of his brain in control of logic.

'What kind of man takes a young girl? You break into my house and do this? You're not human, you're a damn animal, and if you hurt her it'll be the last damn thing you ever regret. Where is she?'

*

In the living room, Nick's words hit like a concussion wave. Anna turned from the window and felt light-headed. Jane gasped. Middleton yelled, 'What the hell is that idiot doing?'

Bennet called for quiet, and they waited. Onscreen, even the fruit machine players captured by Nick's bodycam had turned at his outburst and were captivated.

'Under the Crazy Ninjas,' the voice said.

Someone in the room asked what that meant, but the answer came moments later. Nick's camera bounced towards the young man in a tracksuit, who darted aside as if out of the path of an avalanche. Nick's arms grabbed the fruit machine.

'Mobile phone,' Bennet said as everyone watched Nick bend to pick up something from the carpet where the Crazy Ninjas fruit machine had stood. On a separate radio feed, the tech guy, who was near Bongo Bingo, announced he'd need time to grab the signal.

The moment Nick picked the phone up, it rang. As before, they heard him say hello. As before, it was all they heard. They waited.

And then he ran.

*

'Well, Nick, I suddenly believe you about killing me, which means I'm now scared. You got me worrying you'll get here and hurt me. Better I run now, eh? Better I bury your girl so she can't tell the police anything and just run away to another country and pray you don't find me.'

Nick breathed hard while his heart raced. Outside Bongo Bingo, he turned left and jogged down the street. His clear distress and wild eyes cleared the crowded pavement before him. 'I'm sorry,' he said, the words like acid in his throat. 'You got kids?'

'Did the negotiator teach you to go for "hooks"? So we can have something mutual to chat about and do the bonding thing? We could talk about your kid, so that soon I like her and can't bring myself to hurt her. And then all that guilt makes me let her go and go throw myself under a bus. I've got one kid. Yours. Remember that. And one knife, and I really can't think of much more I need to ruin the rest of your life. Are you at the estate agent's yet?'

Nick pulled up outside a branch of Reeds Rains. 'I'm here. Look, I just meant please understand my emotion. I want my little girl back.'

'Then I can't worry about you, can I? Promise you won't hurt me?'

'What?'

'You need to promise, Nick. I want you to promise never to hurt me.'

He knew he had no choice but to go along with whatever game this animal was playing. So he said it: 'I promise I won't hurt you for taking my daughter.'

'You didn't say never. You might plan to come after me in ten years' time. Do I have to cut and run?'

'I promise I will never hurt you.'

The guy gave a giggle.

'Good. Right, now, memorise the price and location of the house two across and one up on the latest properties. Then go inside and talk to the youngest one. She's got your next instructions. Here's the code for her...'

*

Nick had had the foresight to activate the mobile phone's speaker, so the police could now hear the kidnapper. And he aimed his camera to perfectly capture the advertisement for a two hundred grand detached house in Doncaster. A detective offered to track it and got on his phone to do so. Someone was already trying to learn all about the Reeds Rains staff. Miller and Bennet were in radio contact with various players dotted around Rotherham city centre, who would mobilise depending on where Nick went. Others were on the Internet or their phones, or conferring with each other. So many people, so much activity. Like a military operation. Unwilling to listen, and unable to get near Jane, Anna went for the playroom.

As she passed the toilet, Detective Constable Ella Hicks came out. Anna tried to get past without acknowledging her, but noted the young woman looked pained and was rubbing her swollen belly. So she stopped and asked if everything was okay.

Ella nodded. 'The boss ordered us all burgers. She doesn't have kids, obviously. Now my baby's telling me, *heck no, Mum.'*

Her eyes narrowed as she felt a twinge.

Anna took her arm. 'You should go sit down. Don't overdo things.'

The detective nodded and shuffled away, and Anna put her out of her mind and entered the playroom. She stopped right in the middle and stared at Josie's toys. Some people created shrines for their lost children, left their rooms intact over the years, like time capsules, but that seemed wrong. That would be like clutching on to a lost dream. But the thought of loading up Josie's clothing and toys for a charity shop, of casting all her drawings into the bin, seemed worse.

No. She was determined that wouldn't happen: Josie would get rid of those things herself, as a young woman who'd grown out of them. She felt her clenched fists send sharp nails into her palms, but the pain gave her motivation.

She picked up one of Josie's Paw Patrol colouring books, which had a page of stickers inside. Josie had half coloured in the dog called Rubble. She stared at the picture and felt a mix of anger and sorrow. Cartoon dog and grieving mother: both needed Josie to complete them. Well, she would be back soon to do it.

*

There were only two people in the estate agent's, a middle-aged man and a young receptionist. Nick stopped just inside the doorway, trying to buckle down his roiling emotions. If this woman had his next instructions, she was part of this, and he would have to roll with the pantomime. She seemed to have her act nailed down, the way she smiled at him as he approached. No fear of attack, or arrest. A perfect act. She asked what she could do for him. He wondered if she was the kidnapper's girlfriend. The male was typing away on a computer, oblivious. There was a real temptation to grab this girl, to take his own hostage and… what, swap prisoners? The bizarreness of this whole shebang was becoming dreamlike. He squeezed down on the phone in his hand, like an anchor to keep him in the nightmare lest he forgot what was at stake.

'Sir?'

'A chill wind takes the warmest leaves from the highest trees.'

Even before he heard laughter from the phone in his hand, the girl's puzzled glare told him what he needed to know. He managed to hold back rage until he was clear of the branch and pacing the pavement.

'You piece of shit. What the hell are you playing at? Where's my girl?'

'Okay, Nicky-boy. Calm down. I was testing to see if the cops would swoop if they thought they had one of us. You passed the test so let's get down to the real deal, okay? Are you calm now? Do you want your girl or not?'

He stopped pacing and closed his eyes. It helped. 'I want her back. I've got your money. It's what you want. I'll do what you want.'

'Eight million men were conscripted into the fight against the Germans in the Second World War, as well as many unmarried women. Do you care, Nicky-boy?'

Behind the man's voice, he heard a roaring noise, like a chain-saw. 'What's this got to do with my daughter? Look, please, can I speak to her before I do this? You'll get your money, I promise. Just put my little girl on the line.'

The chainsaw noise continued.

'Family strife, Nick. All those souls drafted into the war left a lot of old people without support, and the government's poverty policies weren't up to the job. We need our old people. They built this world, yet they get overlooked. The problem continues to this day. Do you remember six years ago when you were in the city centre and you walked right past someone collecting for the old? I swore vengeance that day. Now the dues will be paid.'

'Are you listening? Do you want this money or not? Put my daughter on. Please.'

'Go into the Age UK charity shop.'

It was right next door, just feet away. He stepped closer so he could look inside. An old lady was behind the counter and jabbering to the only other occupant, a similarly aged man scanning the cheap books. He didn't approach the door.

'What the hell are you talking about? Where's my daughter?'

'In you go. Let's get serious now. Dues, Nick. Donate the £50,000 to a good cause.'

*

In the living room, puzzled glances were exchanged as Nick said:

'Donate the ransom money to the Age UK shop? All of it?'

'So the house he mentioned?' Bennet said. 'Is that still part of this?'

No one spoke up, which was answer enough. Nick's camera pushed through the doors. Inside, an elderly pair turned to stare at him, and he just about yelled into his phone:

'I'm inside. Look, let me talk to my daughter and I'll do what you want.'

'You're very demanding and antagonistic. Didn't the hostage negotiator warn you about that sort of behaviour? You'll do what I want or you'll have your kid's funeral without a body. You can bury that shoebox as a token. Donate the money to the frail and helpless, right now. All of it.'

Nick went to the counter. His camera displayed a woman obviously spooked. She started to reach for a phone on the counter. Until he dumped a bunch of money before her.

'There's not a chance my money is going to charity,' Middleton said, moving closer. Like Nick, he was shaking with fear. 'It could be a trick. That story about swearing vengeance because Nick didn't donate money? Six years ago? That's surely a lie. Preposterous. No one would be that... You need to look at the people who work there.'

Bennet put up a hand to stop Middleton from crowding the laptops displaying Nick's camera feed, Internet maps and other relevant details. 'All in hand, Mr Middleton. Please, let us handle this.'

'And you need to watch the shop today, to see who comes and goes. Could be that someone is coming later to pick up—'

'Mr Middleton, I—'

'I'm sorry, I'm sorry. I just… do you think it could really be going to charity? What kind of madness is that?'

'If it gets your granddaughter back, so what?' Anna said. Heads turned to see her beyond the shelving room divider, watching. 'You'd prefer it to go into the hands of criminals?'

'I didn't mean it like that, Anna. You're upset, I understand.'

But she wasn't. She was rearranging ornaments on the room divider, and looking no more stressed than someone awaiting news that her husband had deposited money into a bank.

'Let's focus on getting Josie back,' she said.

*

Once burned, twice shy. Nick stood before the old lady at the counter and said, 'Are you part of this?' In a repeat, he saw a frown and heard digital laughter.

You twonk, Nick. What, you think she's the mastermind?' Then, another voice, slightly dulled, as if spoken by a guy further from the phone: *'Stop wasting time, Lee.'*

'Whatever,' the first guy said. *'Nick, leave the shop now that you've done your good deed and let's get you your daughter back.'*

At first he couldn't move. Another kidnapper. Two men. But he knew that already, didn't he? Four people had been clocked in the van that came for Josie. 'Okay. I'm going. You know, we were going to call our daughter Lee at one point. But we changed it to—'

'Now you remember the hostage guy's tricks, eh? Get out the sodding door, Nick.'

*

'Are you going to run that name? A check for criminals named Lee? It sounds like one man slipped up and used the other's real name.'

'Calm down, Mr Middleton,' Bennet said. 'We know what to do.'

Nick's camera made for the exit, but at the door the voice stopped him. It stopped everybody.

'Er, Nick, you seem to have left my money behind.'

'What?'

'Just a joke, Nick. Now you've got to rob an old lady in a charity shop.'

'Why are you doing this?'

'Why do japes exist, Nick? Because they're bloody funny.'

'You arsehole.'

Surely such an insult was at the top of Miller's list of 'barbs' – things you just didn't say to a kidnapper – but nobody was worried this time. Sure enough, the kidnapper's laughter bellowed out of the speakers. One of the detectives tossed down his pen. 'This idiot's just playing with us.'

The second voice said:

'No more games, Baltazar.'

Another laugh.

'Wow, now your police have two names to check. Okay, no more games, Nick. Get my money and get to the train station. Platform 2. Toss this phone down a grate outside. You'll find another in the bin at the train station. And from now on don't say a word unless you have to. No more hinting for the police, or I'll turn your kid inside out. Let's see if I'm joking about that.'

*

'What are you doing?'

Anna spun at the sound of the voice. Bennet was in the kitchen doorway, watching her. Anna was holding the kettle and a small sewing needle, which she tossed on the counter.

'Killing time,' she told the detective. 'This isn't easy for me.'

He nodded and stepped closer, wielding his phone. He showed a picture of a young guy and she instantly recognised the man last seen in a grainy still image from CCTV in a B&B. This was a high-quality face-and-shoulders shot, though: he was surely no more than twenty, ponytail and shaved sides ginger, and had patchy skin with teeth to match. The ginger hair immediately made her picture how Josie might look when his age. Bennet asked if she recognised him.

'No. This is a – what is it called, a mugshot? From the police. So you've arrested this man? Did this man take my daughter?'

He explained. The team watching the B&B for the man known as Dom had decided it was worth risking a peek inside his room. A spare key got them inside, where they fingerprinted a fidget spinner found on the bed and achieved a hit. Bennet just got the news seconds ago. The guy had been arrested for affray a few years back.

'And Dom's his real name. Dominic Watson-Bruce, nineteen years old, from Northampton—'

There was a yelp as Anna, turning to replace the kettle, caught it on the edge of the worktop and dropped it. It hit the floor with a clump and vomited water across her leg.

'Wow, are you okay?' he said, grabbing a tea towel from the worktop.

She snatched it off him.

'Fine, it's not boiling.' Bending to rub at her wet jeans, she added, 'I don't know that name or anyone from Northampton.'

'He gave a home phone number when he was arrested. I just called and got his mother. But she claims he doesn't live there. He lives with his dad, always has done, and she's not heard from him in a week, and she's got no contact number for him or any idea who would.'

She turned to the sink and ran the tea towel under cold water. Still she wouldn't look at him. 'So what happens next?'

'We keep watching the B&B in case he returns. You're sure that leg is okay?'

'Okay. I mean, my leg's okay.'

'Okay. I better get back in the other room. Do you want to come and watch the progress?'

Her back to him as she wrung excess water from the tea towel, she shook her head. 'It's too much to bear. I can't watch it.'

Bennet said he understood, then got out of there, and he did so aware that she hadn't met his eyes since she dropped the kettle. At his mention of the suspect's name, or the location.

*

Nothing in the bin outside Rotherham Central. Nick left behind a lot of puzzled people as he ran past the ticket office, over the bridge across the tracks and down on to Platform 2. Here, he stuck his hands into the only bin he could see and got lucky. An old phone, smeared with drying yoghurt. He couldn't help wonder if that part was intentional.

Nothing happened for the next couple of minutes. Nick scanned faces, seeking someone shiftily watching him. But the problem was that the seven or eight on the platform had watched him rooting through a bin, so all gave him furtive glances. He also watched who entered after him, knowing that both sides, good and bad, might seek to deposit someone close by at all times. Throughout, he said nothing, just in case, somehow, the kidnapper learned of his betrayal.

The phone rang.

'It's 12.18, Nick. The 12.32 to Leeds, that's your train. Once there, you'll go to the Queens Hotel next to the station. Book room 50 and look under the bed. Take what's there and give it to a man who will be sitting in the foyer when you come back down from the room. He's going to leave your next instructions on his seat.'

The caller hung up before Nick could reply. *Withheld number.* He fought the urge to throw the phone. And he kept his emotions in check.

A middle-aged man in a white coat came on to the platform, just as the 12.20 to Meadowhall rolled in. The man tried his best to look casual, but Nick could see his chest heaving as if he'd been running. He knew something was off with the guy, but he turned his eyes away. If this guy was part of it, and he knew Nick knew, it would ruin everything.

Soon everyone who had business in Rotherham or outside it had passed through a pair of sliding doors and the Meadowhall train was ready to depart. Nick looked at the phone and pretended to be reading something, but his peripheral vision caught White Coat taking a bench seat. And watching him.

The phone rang.

*

Anna entered the living room, her eyes on movement beyond the room divider as detectives crowded their technology in their little control centre. She heard Miller give instructions regarding a hotel. Something about Leeds. The number 50. From the speaker, she could hear Nick's heavy breathing, and the public address system announcing a train about to depart. She paused while her mind raced. Leeds and hotels and train stations? What were those bastards making him do? She didn't want to hear it. She certainly couldn't watch it. It was a struggle, though, to detach herself.

She peered through the blinds to see Jane and the FLO still on the garden bench, chatting away and enjoying the sun. Her poor sister, unable to listen to developments and shutting herself away. Jane was spinning her teacup around one finger. Empty.

On speaker, a phone rang. Nick answered.

'On the train, now!' that horrible voice said.

A bustle of activity suddenly, as detectives jumped into new action. They sounded worried. Fearful, Anna backed out of the room and checked her watch. 12.21 p.m.

*

Nick leaped on to the train just before the doors locked shut. He fell against the doors, phone clamped to his ear.

'What are you playing at now? Is this another trick? Don't you want this damn money?'

'New plan, Nicolas.'

Nick froze. Similar accent, but a new voice. Why?

'This train stops at Meadowhall and then terminates at Sheffield. Six minutes to Meadowhall, another ten to the terminus. Sit on the left side, window seat. Enjoy the view. At Meadowhall Interchange, there's a row of lockers. Code 6437. Put the money inside number 15 and take out the new mobile inside, and then you're done. I'll call you again to tell you where your child is after we get the money and get away nice and safe.'

'Who are you? Are you the one who's got my daughter?'

The caller hung up. Nick got to a seat on wobbly legs. Now he didn't care who heard. He said, 'I hope you got that. Locker 15 at Meadowhall station. Combination number 6437. And this voice was someone new. That's two men who've called, not a woman. Get working on it. How's my wife?'

Then he remembered he couldn't receive, only transmit. The tiny camera sewn into the inside of his T-shirt, his connection to so many protectors, no longer felt like a lifeline. As the train left the station, it became a raft sending him far out to sea. He thumped his chest to try to restore rhythmic breathing. He'd never felt so alienated, or lost, or helplessly weak.

'Anna,' he croaked into air, 'if you're listening, I love you. I love this family and I'm going to put it back together. I'm going to get her back if it's the last thing I do. I promise.'

*

'I have to get some air. I can't listen to this.'

'You can't go out, Mrs Carter. Not yet.'

'I need air.' Anna grabbed her jacket from the peg. 'I'm not under arrest. I'm going to see a friend across the road. I can't be here, listening to *that.*' *That* was the commotion in the living room as detectives scrambled to make sense of what had just happened.

DC Ella Hicks, standing in the hallway, said, 'Nobody should go out. Not yet. Not until we know what's happened.'

'Let me tell you what's happened,' Anna said as she threw her jacket on. 'You people failed. My little lady is gone, and I'm not about to sit and listen to you people run around like headless chickens.'

'But what about your husband? He'll need you here when he gets back.'

Both women heard the living room patio door open, and then raised voices as Jane learned the bad news. She started calling for Anna. Anna quickly opened the front door and darted through.

Moving faster than she should have, and holding her belly to stop it wobbling, Hicks got past her on the path and put up her hand. That clear and universal gesture again. This time it got the recognisable obscene one Anna had avoided offering earlier.

The friend across the road was Mr Parker, a middle-aged man in a wheelchair courtesy of a fall from his roof while tiling. Just before he opened the door to her knock, Anna glanced back to see the young DC in her garden, looking like she couldn't decide what to do.

'Anna? You okay?'

Hicks went back inside. Anna turned to Mr Parker, who asked if Nick was okay, if there was trouble, what the police were doing here, and if there was anything he could do to help. Thankful that the street didn't know about the kidnap yet, she quickly invented a story.

'Oh, we're fine. Nick's workplace got broken into late last night, so he's been in and out of the house all night sorting that. Josie is with friends while we give statements to the police. Everything is fine.' She smiled, gave a sly glance at her watch, stepped inside and closed the door. 'The police are being so nice, and I wanted to make them some of that chargrilled mackerel and sour beetroot you did for us last week. Do you mind if I pick some of your beetroot?'

Of course he didn't. He spun his chair and led, and she had to contain her eagerness to get into his back garden.

*

Ninety seconds later, Nick was still talking to Anna, who wasn't there to hear any of it, when the train rumbled past the New York Stadium and took a small iron bridge across the River Don. That was where it happened.

The phone rang. Nick jammed it to his ear and opened his mouth to speak, but didn't get the chance.

'Don't say a word. Wait. Take the money out of the box, but leave it in the freezer bag. I want you to read out a couple of the serial numbers for me.'

Nick did as instructed. He dropped the box on the floor and held the wrapped cash in one hand, thoroughly disjointed. Serial numbers? He could feel blood pulsing in his neck. Ahead, six rows away, he saw White Coat, peeking at him from behind a guy in a beanie.

But Nick had only just made it on to the train. White Coat must have bombed through the doors in a serious hurry, and that could mean only one thing.

Suddenly, it hit him. White Coat would be taking the money. Minus the box, the cash bundle was small enough to secretly slip to the guy as he walked past. It was all another trick. There was no locker awaiting him at—

'Toss the money and the phone out the window, RIGHT NOW!'

The vehemence in the scream allowed no pause, no deliberation. Nick leaped to his feet and rammed open a sliding portion of the window at the top, and tossed out the package. The phone was right behind, before he'd had chance to realise he was killing his only link to the kidnappers.

In the half-second he got to imprint the lay of the land in his memory, he saw a river, and thick shrubbery along both banks, but he also saw a path running parallel to the water, and on that path was what looked like a quad bike. And then the train was over the bridge and the money was far behind. He didn't see where it landed, whether it was on land or water, and he didn't see anyone near the quad. But he didn't need to.

Face against the window, looking back as the river and the money fell far behind, Nick tried to digest what the hell had just happened.

'Base, it's gone,' he heard someone yell. 'He took a call and just lobbed the money and the phone right out the window, quick as a flash. Bridge over the River Don. Money is in the River Don just past New York Stadium.'

White Coat, who was on his feet and holding a radio by his mouth. Not a kidnapper at all. A police officer. Across ten feet and a dozen heads, both men leaned against glass and stared at each other.

'So where the hell is my daughter?'

*

When Bennet pulled up in the car park at Meadowhall Interchange, Nick walked away from White Coat without a word. He seemed to fall more than climb into the back seat. Bennet climbed in and said, 'Why did you refuse to answer the tactical team's questions?'

'Is my girl dead?'

Bennet turned to face Nick. 'Don't think like that. I told you how this might go down, do you remember?'

'No. What do you mean? You knew this was going to happen?'

'No, nobody knew what would happen. I apologise for being blunt, but we couldn't expect these people to carry your daughter about with them. We believe that once the kidnappers are clear, someone will either call us with details of where to find her, or she'll be let go in a street somewhere. Someone will find her, take her to a police station, and you'll get her back.'

Nick really wanted to believe that, because it made sense, but paranoia created major doubt. 'That's the way it goes, is it? Every single time? No third option?'

Bennet gave a careful, analytical look. 'Stay off the Internet, Nick. Trust me.'

'You mean you promise?'

Bennet started to drive. He didn't answer the question, but said, 'You refused to talk to the tactical team. Why?'

Nick lay down across the back seat and scratched his forehead with all ten fingernails, as if trying to coax away a headache. 'Tactical team. Is that why I don't recognise that guy you stuck on the train? Why did nobody say there were a bunch of strangers following me around? So how many people was it who watched my daughter slip through their fingers?'

Bennet started the car and pulled out of the car park. 'DCI Miller was in joint-command, but we used a ransom kidnap call-out team from the National Crime Agency. They're trained for this kind of surveillance—'

'Forget that. I'll decide how many people I'm suing later. There was a quad bike near the river. What do you know?'

'We're looking for the quad. We'll try to find CCTV, witnesses, the usual. We're going back to all the places you've been. We're working hard to—'

Nick groaned. 'Don't say anything else. Always the political answers. I'm getting tired of it. Just drive me home. My wife will be beside herself and I need to get there.'

'We'll be home soon. Nick, you should have answered Tactical Support's questions. I'm sorry about what happened, and I promise we'll do everything we can to get Josie back home. But now you need to help us with that. From the start, at the bingo club. We saw and we heard most, but pretend I know nothing. It's the little details we need.'

Nick kicked out, catching the back of Bennet's seat. The detective ignored it. 'I want to kill every one of them.'

'Completely understandable. But believe me, a life sentence in a cage is worse, and that's what they've got coming.'

'What if Josie is in a cage and they can't get back to her? Or they just decide it's too risky to go back? If she's tied up and she can't breathe properly and she's got no water and they just abandon her…'

Legs again thumped the driver's seat. Bennet slid the car into the side of the road and turned to face Nick. 'You have to try to relax, hard as that seems. Look, I'll be honest, I don't know for sure if they plan to release your daughter. Not for certain. But they wanted money and they got it. It makes no sense to hurt Josie now.'

'If you say so.'

'Tell me about the callers. You said two men. Did you recognise either voice? Are you sure this wasn't one person?'

'Two men, Bennet. Not some woman doing a damn Darth Vader impression. Look, no more questions from you. You saw the show. You know what I know. Now you talk to me. You tell me what you know and what you're doing to find my daughter and these bastards. And start driving again so I can get back to my wife and make sure she's okay.'

Bennet didn't object. The vehicle started rolling.

'Dominic Watson-Bruce,' Nick said, tasting the name while staring at the man's mugshot on Bennet's phone. 'They were going south and Northampton is a straight run south. So that's where they're going? I want to go there. If they're going to release my daughter, and it's going to happen there, I want to be there for her as soon as possible.'

Bennet said, 'We're not certain this man is in charge of your daughter. He's only nineteen and he's only ever been done for car theft and some petty troublemaking. We think his role was to secure stolen vehicles for the rest of the team. He might even have no idea what the vehicles were for. He might not have many answers. And you said the caller had the Sunderland accent, which this kid doesn't.'

'But Dominic is in Sheffield and you told me the text message Anna got about the Bongo Bingo club was traced to Sheffield. So maybe Anna was right and Josie *is* still here, and this guy's watching over her. The calls being made from a vehicle heading south could be a diversion, because they'll know you can trace the phones.'

'We don't know how many people are involved, or if it's one team, two teams. Josie could be with the south-travellers, or they could be a diversion. I'm sorry, we just don't know. But this Dominic is a petty lawbreaker and not experienced enough to be left in charge of a kidnap victim. And there's no guarantee that the south-travellers are headed to Northampton just because one of their team hails from there.'

Nick knew that but had hoped for a more positive answer. So Josie could basically be anywhere. He gave a frustrated laugh and lay on the seat again.

A moment after handing back Bennet's mobile, it rang.

'Mitigating circumstances, or whatever the lawyers call it,' Nick said. 'What's the least jail time you get for revenge killings? What would happen if I tied them all up in a line and gave Josie a gun and a pound for every decent headshot?'

No answer. Nick raised his head to see the detective with his phone clamped to his ear. Just listening. A few moments later, he hung up and cursed. He pulled the car into the kerb and gave Nick a long glare, clearly reading him.

'What's going on?'

'What *is* going on, Nick? Where's your wife gone?'

'Gone? What do you mean?'

'Right around the time you were on the train, she went across the road to see a neighbour. He says she went to pick beetroot in the backyard. My detective just went to get her back. The beetroot's there. She isn't. Where is she?'

Nick sat up. 'What? She's vanished? Why did you people let her go out? She's not herself. Jesus Christ. Get driving. Get me home.'

Bennet's eyes softened, as if his suspicious tone had been an act designed to make criminals crumble during interview. He got the car moving. 'We'll find her. She seemed to just need to get a break from the house. Nobody knew this was going to happen. Do you have any idea where she would go? Or why?'

'I don't know,' Nick said, but he had a suspicion that Anna was off trying something heroic. Had she figured out something the detectives had missed?

Did she know where Josie was?

*

Bennet drove like a lunatic, but not by a long shot was he the most eager to return. Even before his car had stopped around back of the Carters' bungalow, Nick was out and running. Detectives were in a scramble in his living room, much as he imagined they had been when he escaped the house to confront a child molester. He'd been building up to unloading his anger on Miller, who was top dog and thus responsible for these people and their mistakes, but that changed when he saw Jane pressed into a corner, as if she feared a single step would send one of the frantic detectives barrelling into her. Ignoring Miller, he pushed through the crowd, grabbed Jane's wrist, and dragged her away from the mêlée.

In the bedroom, she hugged him and said, 'I'm so sorry about Josie, Nicky. But they're trying hard to find her. I'm sure she'll be back soon.'

He'd had time to somewhat acclimatise to Josie's disappearance, while Anna's was still a fresh and bleeding wound. 'Thank you. You're right. But what about Anna? Have you any idea where she went? What happened?'

'I didn't see her leave. She was supposed to be across the road with a neighbour, but then I heard she had gone. She's not answering her phone, Nicky. It just rings and goes to voicemail. She knows it's me, so why wouldn't she answer? Oh, where has she gone, Nick?'

Bennet called his name, so he slammed the bedroom door. 'Did she say anything while I was gone? Give any clue? I wonder if she's gone to try to find Josie. Maybe she knows something? Some clue she got when she went to the ransom call? From the man's voice maybe. I felt her attitude changed after that call.'

'Changed? What clue? How would she know something? We all heard the phone call. Those men didn't say anything to her about where Josie is.'

She was right. But he couldn't dispel the idea that Anna had gone to try to find Josie herself. 'Where's your dad?'

'In the kitchen. He's calling people. The police have gone looking, but they wouldn't let us out. But should we go look?'

'I can't.' He really wanted to, but Bennet had already convinced him of what he now told Jane: 'I have to stay here in case those people call about where I can find Josie.'

'Yes, that DCI, Miller, she said that's what will probably happen. They might want to get far away before they say where we can find Josie. Do you think maybe they somehow told Anna where Josie is and that's where she's gone?'

Possible. Bennet had suggested the kidnappers might just release Josie on to the street, but what if their plan had instead been to secretly give a location to Anna? Maybe they'd feared a five-year-old dumped on the street might get snatched again. It was only a theory, but the timeline gave it weight: Anna had run right around the time the money had been delivered.

It would be a dream come true if Anna returned with Josie in her arms, but what if she stumbled into the kidnappers? It didn't bear thinking about, so he pulled the power cable on that train of thought. 'You start calling friends. I'm going to find out if the police know more than they're telling us.'

He got to the living room door when a voice said, 'You two are up to something strange indeed.'

Nabi, the foul detective that Anna had had a problem with. The guy was in her cubbyhole, nice and comfortable, tapping away at the computer and not even having the decency to accuse Nick with his eyes.

'What the hell did you say?'

Nabi didn't even turn. 'I'll get to the bottom of this trickery. That's not what I said, of course, but I'm saying this now. Where's your wife gone?'

Nick started to walk towards him. Aware of this, or suspecting it, Nabi got up and turned.

'Get out of my damn house before I throw you out.'

'Got an anger problem, have we?'

Nick grabbed the guy's arm, or tried to. Nabi slapped away the hand that reached for him, so Nick snaked out his other, but Nabi caught that one by the wrist. And in that position, as if about to dance, both men froze as a voice said:

'You're not giving a good impression here.'

Middleton. He appeared at the kitchen doorway, just inches from both men, who stepped apart like kids giving up a rumble at a teacher's approach. Nick was ready to explode if Middleton said the wrong thing, but, surprisingly, it was Nabi who got his attention.

'Your career rises or falls with your boss, Detective Constable. I heard her tell you to watch your attitude around the victims. I'm a boss, I know the score with insubordinates. Go against her, your superintendent will believe you'll have the same attitude with him if you reach DCI status. Then the chief constable will think you'll be the same as a super. So you'll stop dead, right here, as a constable, with a brick wall ahead and a cliff behind.'

Nabi gave a little laugh and turned to walk away. Middleton did the same, not a word to Nick, and Nick watched him return to the kitchen table and sit. He could hardly believe what had just happened. He wanted to say thank you, but didn't get the chance.

Because the landline rang.

Miller yelled for Nick, who turned so fast into the living room that he bounced painfully off the doorframe. She was standing by the phone, waving him over. She looked haggard, as if stress or lack of sleep was catching up to her. Everyone was watching him.

'Be careful how you answer,' she said as he approached, eyes glued to the phone plugged into a laptop, 'in case it's a neighbour or a reporter, and don't—'

He barely heard: he snatched up the phone and said, 'Anna?'

On speakerphone, they all heard a mechanical voice:

'You have received a text message from 07…'

Anna's number. A message from Anna, delivered by a computer that had no idea of the impact it was about to land.

Hi, babe, it's Anna. You're not her real dad. Sorry about the trick to get our going-away money. Hope YOU have got good pictures of her in your head. XXX.

CHAPTER TEN

'Donna, it's Nick. Is Anna there or have you seen her today? She went out and didn't leave a note.'

'Maybe she finally got sick of you and left, Nick. My John told you, you would end up driving her away. Can't say I blame her. Or she's gone out and just doesn't want you to know where she is. Anyway, no, I haven't seen her.'

Five calls to Anna's friends, and nobody had heard from her today. One hadn't been home and he'd left a message, but the other four had all had the same theme: Anna had probably finally left him. These were the same people Anna had frantically called late in the night about Nick and Josie's disappearance, but follow-up contact by the police appeared to have allayed any worry. None knew about the kidnap and they'd eaten up his lie about Anna going out without leaving a note.

That got him thinking. People drifting apart did that, didn't they? Went places without informing each other. Her friends clearly weren't on his side and if Anna had visited one, well, that wasn't his business, was it? Especially if she'd gone for a heart-to-heart about the unfairness of life. So why would anyone tell him where Anna was even if they knew? He gave serious consideration to a series of house visits, just to make sure nobody was hiding her.

But the police wouldn't let him leave the house. They'd told him not to go anywhere and had taken the car key. He couldn't help but worry that they still suspected him of involvement in Josie's kidnap. He and Anna both.

He didn't understand this suspicion. Back when he'd been suspected of taking Josie, certain points had been raised: how would Josie attend school, or a doctor's, or join any other part of society if Nick tried to keep their location secret? Impossible. And the same points negated the notion that Anna had run away with her daughter. She was certainly smart enough to have set this whole thing up, but also smart enough to realise it would be a fool's errand. Anna had known Nick was innocent because of this, but the police hadn't believed it; now Nick, for the same reason, knew she was blameless here. Again the police had serious doubts, but that wasn't the worst of it. Knowing she was innocent meant also knowing something far worse:

That Anna was now in terrible danger, too.

*

When Miller called him inside with news, Nick felt relief. But it was only partly a desire for information. He was sitting at the garden bench and staring at Josie's toys scattered in the turned earth in the corner. He'd expected to feel joy at seeing his girl's things, like using photographs to remember a great holiday, but they were beginning to heighten his sense of loss instead. So partly it was to get away.

The detective was sitting in the dining/incident room, alone. When Nick sat across from her, she lifted a sheet of paper. An old photocopy of a sale receipt for Anna's scrapped Fiat Punto, dated 19th September 2011, from their paperwork file in the cubbyhole. She was waiting for a response. Some kind of detective tactic, maybe.

'Is this scrapyard connected to the kidnap?' He made an impatient hand gesture for her to get to the point.

She tapped the business title at the top: Watson-Bruce Salvage, with a Northampton address.

His jaw dropped. 'Dominic Watson-Bruce, he knows Anna?'

'It's a family-run business, has been for generations, and the owner, Dominic's father, lives on-site. He's divorced, but Dominic, according to his mother, lives there. Which means he was probably there in September 2011. But Dominic, he's only nineteen, so he would have been eleven back when Anna scrapped her car. A child. But, my friend, this is intriguing because you both lived in London, yet Anna chose to scrap her car sixty miles away.'

'But you think she knows someone from that scrapyard? Whoever took Josie? All she ever told me was that that place came as a recommendation from a friend. I don't know who. I remember thinking it was a long way to go. I had to go with her the second time to drive her back.'

That hit some kind of sweet spot in the detective, he saw. She perked up. Second time?

'She went down the first time about a week earlier. I remember it was the day before the 9/11 ten-year anniversary. When I got back from work, she still had the car, though. She told me the people there had refused to take it because of the hit-and-run that had happened.'

'Ah. That's been mentioned before, see. Tell me.'

A week before Anna's first visit to Watson-Bruce Salvage, two hikers had been killed in Ealing on a remote stretch of road. Young students, mown down by a driver who didn't stop. No cameras, no clues, but three days in the police, after some laboratory magic on paint flecks found on the victims, announced that they were seeking a lido blue Fiat Punto from 2003–2006. Same as Anna's. Anna hadn't known about the Punto enquiry, but mechanics at the scrapyard had and they'd told her she needed to keep the car until it was cleared by police. Five days later, police knocked on her door. After her car was checked and cleared of involvement, she returned to Watson-Bruce Salvage and legally scrapped it. Nick had accompanied her in his car in order to drive her back.

Miller nodded. 'I've had my share of car enquiries. A pain to trace and eliminate. Thankfully I don't have to do such footwork now, a hundred times asking, where were you on so-and-so night. Anyhows, where was Anna on the night of that hit-and-run?'

A question, he said, she had already answered for police in London. Her boss, Marc Eastman, had been driving to a function, some forty miles from the scene of the accident, and he'd called her to pick him up. Although by the time she got there he'd already decided to go by taxi.

'Why Anna?'

She sometimes drove him in her car so he could remain inconspicuous. 'So what's the connection here, Detective? You think when Anna scrapped the car she might have mentioned how rich her dad was? The scrapyard has to be connected, that's what you're getting at. Maybe this Dominic overheard her talk about her dad, then grew up and decided he wanted some of that money. So he got her details from the files. Then he set this whole thing up. Maybe it's a scam the scrapyard has going. Find out who's rich and go rob them or—'

He stopped, already knowing it was a big reach.

Miller shrugged. 'Connected, yes. Your theory… possible. But I should mention that my sergeant told me that Anna reacted to the name Watson-Bruce with shock. He believes she knew the name.'

He couldn't miss the hidden accusation. 'So? I remembered the name. I also reacted with shock, as you just saw. The name is memorable because of the story about the hit-and-run. What are *you* saying it means?'

'Again, please, why did Anna scrap the car?'

He didn't know where this was going, but he gave an answer.

'She got disillusioned with London after she almost got car-jacked in the street. She was driving home and someone cut in front and tried to steal her car. He threatened her with a knife, but she managed to drive off. So she wanted to scrap it. Bad memories maybe. Your point?'

'Long way to go to scrap the car. Way out of London.'

'I told you. She got a recommendation. Your point?'

'Why did you leave London?'

He snorted with impatience. 'We were thinking about kids, about a family, and London's too expensive and too hectic. I'm sure Anna told your people this. What's the relevance of any of this?'

'Well, Nick, I apologise if it sounds like I'm interrogating you. Kids, family – the same story Anna's father told one of my detectives. But Anna herself told my people a different story. She said her boss, Marc Eastman, the MP, kicked up a stink with some comment he made about Bovine TB. I looked online for it. It seems farmers get no compensation for killing their affected sheep, pigs and goats, and he wanted that to change. He was accused of trying to increase the animal kill rate. Anna told my detectives she left her job because of this backlash, which wasn't restricted to a bashing in the media. Threats. Personal threats. Some of those animal welfare groups can be quite vindictive, see. Did she ever mention that to you?'

He was puzzled. 'Well, yeah, I knew about that. But she didn't often talk about her job and never really made it out to be a big deal. But I know once she'd left that job, she didn't want to be associated with it. So… is this important? Are you saying this could be about all that animal culling stuff? Some animal rights idiot took my daughter? But it's been eight years.'

She rocked back slightly, as if his words had physical weight. 'It's one thing, Nick, to not talk shop about new policies on unemployment or whatever. Quite something else to not tell your family you were reading death threat letters. It seems this was the reason she changed her name. It affected her that much. Did she tell you why she changed her name?'

Puzzlement was giving over to worry. 'Why is that your biggest concern? That she downplayed this animal rights stuff?

She probably downplayed it so as not to worry me or her family. She told me she wanted to change her name because her dad was angry she'd tossed the job, so if it was because of threats from silly activists, it was to avoid worrying me or her parents. Look, leaving London was because of a combination of things, that included. DCI Miller, I don't like where this is going. You're not looking for some freaked-out activist with an eight-year grudge, because you don't think this is about all that, do you?'

'I don't know what to think, my friend.'

'I disagree. You believe that text from her phone, even though one of the kidnappers also sent a stupid text from my phone. You believe it and you think she went AWOL, so the police don't find out about a dodgy connection to Dominic. So give it to me straight. You think she got this Dominic to help her set this kidnap up.'

In her eyes was a subtle intensity that unnerved him. He could imagine criminals wilting before her in interrogation rooms.

'She ran away from us all, Nick. Right when you were dumping the money, when everybody was looking elsewhere.'

Worry and suspicion were firing up anger, but he dampened it. 'She ran when she heard that name, but not for the reason you think. Not because she's involved in this. She ran because she thinks she knows who took Josie. How can you not see that? How the hell did you become a detective?'

In her eyes there seemed to be sorrow – for him. As if she felt he was naïve, or just stupid. But he suddenly didn't care. Right then, as he was saying it, he knew the truth.

'That's it. Jesus Christ, that's where she's gone. That scrapyard.'

He stood up. She copied. 'You're staying here, Nick.'

He realised the detective had already made plans to visit Watson-Bruce Salvage in search of Anna. And Josie.

'*You* think she's hiding out there. With my daughter and fifty grand, preparing for a new life. *I* think hearing the name

Watson-Bruce told Anna exactly who's got our daughter and she's gone to that scrapyard to save her. Doesn't matter which, because Josie's there either way. So you're going to take me with you. Or I go on my own. Also doesn't matter which. Because I'm going either way.'

*

Jane was in the playroom, trying to kill time by working out a jigsaw by feel alone, when Nick entered to say goodbye to her. And: 'I promise I'll get Josie back.'

She held out her hand for his. 'Don't blame yourself, Nicky.'

'Someone needs to. I should have stopped them taking her. It wasn't like I was asleep and they sneaked in. I confronted them. I had a chance to stop this.'

'And you were lucky you didn't get killed. At least Josie will have a father to come back to.'

They hugged. As he turned, he found Middleton watching from a doorway for a second time that day. This time Anna's father didn't vanish, though. He waved his mobile. 'I've just had a call, Jane. A break-in at my garage. I need to go talk to the security company. Will you be okay here?'

She nodded. 'There are still people to call. I need to be here when Josie comes back. And Anna.'

He nodded. And left without a word. His car was pulling away as Nick exited the house.

On the pavement, Nick stopped to take in the empty spaces on the street, where some of the visitors to the house had parked. But those people had gone now: the Family Liaison Officer, the search team, the forensics team; one by one they had left, probably to continue their jobs at a station or lab. And the foul detective, Nabi, had been sent away by his boss to chase up a dangling end on some other investigation. Their absence at the house, the settling quiet in the rooms, had begun to give a feeling of wind-down, of finality, like a stabling of the air. Like the endgame. He couldn't shake the feeling that this trip to the scrapyard, where answers, and his family, might be kept, would be where that stable air was disrupted, and the storm would open up to play out the final act in this drama. Closure was drawing close.

But a happy ending wasn't guaranteed.

CHAPTER ELEVEN

A few miles outside Northampton was Harpole, and half a mile north of it was Watson-Bruce Salvage, nestled in woods and fields and boxed in by a hill and two roads that met in an L-shape. Apart from a desert oasis of running liquid gold, the last thing Nick expected to see on the smaller of those two tracks was what they came across in a large lay-by around a bend.

Four, he counted: vans. Six: cars. Four: motorbikes, two of them off-road machines, and like their riders conspicuous because they didn't have Northamptonshire Police livery.

'A raid?' Nick said, shocked, but happy. A blitz attack on the scrapyard would give the kidnappers no time to… hurt Josie or Anna. Miller affirmed as the DS slipped the car in behind a van. But that was all she gave him apart from an order to stay in the vehicle. She and Bennet got out to meet an approaching man clad in not much less than full riot gear. Nick buzzed with energy and impatience, knowing Josie could be just a few hundred metres away, but he stayed seated. They could easily have refused to bring him and he didn't want to be sent away now. Not that he would have gone.

Miller was back a couple of minutes later, with some rules.

'Okay, I'm not the boss here today. We've enlisted another police force, but it's their old show, and we can't be ungrateful. They'll secure the site before we go in. They'll let you in afterwards, my friend, but only if you stay by my side. They'll strike quickly to preserve evidence, then call us in.'

'Josie?'

'They know about Josie. But we still have to wait. And they can't go in just yet, I'm afraid.'

He'd remained calm and patient on the way down, partly out of fear that rushing might mean finding Josie dead all the sooner. Now, though, with the scrapyard within reach, with Josie minutes from being in her father's embrace, Nick felt all his pulsating impatience and rage bubbling up. He could have sat still more easily on burning coals. So:

'Why?' he hissed. 'We're right here.'

'Apologies. But please be calm. We have to wait because there's another site.'

'What?'

'The entire Watson-Bruce clan, they've been involved in the scrap trade for ever. And petty crime. The chap who opened this place, like decades ago, one of his kids runs it now. Robert Watson-Bruce. A daughter called Rhona runs another scrapyard, which is way up north. I only just learned this, sorry. That other scrapyard is in Sunderland.'

Sunderland. A solid connection there, which decreased the chances that Watson-Bruce Salvage was a red herring; but Nick could only focus on the fear that—

'Josie might be up there, is that what you're saying? A hundred miles away?'

'We don't know. I'm sorry. Northumbria Police have a team tasked with storming that place. Both teams are to go together, and we're having to wait for things to be ready up that end. We really should be grateful, my friend, because this has all moved very quickly.'

'Because my daughter's in danger.' He grabbed Bennet's iPad from the empty driver's seat. He'd earlier been shown a series of aerial photographs of the site, with Xs to mark intriguing spots. Three of those had been walls of smashed cars, but there were a couple of outhouses, a metal shed by a stream, and the main house, where the owners lived. And what Nick looked at now: a rotting old caravan in a shrubbery-infested corner. It looked abandoned, except that it was connected to a generator and gas tanks.

Suddenly, he was certain Josie was being kept there. But that location was at the far end of the site, easily two hundred metres from the entrance. Not even trained cops on motorbikes could get there quick enough to stop someone slicing Josie's throat, and Anna's, when they heard the front gate booted in.

'Let me go in alone. I'll sneak in, and I'll say I ran from you, so no one gets in trouble. I'll get into that caravan before – why not?'

She'd been slowly shaking her head. 'I know you feel a bit impotent, but we need to preserve evidence, especially if Josie isn't present. These people cannot be allowed a chance to destroy that evidence. So both sites go down at once. After that, we'll go in. You're not here, Nick, to kick open doors. You're here so Josie, if she's here, can ride home right there on the comfy back seat with her dad instead of a bunch of strangers.'

Nick didn't miss that she hadn't painted Anna on to that comfy back seat. 'So it's nothing to do with needing me to negotiate with my wife in case of some stand-off?'

Miller's lack of answer was answer enough.

*

The team way up in Fatfield, Sunderland was ready to rock, so the order came through and engines kicked into life. The bikes were faster, but they held back bar one, whose rider would determine if the gate was locked, and if it was, a van would change that. It was only a thirty-second trip.

The compound was inside a flimsy corrugated iron fence held up by wooden posts, the gate thick and sturdy but also secured only by wood driven into earth. But there was no need to smash it open.

As the strike team rounded the last corner, a mechanic, who'd just slipped out for a cigarette, froze and watched what seemed like an entire police force bearing down on him. Tyres screeched, doors opened, and an army emerged. Miller's car pulled into the other side of the road.

The shocked employee was a bearded young man, big, muscles upon muscles, as if he'd personally hoisted every wreck into the yard from the corners of Britain. He stood before the open gate like Hercules guarding the entrance to Heaven, arms folded, as if his untold thirteenth labour was to stop anyone from entering. But he stepped aside as officers got close. And he said nothing as they pushed through the gate and ran inside, followed by cars and vans and bikes. He was approached by an officer with paperwork. Miller exited the car and accompanied someone inside the scrapyard.

Nick felt like a guy sidelined at a party. He watched the gateway and prayed a police officer would emerge with Anna, with Josie in her arms.

*

'Nabi didn't turn up at the station,' Bennet said, which made Nick look up. But the DS was on his phone, probably to his boss, who was still inside the scrapyard. 'I don't know. I'll have someone call him.'

'Why are you talking about him?' Nick snapped. 'Forget him. What's going on inside there?'

Bennet held up a hand for silence. Nick returned his eyes to the carpet and tried not to let the wait burn him up.

Bennet signed off and said Nick's name. Nick didn't look up.

'My boss just got news. The phone you tossed in the River Don has been analysed. The first male caller was somewhere close to Bongo Bingo, but moving away, towards Sheffield. It was tracked by a number of cell towers. The final tower was only a mile from your home. We think he was the man Anna must have met when she ran.'

'Don't say it like that. Like it was all part of her plan.'

'The second caller, who contacted you at the train station, must have been the quad rider. You were transferred to him because he needed pinpoint timing to get you to toss the money from the train at the right moment.'

'So, what, three teams now?'

'I don't think so. Just two. I would guess that the female caller is being directed by ringleaders here at ground zero because she can make calls on the move. That way we're looking further south while the main players operate up here. A distraction. Both males were in Rotherham city centre originally. One stayed behind. Just the quad rider. CCTV covering your garden showed four perpetrators and there's no reason to believe we're dealing with a larger number.'

'Have you found that damn quad? They don't exactly blend in.'

'It must have transferred to a larger vehicle. We're on the CCTV and seeking witnesses. But it all takes time, Nick.'

Time. Time was something he could feel eroding his mind from the inside out, like acidic cerebrospinal fluid.

Bennet said, 'These traces are going – Wow, Nick, what are you doing? Stay in the car.'

'I need a piss,' Nick said as he kicked open the door and got out.

A lot of woodland had been erased for the salvage yard. Just inside was a shipping container turned into an office, and there was a dirt tennis court behind it. A wide dirt track led to a large open area split into a grid by short rows of cars stacked high, like walls. The rows might have denoted an orderliness upheld at the start of trading, but deeper in it was obvious to spot where laziness and space-saving became the order of the day. The ground was littered with fragments of cars, the aisles were no longer ruler straight, and here and there loose cars lurked like the homeless.

In places walls of cars had toppled and vehicles had been left overturned and smashed. At the back were crushed vehicles and mountainous metal hills.

The high-definition aerial map Nick had studied had also shown him that the line of trees running up to the compound along the side of the road was thin. Behind, a stream that ran parallel right up to the compound wall, then veered left to follow it. The Watson-Bruce clan had utilised as much ground as they could.

He started to walk across the road, towards the trees. He glanced back to see Bennet climbing out of the car. The detective jerked a thumb towards the bushes on the other side of the road.

'Don't play about, Nick. Piss this side.'

Probably not the first time a police officer had heard such a line from a guy planning to make a break for it. He wasn't about to be surprised today.

'Stop, Nick. Come on, man.'

Nick was in the trees a second later, just feet from the iron fencing. Eight steps later the trees vanished, so abruptly he almost sailed out into the river. The bank was barely wide enough for him. He stumbled along, water a foot to his left, the sagging corrugated fence a foot to his right. He could clearly hear the raid taking place: police yelling for people to stop, come out, put that down, and their targets bellowing their confusion.

A hundred metres along, by which time his ankles were burning because of the sloped, summer-hardened earth, the fence and the river turned sharply right, and immediately around the corner he found a section of the barrier that had been broken and replaced by wood. And not set properly. One side leaned inwards, creating a V-shape that he was able to step through.

The mêlée he'd imagined taking place inside had calmed. Nobody was running, nobody was being pinned down. He couldn't hear the whine of bikes on the hunt across fields. It wasn't a drugs cartel stronghold, after all. Men in grimy coveralls were standing around, talking to the police, while other police strolled here and there, looking into nooks and crannies. Some way ahead, one of the outhouses had its door open and there was an officer in the doorway. Beyond that he could see the house, which looked like it was made of corrugated iron painted blue, and this had a police presence outside, too.

But closer: the caravan. A half-naked guy so tanned he looked like a tree stump sculpture was in the doorway, shaking his head at two officers standing before him. He seemed to be reluctant to let them inside.

It was all the stimulus Nick needed.

He rushed that way. Someone shouted for him to stop. Hearing this, the two officers at the caravan turned his way, then stepped into his path. He knew he probably looked like a madman.

'Where's my daughter, you bastard,' he yelled, just feet away now. He felt he had the momentum to power through police, tree sculpture and door without missing a beat. But it didn't happen.

The wall of police met him and he stopped dead. His feet skidded on the dry earth, like a cartoon character building up to a sprint off the line. 'No! Get off me. My daughter might be in there!'

But they didn't get off. He was lifted by powerful arms. He of the scaly brown skin looked on with puzzlement, but not a shred of fear. One of Nick's flailing arms got free and accidentally hit flesh. The next instant, he found himself face down in the dirt, hands behind his back and someone's knee in his spine. Over all the noise he was making, and the orders to calm down, and the vocal confusion of Mister Wooden, Nick actually heard the click of handcuffs snapping on to his wrists. But, worse than all of that, he noticed movement through one of the caravan's windows. A police officer, already inside with Oak Man, who hadn't refused entry at all.

Which meant he had nothing to hide.

'Anna and Josie aren't here,' he heard a female shout. He turned his head, cheek scraping against the arid land. Miller, of course, approaching in that casual and patient way of hers. The officers released him and he got to his knees. The cuffs were removed as Miller squatted before him.

'Dominic Watson-Bruce isn't here, either. Nor is his father, who is off abroad on holiday. No one claims to know where they are or when they'll be back, and no one knows anything about a kidnapped girl. Apologies, but we didn't expect to find your family here, Nick. But we did find something we expected.'

*

Once the strike team had determined that there wasn't a kidnapped child on the premises, although there were some illegal aliens, Miller and her crony had entered the main office to speak with the boss. They came back with a pencil-drawn map of the compound. The two detectives and Nick, free now of his handcuffs, started walking through the maze of walls of cars, and around lonesome vehicles abandoned like lepers. Near the eastern fence, top end, was Zone M-12: a stack of smashed cars eight wide and three high, all missing tyres, windows and doors. No plates, either, but up close he could see registration marks painted in small script onto flanks or bonnets. The pile of wreckage, the scrabbly earth and the burning sun gave an apocalyptic feel to the scene, like something from a Mad Max movie. Bennet approached the middle of the wall and pointed at a blue car in the middle row. Dented to hell, roof half-crushed under the weight of the vehicle above, and Nick stared for a few seconds without realising what he was seeing. Until he noted the registration scrawled on the askew bonnet.

It didn't make sense. 'You came here for this? Why? What's going on?'

Bennet didn't answer. He slipped alongside the Venga beneath the blue car. Nick turned to Miller, demanding an answer with his eyes.

'Yes, Nick, I'm sorry, but we came here for the car. We need to confirm that this is your wife's old Fiat Punto.'

Nick squeezed into the small gap between the Venga and its neighbour and looked inside the Punto. Bennet was on the other side, each man's head visible across the seats. The steering wheel was gone, perhaps sold on at some point. It was weird to see this car again after so many years, and somewhat sad to think that it hadn't been crushed and turned into Pepsi cans, but had been left to rot. He'd driven this thing in just summer shorts, but now didn't even want to touch it.

Bennet reached inside and pulled the bonnet release lever.

There was a dead rat in the passenger footwell, fur matted to the carp— 'Hang on, this isn't Anna's car. The carpet.'

'What about the carpet?' Bennet said.

'A couple of days before we scrapped it. We had some painting gear in a bag. My foot broke the lid of a bottle of turps. It bleached a big piece of the carpet on this passenger side. There's no mark here.'

Bennet was tall enough to see this over the centre console. He shrugged. 'It actually makes sense.'

But not to Nick. 'So why are we here? Someone start explaining.'

Bennet looked at Miller, who was by the front of the car. Nick looked, too, but she said nothing, and a moment later she disappeared behind the bonnet as she raised it.

'Tell me!' Now he was almost dizzy with confusion. 'I want to know what's going on. Right now.'

Bennet reached across to slap a sheet of paper on to the passenger seat. 'We got this from the DVLA.' It was a certificate of destruction. He pointed at the Vehicle Identification Number. Nick looked down at a little metal plate near where the passenger seat was fixed to the floor. The VIN, stamped into the metal, matched the one listed on the certificate. No two cars had the same 17-character code. And the customer's name was Anna Middleton, with her old London address. One Fiat Punto scrapped by the issuing establishment of Watson-Bruce Salvage. There was also a small sale receipt stapled to the certificate, and the registration number there matched. Sale of one 05 Fiat Punto from Anna Middleton to Watson-Bruce Salvage. It was Anna's car. He was puzzled by the carpet. No bleach stain. Just the rat.

Bennet's finger touched the date printed on the destruction certificate. Same as the sale receipt: 19th September 2011.

Nick said, 'The date she scrapped it. So? Look, I'm getting a headache.'

Bennet reached out to him, a car key on a card tag dangling from his fingers. Nick took it. He recognised it. In handwriting the tag simply listed make and model, and a tiny printed number: 1051.

Bennet said, 'These key tags are from a book. Sheets of them, serrated, and each tag is numbered, so you tear them off in order. This is the one after.'

Bennet held out another key, which Nick took. This tag listed make and model, but also registration, and the date. A Renault Mégane, 2003, tag number 1052.

But the date was 12th September 2011.

'You're saying Anna sold her car before the 12th? You're saying she sold it on that first occasion when she came down? No, she drove it back. She had it another week or so. The damn police came to look at it, remember.'

'And you spilled a bottle of turps in it,' Bennet said.

Miller stepped into the dim little corridor created by two towers of cars. 'Well, the police investigating the hit-and-run on Horsenden Lane North in Greenford were checking all blue Puntos within a whole bunch of miles of that area. It was a long process, just like it's been for us – you know, the Volkswagen Passats? It's a simple job, really. No need for the cars to be whipped off to the lab. No time for that, either. A lot of cars. If a car slams into three hundred and fifty pounds of stationary meat and bones, well, there will be damage, and blood. And if the registration on the car matches the one registered to the owner, well, why check the VIN?'

Nick remembered the policemen who came all those years ago; remembered that they'd been gone fifteen minutes later. Understandable: respectable working woman with an alibi, paperwork in order, no damage to the car, no blood – no reason for doubt. His chest seemed to shrink, painfully compressing his heart.

'Anna sold her car on the 10th, five days after that hit-and-run. The scrapyard held off with the paperwork until the 19th. Nick, apologies, but it took the police ten days to get to Anna's car. The 15th.'

He fell back against the ruined Fiesta behind and had to grab rusty metal to prevent a collapse to the hard dirt. The 15th. Five days after she sold it. 'But she – she didn't sell… she… drove it home.'

'Same registration plates, same make and colour, and soon afterwards to receive a bleach stain, but that, I'm afraid, was not Anna's Fiat Punto. The police couldn't be allowed to get near Anna's car. Because hers had killed two hikers.'

CHAPTER TWELVE

He was shaking his head, unable to believe, or even understand. He was sure he'd misheard, or misread, or dreamed the whole day. Bennet stared him dead in the eye as he reached a long arm through the car and laid a hand on Nick's shoulder.

'Look here,' Miller said.

He slipped out of the gloom, into the burning sun, and to the front of the car. Inside the engine bay, the detective was shining a torch on to the old engine. He could clearly see faint little stains, and she illuminated some on the broken grille, too.

Blood.

He didn't want to believe it, but everything made sense. On the night of the hit-and-run, Anna had returned home in a frightful state. She had gone out to pick up her boss, Marc Eastman, to take him to a stuffy function, but afterwards, according to her, a man with a knife had threatened her for her car.

For two days she had been reserved and nervous, confined to the house, barely eating, napping in the day a lot, and talking about leaving the city. Strange half-asleep mumblings about a fresh start soon became a sincere desire to leave London. Wildly in love and eager to please, Nick had agreed that getting out of London would be a good fresh start for them both. Aided by her father, who'd bought her a house in Sheffield to guarantee that his daughter – and the child she planned to have – remained close, she and Nick had been packed and gone within two weeks. But not because goat lovers swore vengeance, or because a thief with a blade proved the city had dangerous streets.

Anna had fled because she'd killed a pair of hikers on a dark road.

Bennet was suddenly by his side again, giving the dead eye. 'Why take the car out of the city, Nick, when London has a thousand scrapyards? A connection. By Anna's reaction to the name, I knew that connection wasn't anything as lowly as simply scrapping her car here based on a friend's recommendation. Something bigger. Something she couldn't tell the police. Something that propelled her to run today. Normally we would assume that connection was a person. But she scrapped a perfectly good car based on some robbery attempt story never reported to the police. She scrapped it right around the time that police were looking into similar cars because of a hit-and-run. And then she left the city under a new name.'

Hearing it like that, it all seemed so obvious. But still Nick refused to believe it.

Miller spoke next. 'Nick, once Anna's car was cleared by the London police, that was the end of their interest in it. They didn't know she later scrapped it and drove way out of the city to do so. They didn't know she'd been a shivering wreck after an incident on the night of the hit-and-run. And of course they couldn't possibly know that someone from that scrapyard would kidnap her daughter eight years later.'

Back to Bennet. 'The people who took her know what she did. They knew about the swapped cars because they set it up and fudged the paperwork, which was the final piece of evidence we needed in order to be sure of our suspicions. The kidnappers took Josie because of the hit-and-run.'

They were both crowding him, like a bully tag team. Miller's turn: 'It's why Anna ran away. She couldn't tell us what she knew, because, well, the truth couldn't come out. But if Anna could get away while we were distracted, maybe she could get to these people and get Josie back without anyone knowing anything about what happened in the past. And the kidnappers must have told her how to do this somehow. Whatever it is they want, it's more than just money.' She put her hand on his arm. 'Nick, apologies, but do you understand all of what I just said?'

His head was clear enough now that pieces were tumbling into place. He believed. But right now Anna's position as a *double-killer* didn't even matter as Miller's claim sought the spotlight. *More than just money.* It gave him a feeling of deadness inside.

'You're saying this is about *dues* after all. But not mine. These people want Anna alone so they can kill her. Both of them. My wife and my daughter. It's payback.'

*

On the drive back, while Nick was still trying to accept recent bombshells, Bennet got a call from a colleague and relayed it to the DCI. 'Something perhaps we should consider connected: Larry Middleton's home garage was broken into a short while ago. The security company called him when the alarm went off. He says nothing looks to have been stolen, but the place is a mess, as if someone was looking for something. Any other day, I'd discount it, but…'

Nick realised that Anna's father and sister would be awaiting news. He didn't have a number for either of them in his head, but Middleton's mobile was listed on the website for his casual dining restaurant in Sheffield because he liked all customer feedback to go through him. He asked Bennet for use of his phone.

'*DS Bennet, where are you?*' Middleton answered. He must have stored the DS's number. '*Anna left a secret message for Jane. What's happened down there?*'

'What? What mess… explain that.'

'*Nick? What's happened down there?*'

Nick blurted a flash version – minus the part about dead hikers and cloned cars – so he could quickly return to Middleton's shocking revelation. For the second time, he was careful not to say something that would alert the listening detectives.

'*The message said, "Trust me, don't tell police. I know what they want. I'm going to get Josie back." Do you know what she's doing, Nick? This looks planned. Did anyone forget there's a little girl's life at stake?*'

Trust me, don't tell the police – it gave weight to the theory that Anna had escaped the house in order to fix this problem alone. And preserve her terrible secret. Somehow, he managed to sink lower.

'No one forgot. That's our daughter. My daughter,' Nick said. 'Anna's just trying to find her. Where was the… where was it?'

'*It was Braille. She punched little holes in some stickers and put them on the handle of the kettle. Jane knew as soon as she picked it up. It was quite creative. No one but Jane would have had a clue. She wanted us to not worry, I think. Though Lord knows why she didn't just tell us.*'

'You just answered the phone by trying to tell the police, that's why.' That line, although disclosing nothing, made the detectives cock their ears.

'*Nick, do you know where she is? If you do, you must tell the police.*'

'I don't know.' He could hear a car engine in the background. 'Where are you?'

'*Just arriving back there. Jane called me about the message. My garage was burgled and I had to go check.*'

'Tell me about how Jane hurt her foot again?'

There was nothing wrong with Jane's foot of course, and Nick hung up before Middleton could voice his puzzlement at a line meant mainly for the detectives to hear. Then, with the phone still clamped to his ear to make the detectives think he was listening to a story, he sent Anna's father a text by feel alone:

Meet me at Sir Jack, Aston

Once sent, he deleted it, said goodbye to a dead line, and handed the phone back. He prayed Middleton wouldn't call back or send a return text.

A little later, Miller signalled to leave the M1 and take the A630 east. Nick sat up. When the traffic slowed at the end of the slip road to join the Catcliffe roundabout, he threw his door open. No line about needing to urinate this time: he simply powered his legs and vanished into the trees.

He heard his name shouted, and then honking horns that suggested the detectives had blocked the road by exiting their car. But Miller was in heels, Bennet was too big and unstable, and their desire to catch him fell far short of his determination to find his wife.

HIKING COUPLE KILLED IN HIT-AND-RUN

Joanne Padley, twenty-one, and her boyfriend Jon Adams, twenty-three, were killed when struck by a car that failed to stop while they hiked the Capital Ring in Greenford on the 5th of September.

The hikers had been partway through a week-long trek of the Capital Ring, a series of walking trails surrounding central London. That night, walk number nine, Greenford to South Kenton, but in reverse. They drank at the Ballot Box, an old pub on Horsenden Lane North, and walked south along the lane, somewhat parallel to the Capital Ring, planning to regain the trail at the canal bridge.

But about four hundred metres from the pub they were hit by a car that failed to stop. CCTV in the local area has so far proved unable to help, but forensic scientists have analysed paint flecks found on the bodies and the police have released information

that they wish to trace lido blue Fiat Puntos registered between
September 2004 (54 plate) and March 2006 (06 plate).
    Anyone with information should call either…

'You think Anna was driving? Preposterous?' Middleton said.
'Can't be,' Jane wheezed.

Thankfully, Middleton hadn't brought the police to the
meeting at Sir Jack's restaurant. During the wait, Nick had
thought hard about how best to tell his tale, and in the end he
decided to get the worst of it out early. He'd rushed to the car and
jumped in the back before it had fully stopped, and immediately
unloaded:

'The police think Anna was involved in a hit-and-run killing.'

Jane had uttered her shock, her puzzlement, and her absolute
disbelief. Middleton, though, had said nothing until he was parked
up. And then he'd told Nick that he'd had two calls from Detective
Bennet, which he'd ignored until after he spoke to Nick. He'd
got Jane calmed down then ordered Nick to explain. Nick had
snatched up Middleton's mobile from the centre console, already
planning to use the Internet to prove his case.

Middleton had read the newspaper article aloud for Jane. Twice.
Then came a period of silence as Anna's family sought reasons to
disbelieve the old news story. Jane had been first to submit to
acceptance. She had started to cry. This seemed to tip the scales
for Middleton, whose head had slumped forward.

Now, he said, 'The carjacking story was a lie?'

Nick took the mobile out of Middleton's limp hand and said,
'I think it was to explain how shaky she was that night. How
scared. She came home, utterly distraught. I couldn't really get
much out of her at first. Just the basics. Some guys cut in front
of her and tried to steal her car. She kept saying she didn't want
to talk about it. She made me promise not to bring it up again.
Even today we don't mention it.'

'It explains why she didn't want the police involved,' Middleton said. 'I hate to say it, but I remember thinking how weak I considered her because of it. A man tries to rob her, and she's distraught for days, and then decides she needs to get out of London. And throw away her job.'

But Jane was silent. Nick put his hand on her shoulder. It made her jump and prompted: 'She told me that she wanted to have children and bring them up in a quieter city. But I thought…'

He didn't know what to say. Middleton broke the silence again. 'So this is why Anna ran. Because she thinks the police will arrest her. Do you think she hopes to solve this herself? That she can get Josie back and the police will never know what she did?'

'Yes,' Nick said.

'This hit-and-run. So many years ago. Why now? How is this connected to my granddaughter being taken?'

'The police think Dominic Watson-Bruce knows what Anna did. Somehow he found out, and he contacted a family member or friend of one of the… hikers.' He was careful not to use the word *dead*. Never again.

'And these people, they heard his wild tale and decided, rather than expose her, they would threaten Anna for money to get some kind of revenge?' He was shaking his head, totally unconvinced. It was indeed a bizarre story. But his next words were delivered quietly, his face grim, and Nick knew Middleton had suddenly reversed his denial. 'Was this why they kidnapped my granddaughter? Was this so that I would be forced to pay? They knew I had money and they chose that instead. So I caused this after all.'

'It's not just about money.'

This was the part he had been least looking forward to, even over telling Jane and Middleton that their family member was a killer.

'The money might have been Dominic's pay for information, for help, but they got the money. And still they got Anna to run.'

Both were intent on him, even though Jane's eyes saw nothing. He took a deep breath.

'I think they want her to do something. I think taking Josie was to make sure she did it. I think the police turned up and ruined their plan, so they got a secret message to her somehow, somewhere. She ran right around the time I delivered the money. She didn't wait. Her message to Jane said she knew what they wanted. She waited until everyone was distracted by following the money, and that's when she ran. Because she had to do this alone. And they wanted her alone.'

Middleton almost shrieked. 'You're talking about revenge, aren't you? They've fooled Anna into thinking she can get Josie back, but that isn't it. She's running into a trap. They want to hurt her. They want payback for killing their children.'

Nick had, of course, had the same black thought: how better to exact retribution than to make Anna suffer the loss of a child – an eye for an eye – before killing her? But Miller and Bennet had quickly shut down that theory and he now tried to calm Middleton and Jane with the detectives' reasoning:

'I don't think so. If it was revenge, they could have got to Anna anytime. They could have killed her when they broke into the house. They could have run her down in the road, just like she…' He stopped himself before he could say it. 'No, they told Anna where to meet them. They want her to do something for them. They must have told her what in their secret message. And that's why I need your help.'

Middleton turned to look at him for the first time since parking up. 'What help? Is this why you wanted this damn silly secret meet? You don't want the police to know because you think you can make everything all right. You think you can save everybody. But keeping the police out of this puts my daughter and grand-daughter in danger, you fool. What can *you* do?'

That final sentence had been almost spat out in contempt. Nick paused a second to let rising anger subside. 'Look, I know I'm not the ideal man for Anna in your eyes. I'm just some grunt with no desire to rule the world. I'm not obsessed with money and power and I don't want people to bow at my feet. You think Anna can't cope without you because she failed in London, and that I'm not the right person to look after her, even though we've been fine for years. If only she'd married a judge or famous novelist, eh? I don't care what you think. All that matters to me—'

'And what about what matters to me? I don't want you making things worse by—'

Jane had been silent for a time, but no longer. 'Stop this, you two,' she yelled. 'It ends now between you. I heard what Nick said to you back at the house and he's right, Father. You cut her off thinking she'd regret her decision to settle down. It's not going to happen. Josie is the best thing that ever happened to her, to any of us. And even if she left Nick, she's not going to suddenly decide to start a career. Stop blaming Nick because Anna didn't become the daughter you wanted. And you, Nick, stop blaming Father for finding it hard to accept that Anna chose a different path. Both of you! Fighting when Josie and Anna are out there somewhere and in danger. I'm sick of it!'

That silenced both men. Jane rubbed her chest in a calming motion, and wiped a tear away. 'I agree with him, Father. He wants to find Anna before the police do. There's a chance this is all just wrong. We need to hear Anna's story before she gets arrested. I think we'd all prefer to see her without being surrounded by police and solicitors. Especially if it's going to be the last time alone as a family.'

Middleton rubbed his forehead. Nick tried to eject an image of Anna staring at him through the iron bars of a cell as he was forced to walk away – back to an empty home.

Jane said, 'Nick, what message are you talking about? You said they got a secret message to Anna.'

Middleton said nothing. His chest rose and fell fast. Nick took it as willingness to hear him out, so he said, 'I think their message gave her the idea for the one she left you.'

Despite her blindness, Jane actually turned in her seat, as if to stare at him. 'Braille?'

*

Nick picked up the phone, just as Anna had, and immediately felt stickiness on his fingers. From the inside of the handle. He saw a slight residue, as if from a now-gone sticker. He handed the phone to Jane, standing in the phone box doorway, who ran her fingers along the hard plastic. Behind her, Middleton paced on the pavement.

'My God,' Jane said. 'There was a sticker here. Just like on the kettle. But the message is gone.'

She bent down and ran a hand across the floor. Before Nick could process why, she stood up, and in her fingers was something. Black, the same colour as the receiver. Jane started to unfold it. A little scrap of black tape, scrunched up, and discarded. He saw lumps and bumps, and he just knew. Her fingers ran over its surface.

'Is it Braille?' he said, all urgency. 'What does it say?'

She ignored him, dropped the scrap of tape, and started to feel under the shelf.

'Silence. Under shelf,' she said. And then, 'More stickiness. But there's nothing here.'

And he believed that, because Jane had a far more sensitive touch. But still he ran his own hands over the underside of the shelf, hoping she was wrong. She wasn't. No message, and nothing else on the floor. His shoulders slumped. He'd been hoping to find a clue to her location. An idea of what the hell these bastards wanted from Anna. Failure put a painful void in his gut.

'A bigger message,' Jane said. 'Something that wouldn't fit on the handle. But how would they have known to do that?'

Because they knew all about Anna and her family.

'They must have returned here to get rid of the message,' he said. 'Jesus.'

'But what do they want? They got the money. What can they want from us, Nick? Is this something to do with the burglary at Father's garage?'

Nick hadn't connected that event to this, but it had caused DS Bennet to wonder. And the burglary had occurred not long after Anna vanished. *Any other day…* Prompted by elevating hope, Nick remembered a line from Anna's secret message to Jane.

I know what they want. I'm going to get Josie back.

*

Nick stepped inside carefully. He needed to be quick, because he knew the police were sending someone to fingerprint the busted door. But he also needed Middleton out of the way.

Amongst various items strewn around the garage floor, Nick noticed his lucky milk bottle, broken into a thousand pieces. He didn't care: it couldn't be deemed to have any power if Josie and Anna were still missing.

He picked up a piece of the glass. 'I'm still keeping this. Have you got a small box and a dustpan and brush?'

Middleton had doubted the kidnappers had busted into his garage. The whole street knew he had money and a busy outdoor life but no wife and a daughter who wouldn't be very good at providing a description: no secret, then, that his property was often unattended. If what the kidnappers wanted was in his garage, they could have broken in anytime. So why take Josie and then come kick in the door anyway? Plus, there was nothing of worth, nor was there anything missing.

Sold. Nick had agreed with the older man's theory, but asked to see the garage anyway. By the time they'd arrived, he was doubtful. Once inside, and looking at nothing but junk across the floor, he was certain he was on a wild goose chase.

And then he spotted something.

When Middleton was gone, Nick picked up the item that had caught his attention. Right then he knew where this whole mess would end, although he had no idea what treasure could be at the end of this rainbow. Jane was by the door, watching but not. But she heard the slight scrape of something dropping to the floor.

She asked.

He lied: nothing. But then he said, 'Tell your dad I'm sorry.'

'What do you mean? Sorry for what?'

*

'He said he's sorry for taking your car,' Jane said sixty seconds later, when her father was by her side in the driveway and he was staring at a blank space where his forty-grand Jaguar wasn't.

'That bastard,' Middleton hissed. 'What did he say? Did he find something?'

'He picked something up.'

Because standing in the bare driveway, despite it being part of her home, was like being adrift in a vast ocean, she reached for him, meaning to grab an arm with both of hers, to anchor herself. But found the space where he should have been empty. The crunch of gravel told her he was headed back to the garage. Once there herself, she heard the beep of his phone keypad.

'Father, what are you doing? You can't call the police.'

'Anna and that bastard might think they're trying to save Josie, but their damn vigilante ideas might get her hurt.'

'No, don't call the police just yet. Anna will be arrested. Maybe Nick has found something.' She grabbed his arm.

He shrugged it off. 'And I intend to know what. I took a picture.'

'What do you mean?'

What he meant, but didn't say, was that he'd taken pictures of the garage as it lay following the robbery, to document the damage.

Now, he pulled up one he'd taken from roughly this very spot and which captured the entire interior. He held it so he could see picture and subject with only a flick of the eyes.

In this game of spot-the-difference, there was one anomaly. One thing, but not missing, only moved a couple of feet. He stepped inside and picked it up. A velvety A5 folder embossed with JEFFERSON'S, which had been Anna's way back, when she was Marc Eastman's PA. It contained a card key and paperwork for a safety box in a private London bank, where Eastman had insisted she stored sensitive files after his office was burgled. The box hadn't been used since she emptied it and left London; the folder, like other unneeded junk, had gone into a box and made the journey north, but since that day hadn't budged from its dusty spot in the garage. Until it got tossed on the floor as burglars threw things about while seeking valuables.

And it had moved again when Nick picked it up.

CHAPTER THIRTEEN

10.58 a.m.

The moment she picks up the receiver in her left hand, what she feels beneath her fingertips is as potent as a live wire. She takes a deep breath and realisation hits.

'Hello, my master. I am so scared,' she says. She is reminded of the order to hold the receiver in both hands – not so she can't press record on a tape machine, but because one hand needs to hold the receiver while the other slides along what she knows is a Braille message on the inside of the handle. Her heart races.

'Pay careful attention to what you feel. It will help you do the right thing. Remember that any trickery and your kid doesn't see old age.'

With two hands, one to hold the receiver, and one to read, she says nothing.

'So you understand the message I'm giving you. Good.'

She does. The message says:

Silence. Under Shelf.

'I will do whatever you want,' she says, to relay her own message: that she understands. There will be another message under the shelf, because a tiny phone handle offers no room.

'We don't want you to do this. We want your husband to bring the money. Go home and we'll call again.'

Click.

She drops the receiver. She leans on the phone book shelf, gripping it tightly, her fingers feeling beneath. Rubbing. Reading.

Escape the police at 12.25 p.m. Get to Bex Park. Bring your Forcefield. Destroy the messages.

She stands. Picks up the receiver again. Says 'Hello' into it, but this is just cover so she can rip away the ticker tape as she hangs up and withdraws her hand. Both hands come together, mashing the two messages together.

Forcefield.

The bigger message, the size of a postcard, is on paper, so it can be destroyed easily; the smaller, though, is on thick ticker tape so that it can withstand the friction of palms that used the phone before she took hold. This piece of plastic refuses to gel with the paper and skips from her rubbing hands. She sees it tumble to the floor. She cannot retrieve it, because the camera is watching. But it's tiny, scrunched up, and no one will see anything but a piece of litter. She leaves the phone box with the other message squashed in her fist. Carefully punched holes in the paper now ruined by her hands, it will tell no one anything even if they find it on the floor of her already-littered car.

Forcefield.

The shock of it is like an icy lake dousing, but she holds her outward demeanour firm, for the police watching and listening, as she walks back to her car.

Forcefield.

A simple, single word, but all-powerful, and all-encompassing. Because now she knows who took her little lady, and why…

*

Across the road at the end of the alleyway behind her neighbour's home is Bexland Park, and a pedestrian side entrance via a lichgate

just a short way to her left. She takes it. The park is empty because
kids and jobless mothers like herself prefer the park down the
road. This one doesn't have much to offer because it's just a green
the size of a football pitch with benches and a road cutting it in
half, all enclosed in head-high hedge. That means she knows the
Ogres will be able to take her, and nobody will see a thing. But
there is someone here, a council worker with a hedge trimmer.
At least he's far away, his back to her as he pretties up the hedge.
And the noise of his hedge trimmer means he doesn't hear a car zip
quickly inside as she approaches the road slicing the park in two.
Some drivers use the road through as a shortcut, and the vehicle
certainly has the speed to suggest it isn't going to stop. Until it
does with a screech of tyres right before her.

No chance to back out now. But she wouldn't anyway. High
trees around the edge of the park seem to lock her in with the car,
casting gloomy shadows and creating just the sort of scene a novelist might imagine for a kidnap. But she knows she would let this
happen even if it were one of Jane's burning beaches full of bathers.
That car, no matter the dangers it might hold, is the portal to Josie.

A back door opens and a man in a baseball cap pulled low
steps out. She can see only his mouth, which makes big horse-like
chewing motions. With no face to look at, her eyes drop to his
hands. Clothing, which he drops to the ground.

She instantly recognises Josie's Daffy Duck pyjamas…

A moan escapes as she stumbles forward and bends to grab
Josie's clothing. She knows it's a trick to get her close, because
they're right at his feet, but what she knows and he doesn't is that
no trick is needed. She is going through the portal, no matter
what, but she is desperate to do so with Josie's belongings in her
arms. No special necklace here, so thankfully her little girl might
have been allowed to keep it.

Ball Cap grabs her ponytail and yanks her up. His other hand
slaps over her mouth to stifle a scream that was never part of the

plan. He turns and forces her into the car, grunting with exertion he doesn't have to use. She sprawls across the back seat. In a flash of a second before he's inside, on top of her, forcing her head down, she glimpses the back of the driver's head: ginger hair with shaved sides.

The door slams. The car jumps into action. Already, she is closer to Josie, and tension disperses like smoke in the wind. Ball Cap is unaware of this and forces her off the seat, into a lying position on the floor, face down. Her nose thuds the carpet, and it's this impact that ejects a yelp from her lips. Ball Cap, though, misreads yet again and jams his feet hard into her back and tells her she's going nowhere. Amid the maelstrom of emotions, her brain finds opportunity to recognise the same thick northern accent from the phone calls.

At first, the engine is loud, the turns sharp, but soon everything calms down as the vehicle exits a perceived danger zone. Ball Cap starts to speak around a wad of gum in his mouth.

'No police, you silly mare. Remember?'

'Where's my daughter? A neighbour called the police. I'm sorry.'

'You didn't half cause a hassle, woman. You were supposed to wake up in the morning to find a nice little note in your girl's bed, and then we'd go do this all quiet, no problem. But your bloke, what the hell was he doing up? Who's awake at that time of the morning, eh?' He seems to find this funny. 'And no cops, that was meant to be part of it. Scrambled that one up, too, didn't you? You'd have had your kid by now, so you went and messed up, didn't you? Caused us to get our thinking caps on. Are we going to have any more spanners in the works?'

Josie's pyjamas are still in her hands; she forces them into her face, inhaling her smell. The pain in her nose vanishes.

'That's better,' the other guy, the driver, says. Dominic Watson-Bruce, she remembers. She is glad she hasn't yet seen his face, or him hers.

Ball Cap turns her head with a fist in her hair, so she can see something his other hand is holding close to her face.

'This was a wasted note. I hate waste, so now—'

She sees a piece of paper the size of a postcard. Scrawled words:

WE HAVE YOUR KID. NO POLICE. TELL SCHOOL SHE'S SICK. WILL CALL YOU AT TEN

'—you'll eat it.'

And he's serious because he forces the paper against her mouth, pressing so hard it hurts her gums and lips, and she knows there's no point in trying to refuse. So she opens her mouth, and accepts his rough fingers forcing the paper inside. She blocks her throat with her tongue, unsure if he's going to force the ransom note all the way.

'Don't be a twat,' Dominic says.

Some kind of point proven, Ball Cap releases her and sits up. She spits out the paper. The man seems to drum a beat on her back with his feet, as if to a song in his head. She knows that this journey through the portal will go more easily if she doesn't speak, simply does as she's told, but she needs to know Josie is okay. She means to try to ask about her daughter pleasantly, as if enquiring about how she's adapting to a new school, but the pyjamas Josie was wearing are in her hands, and a terrible fear about what that could mean transforms her enquiry between brain and mouth.

'What have you done to my baby, you bastards? Where is she? Why did you take her pyjamas?'

'We changed her, that's all,' Ball Cap said. 'She said she's not allowed to wear pyjamas once she's up. You think I'm some sort of weirdo?'

That was right, she'd been taught to get dressed as soon as breakfast was over, but surely she wouldn't undress in front of these Ogres. Had they forced her to…?

As if reading her mind, the guy beside her says, 'We haven't harmed her one little bit, okay? As is, it's a kidnap. Imagine if the police happened to burst in and find a naked kid? That's a sexual aspect right there, and you know what that means? Solitary confinement for my own safety. Not a place on earth I wouldn't be hated. Especially for a little girl. Imagine that, everyone everywhere wanting to hurt you. And the prison screws would over-salt every meal I ever had. Think I'm stupid? I can hide from the killers. Can't hide from the salt. So your kid's dressed and she's… let's say she's not unhappy. Except with you, that is. She's annoyed at you. She thinks you sent her to us for being naughty before bedtime.'

Josie had spoken with these Ogres? She was a sociable girl, but…

'I want to see her. I want to see my daughter now.'

Dominic speaks this time. 'Have you got what we want, countess?'

Still, thankfully, she can't see his face, but that word, *countess*, puts an ancient image in her mind: a yelling boy, a runaway bicycle, and herself rushing forward. She shuts it down before the scene can display her performing a mistake.

'Hey, did you hear?' he says.

A spike pierces her heart, worse than any pain she could have imagined. Here, she will be forced to say *no*. She can get it, she will say. She will promise to get it. But if they are expecting to take hold of the *Forcefield* right now, and they can't… Josie could suffer the consequences.

The kidnapper stamps her back hard enough to hurt. 'Hey, answer. It's the cop shop where you have the right to remain silent, not here. Here you have the right to watch your kid's eyes get flushed down the bog.'

'I keep it stored away at my father's!' she yells. 'Please, I will get it. All I want is my daughter. You can have it, I promise.

There won't be any tricks. Please. My little lady. She's everything to me.'

Silence for a second. She imagines the Ogres looking at each other. Trying to decide what to do. They will believe her, or they won't and Josie will suffer.

'Think this is bullshit?'

Dominic's question, so Ball Cap is the man in control of her very world. If he says yes, Josie will—

'Doubt it. She knows we'd send her a bone a day in the post for a year.'

'People only have two hundred odd bones, not three hundred and sixty-five.'

'Babies and kids have more.'

'What, three hundred and sixty-five exactly? That don't make sense. Where do these bones go?'

'Go? I don't know. Maybe they shed them. I read it. So where is this thing?'

Silence. Then another stamp on her back, and she realises the final question was for her.

'My father's garage. At his house. I can get it. I will get it, I promise.' Again, she's survived a terrible and dangerous moment, but something inside her decides to push: 'But not until I see my daughter. You have to take me to her.'

'You can see a piece of her every day for a year,' Ball Cap says. She fights the urge to argue.

'Internet says here,' Dominic says, 'that babies have three hundred. Not three hundred and sixty-five.'

'Aha, good point. Give me your phone.'

This time she knows the words are for her. Before she can respond, though, his hands are on her. She buries her face in Josie's pyjamas and expects his fingers to go between her legs, and she doesn't even care because it might mellow him. But they don't. They quickly find the phone and retreat.

'You should have got that straight away,' Dominic says. 'What if she called the police? Open line, could have been tracing it all this time.'

'Nah, it's not on call. Anyway, you'll like this cool idea I just had. So, missus, we're gonna go get this damn Forcefield thing. Tell me about the place. Everything a burglar needs to know to get in there. Me and you are going in. Miss out a vicious guard dog and I'll feed your kid to my own dog.'

She hears a crackling sound she can't recognise. Then his fingers are back, but in her hair this time. He turns her head. Something before her eyes, which he wants her to look at. So she looks, to keep him mellow.

A laminated sheet of paper, creased, rippled, old, like a keep-sake. A newspaper article: the *Sunderland Echo*. The headline is: 'Arsonist Strikes Again.'

Before she can read more, it's gone. Pre-empting him, she turns her face. Back to the pyjamas. Back to Josie.

'That's me. Six infernos in parked cars, and six dead kids left by shopping mothers. Snuffing out little kids gives me a buzz. So don't think I don't have it in me to kill your kid. Okay? You mess this up, try any tricks, I'll go and snap her bones until she's got five hundred, never mind three hundred and sixty-five.'

CHAPTER FOURTEEN

The sneezing noise seemed to wake him up. But all was still black. His head was heavy and he couldn't lift it. He felt something on top of him, some kind of thick, coarse fabric, like the underside of a carpet. That sneezing noise again. Somewhere here in the dark with him.

'Josie?' he tried to shout, but it came out only as a croak.

'Daddy, I don't like this dark. Where is this place?'

He had no idea, was aware only of a rumbling noise, a vibration, and the heavy carpet, and the dark.

And Josie. He could hear his girl crying.

'Josie, are you all right, choc?' he said, maximum effort into making the words sound no different to all the times he'd returned from work to high-five his daughter.

'I'm sorry for being naughty, Daddy. Can I go back to my bedroom?'

He couldn't stop a moan emerging from between his lips. He tried to get up, again, but couldn't.

'Mummy didn't mean to shout and send you to bed, Josie. Everything is okay.' But it wasn't. He could remember high-fiving Josie after work, but he had no idea how he'd got to wherever this place was.

'A man carried me out of bed. He said to keep quiet. Is it all right to talk now? I don't like it here. I want my bedroom. Is this a bed sheet? It's too heavy. Get it off.'

He remembered a portion. Shapes. Men. Darkness. Josie. They took Josie, and now they'd taken him, too. That in mind, the rumbling and vibrating made sense, even if little else did. A vehicle, something big, like a van. Maybe a carpet van. He and Josie, taken in a van.

'I want to turn the light on. Turn it on, please, Daddy.'

'We can't just yet, Josie. Because… you remember, the earthquake at Blackgate Prison?'

'Yes. From *Batman*. Did we have an earthquake?'

No more portions would come, but Batman was there. In his high-five voice, he said, 'Well, Josie, you went to bed without a story. So instead of reading a *Batman* comic to you, I thought we'd play a game like that.'

'A Batman game?' The distress was leaving Josie's tone, which was beautiful to hear. 'So this is Blacky Prison? Are we prisoners?'

'We are. Oh no, we're captured. Just a couple of visitors who got caught up in it. You remember, lots of prisoners escaped in the comic when Blackgate Prison was in the earthquake? Like Joker and Riddler.'

'Is that the noise and the shaking? Is this an earthquake? Is the prison broken?'

He felt his head swim and for a second he forgot what he was in the middle of, but it came back quickly, like an old TV's signal after a burst of thunder. 'Prison. Yes, the prison. It's broken. We're trapped prisoners under rubble. But we'll get out soon.'

'I want out now. I don't like this game.'

He heard sniffling. 'But it's a good game, Josie. Please play it with me. Daddy loves this game. There will be a reward if you get out. You can ride a horse. I'll take you on a horse every day for a week. No, a bouncy castle, I'll buy a bouncy castle. And the game will be over soon.'

Josie's sniffling stopped. 'When Batman rescues us? It's stopped quaking. Listen, Dad.'

The next part was hard to say, not least because his head was beginning to cloud again. He knew he wouldn't have the strength to stop whoever came to open the van doors. He had weakly failed to help his daughter earlier, and soon he'd be forced to watch again as dangerous people took Josie for a second time. And *soon* it would be, because the ceased noise and vibration meant the vehicle had stopped.

'Josie, listen quick. Batman can't get through all this rubble to rescue us just yet. So some men are going to take us out. They've been gassed with Scarecrow's Fear Gas, so they might be a bit rough and shouting. Just close your eyes and try not to let it worry you. And they'll take us to another place. No matter how bad they shout, or even if it hurts a little, just remember it's a game and soon it will be all over. Soon we'll be rescued. Can you do that?'

'And Batman will find us there? He'll put these baddies in Arkham Asylum?'

This Batman is going to kill them, he wanted to shout.

A grinding metal noise, and bright light stung his eyes—

*

—which pulsed red and blue in the night, lighting up his rear-view. Snapped awake from a nightmare memory by a single blare of the siren, Nick realised he was doing over a hundred miles an hour, leaving behind everybody except the police.

He veered left, crossed two lanes and slipped into the hard shoulder. Upon stopping, he got out of the car. A police officer in a bright yellow jacket ordered him back inside, but wanted his arms sticking out the window. He did as instructed, and the officer finally decided it was safe to approach. But he stayed out of arm's reach.

They went through the motions: *licence, registration, not my car, borrowed it, hand me the keys and sit right there, sir.* Nick looked round to see the other officer on the car radio, probably running his name and the car's registration. They would find out about his one-year driving ban seventeen years ago, but that would be no cause for concern and hopefully he'd be behind the wheel again soon. His only worry was that Anna's dad, when called, would say his car had been stolen. If that happened, he would have to make a run for it. Somehow.

The guy on the radio waved his comrade over, but he was back quickly with fresh orders for Nick. Out of the car. Turn around. Nick said nothing until he felt handcuffs snapping on. 'Hang on a mo, the guy who owns the car is my father-in-law, and he's a bit of a twat.'

'Be quiet. And listen carefully, pal, okay? Nicolas Carter, I'm arresting you on suspicion of cruelty to a child—'

'What?'

The caution came as he was led to the police car. He was put in the rear, hands cuffed behind him. Throughout, he demanded answers. He got one not long after the driver got out of the car to take a call on his mobile radio. Nick had a serious sinking feeling, but sixty seconds later found himself standing on the hard shoulder and no longer in handcuffs. He was given a ringing mobile phone. By now he was thoroughly puzzled and wondering if he'd had a false awakening.

'Nick?' said a voice he recognised.

'DCI Miller. Did you arrange for me to be arrested?'

'Ah, apologies. I had to put you on the system when you went missing overnight. I guess I forgot to take you off, my friend. What are you doing on the M1?'

'Forget that. What's this horse crap about cruelty to a child?'

'Only way I could put you on the system. As a wanted man. I'll get rid of it. So, your presence halfway down the M1?'

'I'm lucky these guys didn't hammer me. Cruelty to a child! What the hell?'

'Like I said, apologies. M1?'

'I'm just out driving to clear my head. Against the law, is it?'

'Perhaps on your way to Nuthall to search?'

'Detective Miller, why don't you tell me some good news, if you can? Any likelihood in the far future of finding my daughter?'

'We have a couple of updates,' she said, sounding more serious now. 'Now, without proof of the involvement of the families of the hikers killed way back, all we can do is put them under surveillance. That's been ongoing most of the day and I'm hearing nothing untoward is occurring. There's certainly nothing suggesting your family is in that neck of the woods. If that changes, I'll know instantly. But my gut is ruling them out.'

Nick's gut turned at that news. It was good and bad all at the same time. But Miller continued before he really had time to process the information.

'Remember I told you that the Watson-Bruce clan, a couple of them run scrapyards? Well, the chap who started it all had three children. Another daughter, see. This lass isn't in the scrap trade, my friend. She's like the white sheep of that family. She got away from them. Moved away to find a better life. And she's managed to keep her family history out of the limelight. She took her husband's surname when she married, and this was way before he stepped into the Westminster limelight.'

Nick felt a realisation – based on that term *Westminster limelight* – touching the tip of his tongue, but it surfaced no further. Miller gave a push:

'Her name is Iliana. Iliana Eastman.'

Iliana Eastman – Marc Eastman's wife and aide. Shock had a texture and a weight in his belly. 'Eastman… Marc Eastman helped Anna cover up the hit-and-run? That's what you're saying?'

'Well, that idea doesn't sit well with me. The current Secretary of State for Education burying such a crime? No. See, I'd much rather bet on Anna turning to Iliana, if they're friends. I can see her fearing the story could harm her husband. Shadowy as she is and all, and obsessed with the power he's got, and the power she's got over him. Yeah, I can see her doing this for her husband, perhaps even without his knowledge. He's getting some grief at the minute because a newspaper is trying to discredit him with this Witches of Eastman story. The country has learned about three affairs so far that he's had over the last twenty years, but his wife has stuck by him and that proves a tight bond. Perhaps tight enough that she would cover up a hit-and-run by his caseworker to avoid negative splashback.'

'But Josie… how is that connected…'

Her voice now got a little higher, her tone a little desperate. 'Now let's not assume anything, my friend. I called down south and the chaps there don't have any evidence that Eastman or his wife are being targeted, any more so than politicians usually are, that is. But I'm sending someone down there on the quiet to watch them, see if they show any signs of duress. Just don't let your mind run rampant, Nick. Dominic and the rest of her family, I told you she abandoned them.'

His thoughts seemed bogged down in quicksand, not running rampant. But her warning had the opposite effect as he realised what she was trying to prevent him from doing.

'Are you saying Eastman and his wife and her family could all be involved in the kidnap?'

'Nick, please, no. I just told you Eastman's wife has nothing to do with her family. I just told you not to jump to conclusions. There's no evidence—'

'No evidence they're being targeted, that's what you said. And if they're not givers, they're takers.'

'No obvious evidence, which is why I'm sending someone for a watch on the quiet.'

'On the quiet? You need to arrest this guy, both of them. Get Eastman and his wife in a police station and get their stories. What good will just watching do?'

'I can't just start investigating someone like Marc Eastman. Nick. Apologies there, but I'd be sidelined in a flash. There's not even nearly enough evidence—'

'There's Dominic!'

'Nick, he's just a nephew, just part of a family she left years ago. Not nearly enough evidence, my friend. And think about what Eastman or his wife have to gain from this? Nothing but money, and that's too much to risk, and they have enough of it already. But I am considering everything, my friend, believe me. Until I get back to you, do nothing and leave this with me.'

Something the DCI had said about Eastman's wife and loyalty put a terrible thought in his head. 'Did my wife have an affair with this guy? I met her not long after she started working for him. But was she still sleeping with him even when I came along?'

'I go with evidence, Nick, and, well, none points that way. There's nothing to suggest Anna ever connected sexually with Marc Eastman. Why such a random idea?'

It wasn't random, though. A sexual bond could create unbreakable loyalty, as with Eastman's wife forgiving her husband's affairs, and agreeing to help him help Anna bury a crime. Eastman would have needed a high dose of loyalty towards Anna in order to risk everything by protecting her. And how else would he have developed such devotion? He explained this to the DCI, who again jumped on her evidence mantra.

Then added: 'So, I repeat, remove such thoughts from your skull. Now back to you, Nick. I don't like you being out there. You can't be thinking straight, okay? If you're not coming on home, then I want you to tread carefully.'

And then she was gone, leaving him replaying her final sentence in his head. She could have ordered the police to return him to Sheffield, but she hadn't. Instead, she'd warned him to be careful. As if she knew he was on a mission... and was permitting it. Maybe even condoning it.

Miller's information, and her warning, had him straddling a fence, unable to pick a side. Were Eastman and his wife victims too, like Anna? Were they connected at all?

Still a little spellbound by this latest scene in his life, Nick handed the mobile back to the police officer. He still half-expected to be arrested for car theft, but instead he was told to have a good day and to watch his speed, then left alone out there.

He did neither.

*

After what seemed like hours stuffed into the floor of the car, with the man's stinking feet on her back and rock music pounding her head, and sometimes his voice telling her things, she felt a slowing, and a turning to the left. The constant speed and lack of outside sound had told her they were on the motorway, heading south she knew. But no more. They were turning off. Her heart vibrated like crazy with mixed emotions, because they had promised her something, and this could be it, but also because it could all have been a lie.

A minute later there was another turn, to the right this time, which made her worry they were hitting the motorway again. But the car slowed, made another couple of sharp turns, and then she felt the light dim slightly, as if they'd gone under a bridge.

'Up,' Ball Cap said.

She sat, wincing against the daylight because she'd had her face buried in Josie's pyjamas for so long, even though it was subdued.

In the driver's seat, Dominic turned to look at her. It was the first time he had really shown his face, and she had been dreading the moment in case he recognised her through the extra wrinkles and fat on her face. But she surprised herself by glaring him dead in the eye. She failed to spot something familiar in his features. He was the same only in name. Even that had changed for Anna.

He failed, too. She could see it right there in his eyes: not a hint of recognition, for which she was glad. But, fearful that his brain would make a connection in the next few seconds, she lowered her eyes to his throat. And wished she hadn't.

He wore a necklace she recognised. The sight of it made her eyes grow wide in shock, and she closed them so he wouldn't see fresh distress and fathom the reason.

'There you go. Have maybe your last look, if you stuff us,' he said. Then turned away.

That was when she noticed her surroundings. Not a bridge or a tunnel or a building that had cut out the light, she saw. Lorries with big trailers surrounded them, their high sides blocking the sun. Her thought: a lorry park at a Services.

Ball Cap put his hand on her neck, used it to turn her head towards him. No, not him. The window behind him. They were parked at the back of two articulated lorries that created a high corridor ten feet wide. As she watched, a van moved into view at the other end and a side door slid open.

'Oh my god. J—'

'Calm down,' Ball Cap said.

She reached for the door, but his free hand grabbed her pony-tail, both grips locking her in place. She shut her muscles down because she knew the van could escape long before she reached the end of the corridor.

She couldn't believe it. There was Josie, on her knees in the back of the van. Her little lady. She didn't look hurt or tied up, but Anna got only enough of a glimpse to know it was her, and then the sliding door shut, and the van pulled away, out of her view.

'There. A movie clip. Now you want to see the whole film, don't you?'

Ball Cap started to stuff her down on to the floor again, pony-tail and neck in his hands, but she struggled. He let go of her hand and clamped it over her mouth, shutting off her air, and promised he'd— 'Bury both of you right here if you don't quit it, woman.'

The fight went right out of her, but not because of his threat. If she wanted Josie back, there was only one way to do it. Do what these people wanted. She had given in to them all the way so far, so why change that now, especially after they'd followed through with a promise to show her that Josie was alive? Do as they say, give them her Forcefield, and surely they would also follow through with their promise to free her daughter.

'Let's just get driving,' she snapped as she laid her head on Josie's pyjamas again. 'We're wasting time.'

*

When the satnav said he'd arrived, Nick parked and shut everything off. Absently, he reached for the glovebox and a photo of all three of them, himself, Josie and Anna, at a country park picnic table. Only when he saw no picture did he remember that he was in Middleton's car. But he did see a half-empty bag of roasted nuts and his stomach immediately grumbled. He slammed the lid and started gorging.

It was late and he knew nothing was going to happen overnight, so he put the seat back and tried to relax. It wouldn't happen. And it was cold. He went to the boot, hoping to find a coat or blanket, but what he found was a box wrapped in flowery paper. A tag said…

Happy Birthday, Eldest. From Dad

A birthday present for Anna. The shape was unmistakable: alcohol! He snatched it up. Randomly, his mind flipped through history – had Eastman ever bought Anna a birthday present? With a secret love note, perhaps in Braille so nobody else could read it?

Back in the driver's seat, paranoia fading, Nick tore a strip of the paper away before he caught himself. Beneath, he saw part of two words:

EGA CHA

It was as low as he'd felt for hours. Sitting in a stolen car, about to drink wine bought for his wife's ruined birthday, and wondering still if she'd had an affair with her boss while he'd been dating her.

His mind turned to his daydream on the motorway, when his brain had decided he could cope with a return of some memories from last night. Before, he had lied to DS Bennet when he'd said he didn't remember anything else about being taken by masked men, but that had been because he'd believed he'd lain in that van and let panic overcome him, let his daughter down with inaction. But now he knew he had talked to Josie; he had tried his hardest to comfort her, to dispel her fears. Tied up, drugged, words had been all he could offer. And now he felt he had done as much as he could. Not enough, of course, but the limit of his ability.

So he hadn't been weak at all. He'd shown strength, and he needed to show it again tomorrow. And the day after, and for the rest of his life.

Including right now.

He pressed the torn paper back into place and put the bottle on the floor. He was about to put it under the mat, so it wouldn't call to him, but backtracked. No, let it stare at him. Let it call, tempt, cajole, threaten. He was stronger.

He remembered the framed quote in his kitchen, which he'd never before thought about. Author Josh Jameson's belief that sometimes it was wise to give up, if the chips were stacked against you, but sometimes you needed to dip into reserves and push on.

'I will not close the book.'

*

The next leg was long, no stops. It gave her time to think. She tried to remember Miller's instructions on how to talk to captors. She replayed everything Ball Cap had said to her, trying to get a read on his personality so she could work out tactics for conversing with him later. But soon after something happened that dissolved her belief that Ball Cap was the leader of the pair.

He tapped her head with his foot. 'What is it these guys are after? Why's it called the Forcefield?'

Not 'us'. 'These guys.' And delivered in a whisper. Was he just some kind of helper, unaware of what was going on?

She got her answer when Dominic said, 'Hey, man, you were told not to ask about that. You're not supposed to know, that's why we call it the Forcefield.'

'I thought that was in case the cops were listening.' She felt him shift close. This time his breath was right by her ear. 'Come on, tell me. What is it they want? What's this lark about?'

She didn't want to antagonise him, but also didn't want to tell the truth, not if he didn't know already. So something cryptic, thus safe, slipped out:

'Immortality.'

'Dude, Jesus, I told you not to ask her,' Dominic said.

That feeling of proximity was gone. The feet were on her back again. The car rolled on. The minutes trickled by.

The next time the car stopped, it did so for a long time. She knew they had arrived. But nobody said anything. She felt the daylight losing control to darkness. Dominic shut off the radio. He announced he was going for food and got out. Now, she knew, Ball Cap could do what he wanted. He could go between her legs, or he could insist on that answer he so wanted. But he did nothing, said nothing. Dominic returned with what smelled like fish and chips and both men ate noisily and talked about nothing that mattered to her. She wanted food but didn't ask. Weirdly, though, upon the heels of this thought, Dominic said, 'Hey, don't scoff the lot. Some of that was for her.'

'She's had paper.' Just a joke because chips pattered to the carpet by her face. She couldn't move her arms because they were jammed by her sides. Rather than eat like a dog, she didn't eat.

'Hey, don't waste it,' Ball Cap said. 'You don't want to try a daring escape and find you're out of energy.'

She let a few minutes go by so he wouldn't think she had an escape plan, then ate. Not long after that, Dominic said the words *Boot time* and Ball Cap tapped her head with his foot.

'It's late, missus, and we need sleep. I can either sleep on top of you, or you can go in the boot.'

'Don't mess around,' Dominic said.

'And I sleep naked. So, me on top or the boot?'

She wanted neither. 'I won't run. I came to you. I want my daughter back.'

'I know you won't run. You'll be in the boot. Or under me.'

'Boot,' she croaked.

She heard a thump. Ball Cap grabbed her ponytail and lifted her up. She fought to get her arms under her and struggled to her knees. Ball Cap had collapsed part of the seat to expose the boot. In the darkness of the car, it was a black mouth she didn't want any part of.

'What are you, a vampire? I invite you into my boot.' He swept a hand like a concierge displaying the penthouse suite.

She climbed over the back seat, into the black mouth. The carpet was rough and smelled of timber, and the fibres were studded with a billion splinters. He told her to lie with her back to him, hands behind her. She did and he slipped a piece of fabric around her wrists.

Then his weight was on her and she feared he was going to kiss her good night, but he reached out to prop an electronic tablet against the rear of the car, right in front of her face. On the screen was a paused YouTube video called *Hilarious Cats*.

'Dead funny, that. Don't laugh too loud, okay? Oh, and if you scream for help, your kid will end up doing the same.'

He shut the mouth. Thankfully, the tablet prevented total blackness. Behind the wall, she heard Ball Cap shifting about, getting comfortable. She heard the click of the driver's seat reclining as Dominic prepared for bed, too.

As the two men settled, she closed her eyes and said, 'I will turn the page.'

CHAPTER FIFTEEN

Afterwards, she got thanked for her concern, but it wasn't for the child. It was because she couldn't fathom the horror of letting someone else get hurt by her car.

Before all that, though, the boy, still shaking after nearly racing his runaway pushbike into her Punto, holds out his hand and she shakes it. He thanks her for rushing forward and stopping his bike. She tells him to be careful in future. Running a hand through his floppy ginger hair, he remarks that kids are tough and he would have been fine. He's a good-looking boy and she hopes to have one like him if she can't strike lucky with a daughter. Far from here, though. And when she gets her life back on track, and these demons from her mind.

Perhaps sensing that he's being rude, he says, 'I'm lucky you was here, countess. I was gonna have a smash.' Thankfully, he doesn't ask why she's here. 'Maybe you should never leave and make sure nothing else happens to me.'

'I can't. I have to go soon. But I have something for you. A present…'

She was snapped out of the dream – the nightmare – by Ball Cap shaking her. Daylight streamed into the mouth. Amazingly, she had slept until morning. Deep enough to slip back into a dark period of her life.

'Hey, what's this?' he said as he snatched up the electronic tablet.

'No, don't you look at that.'

But he sat back and looked, and he showed Dominic, who was rubbing sweet sleep from his face.

'Put it down. Don't you look at it.'

'Mess this up and pictures are all you'll have left,' he said, turning the tablet so she could see him tap the picture of Josie.

In the night, strangely not in the mood to watch cats falling off walls, she had logged in to Facebook, using her nose to cycle through pictures of Josie. But then she must have fallen asleep with one still onscreen.

He tossed the tablet aside and ordered her out. He watched her struggle, laughing, until Dominic told him to untie her and stop messing about.

Seated and trying to ignore the pain from arms locked behind her all night, she was ordered to wash and given a packet of baby wet wipes. Dominic was reading a newspaper, but Ball Cap watched her scrape away tear residue and dirt from the boot. She realised she hadn't showered since the morning of the day before yesterday, just before taking Josie to school. This time, for the first time since the nightmare kick-started, picturing her little lady didn't come with a wave of dread. She knew what that meant.

'Hey! I said: you didn't try to run, then?'

'I want my daughter,' she said with confidence borne of the knowledge that she would have her Josie back soon. She looked into his eyes. 'You could even send me for breakfast.'

He laughed. 'Comb your hair. You look like a whore who had a killer night.'

He gave her a plastic chip shop fork with hardened grease on it. She dragged it through tangles and knots, while reminding herself that she had only to follow some simple rules, and give these people what they wanted, and then soak up a magnificent, delicious reunion with her—

'Hey! Snap out of it. I said put this on.'

He was holding clothing pulled from a plastic supermarket bag. Black trousers and a suit jacket. He was grinning.

'That's right. This is your changing room.'

So, there in the cramped back seat, with the Ball Cap bastard watching and making no attempt to pretend he wasn't, she stripped out of her dirty clothing. But before she could drag on the trousers to cover her underwear, he plucked out a final pair of items from the bag. She knew what was coming even before she saw knickers and a bra in his hands. She wanted to protest that hers were fine, but knew these people hadn't brought them because they wanted her fresh. So she didn't bother. She took hers off and put on the new stuff, knickers first.

'Hang on, let me help with that,' he said when she tried to put the bra on. She ignored him. Once done, she quickly got into the trousers and suit jacket, which thankfully buttoned up above her bra.

Afterwards, he held up a pair of shoes. But he only gave her one; the second he insisted on putting on himself. She put her eyes out the window as he slipped it on to her foot. He patted her instep when it was done.

Next he reached over the passenger seat and ripped the sun visor right off the roof, which made Dominic swear. He turned his head, angry, and she got another look at the necklace he wore. She wanted to tear his eyes, oh so in range of her nails, right out of his head.

The sun visor, which had a mirror, got dumped in her lap along with a few make-up items.

'I'll help with the lipstick,' he said.

And he did.

'Now sit back and relax,' he said afterwards. 'We've got twenty minutes until 9 a.m.'

'What?' she snapped. 'We waited all night because of that? It's a twenty-four-hour establishment, you damn idiots.'

She'd blurted the insult in anger, because this error had kept her away from Josie for hours, but now fear flooded in as she worried about repercussions. But both men just looked at her. Ball Cap punched the back of the seat, just inches from her. 'Why didn't you know that?' he asked his pal. 'We just sat here all night.'

'So go now,' Dominic said, turning back to his paper.

She shrank back as Ball Cap reached past her to grab the door handle, but paused like that. 'In and out. I say this takes half an hour tops. Any longer, bad news. Do I need to remind you of what happens if you run or anything? Do I?'

She shook her head. 'I won't run. I want my little lady.'

He opened the door. And that was it. She got out. Free. She looked around, seeking the van she had seen yesterday. But Josie was probably miles away in case she called the police. With no other choice – not that she would have taken another – she virtually ran down the side road, and out into a blizzard of pedestrians on the Strand in Westminster, London.

*

Jefferson's was down a nondescript side street off the major London thoroughfare, tucked nicely away because it didn't need or wish to advertise. The kind of people who banked there went looking for it.

The perks of banking here included access to executive lounges in hundreds of airports, major discounts on fine wines across the city, and a Breitling watch with personal locator beacon, because clients of Jefferson's didn't holiday in Blackpool. And since many were international and didn't keep to British working hours, there was a concierge in reception twenty-four hours a day.

Anna swiped in with the keycard from her father's garage. Ahead, across a marble floor, the white-suited concierge rose from behind his desk and straightened his tie with a smile. She started towards him, telling herself that she needn't worry about her demeanour, because often the rich were quirky, and this guy was paid not to ask questions about—

He lost that smile in the quarter-second before she heard a bang behind her.

She whirled to see a man at the door, having just caught it before closing. Dishevelled, anxious, with distressed eyes and rapid breathing.

'Nick. My God, what—'

He rushed in and grabbed her arm.

'Ma'am, do you know this man?'

Over her shock, she turned to the concierge, who was walking around his desk.

'Yes,' she said. 'It's fine. Thank you.'

He didn't look like he believed this, but he was paid not to ask questions of the quirky rich. The guy simply nodded as Nick guided Anna down a short corridor bearing the toilets. He pushed open the door of the Gents and virtually dragged her inside.

Still in shock, she didn't manage to form a question until they were in a cubicle and the door was locked.

'How did you know?'

He seemed calmer now they were alone. 'It is revenge?'

'You can't be here, Nick. This will ruin things. How did you know where I was?'

The panic came back into his face. 'Do you know where Josie is? Was she ever at the scrapyard?'

Scrapyard? He'd been *there*, too? She sat on the closed toilet lid, legs weak, goosepimples on the back of her shoulders. She knew he knew it all. He glared down at her, his face part anxiety and part anger and part terror. But he knew she was suffering too, because he took her hands and knelt before her. Jefferson's didn't have cramped toilet cubicles.

'I know, Anna. I know it all. I know about the hit-and-run. It's why you needed to leave London so quickly. I know about the cloned car. I don't know how you arranged it all, but I know. Is this about revenge? Someone connected to those people you killed? Did they take Josie to get revenge? But what are you doing here? Is there something here they want? A secret money stash? What? Talk to me.'

Still in shock, she touched his face, as if to confirm he was really there, and to give herself time to catch her breath. He waited.

'Yes, I did that. It was me. Do you hate me? I killed them, I killed those two people, and I didn't tell the police. I couldn't. The families have had no answers because of me. But I hid that secret for us. We were going to get married. We wanted children. I hid it for us.' She averted her eyes. 'And for *him*, God knows why,' she added with clear distaste.

'Him? Who? Eastman?'

So he really did know it all.

'Was this about revenge? What's here in this bank that the kidnappers want, Anna?'

She gripped his hands tighter. So, he didn't know it all, and now she had the added problem of having to dump another crushing weight on him. But his hands were warm and comforting and she wanted to unload, needed to after all these years, and there was no person on the planet, not even Jane, she would rather confide in.

'It's not about revenge. But it is about that night.'

'Anna, right now I don't care that you hid it away. I understand why, and I'll help you come to terms with it—'

'But the police know, Nick. That detective, Bennet, he told me they knew about Watson-Bruce Salvage. I knew then that the police would eventually find out about the… accident. That's how you know, isn't it? You went there with the police, didn't you? They know everything, don't they? They're going to take me away from Josie.'

'Yes, they know, but we'll get through it. Why is that hit-and-run connected to Josie's kidnap, Anna? What's here in this bank that they want? Is it money?'

'I wish this was about money. But it's not.'

CHAPTER SIXTEEN

'Marc called me on his way to Hammersmith Medicines Research, east of there, where he was due to give a dinner speech. He was still reeling from comments he'd made to a local TV news station about Bovine TB, so he wanted to remain inconspicuous. At least, that was what he told me. I mean, I know his wife never goes to functions with him, but he's got a man who drives for him. Sometimes I'd drive him to places, but usually when it was personal and he didn't want to be seen out and about. But this didn't make much sense, since people knew he was giving that speech. But I went along with it when he called me to drive him to the function. And we used my car because people knew his, which I also found strange. I picked him up at a petrol station car park on Western Avenue, about a mile or so from where the hikers got hurt. Western would have taken us just about all the way to the research centre. But about halfway...'

*

Eastman's face lights up white as he pulls out his phone and puts it to his ear.

'Twenty minutes, babe.'

He hangs up, straightens his tie and his hair in the sun visor's mirror – and then spots Anna's shocked face.

'You're meeting a woman? Is that why you're cancelling the speech?'

'Sure, unless you want to take her place,' he says, and strokes her leg.

The shock of it makes her clip the kerb with a front wheel. She grips the steering wheel and watches the road.

'Mr Eastman, I don't think that's a good idea.'

'Meeting her or *this*,' he slurs, and touches her again.

'Stop that,' she says. He's never shown sexual interest in her before and it throws her brain. But then she's never seen him this out of it, or ever been alone with him when he's drunk.

'What about the speech? You can't just not turn up,' she says, and while in part she means that, she's mostly trying to get his thoughts off her legs. Next time, trousers instead of a dress.

'Already called them. Stomach bug. It's up near All Hallows Church, so take the next north on Greenford Road.'

He returns to the mirror. Hair, tie, and teeth. He glances at her legs again. She only wore the dress in case he decided to take her to the function, and now regrets it. She tells him he shouldn't drink any more at the function, and silently considers telling him the function might be a bad idea if reporters will be present.

So worried is she by his scrutiny, she misses the turn north on to Greenford Road. In the midst of sending a text message somewhere, he tells her to take the next left. She enjoys the next part of the ride in silence.

Horsenden Lane North. They ride over the train tracks, through an estate, and then north still over the canal. The road cuts through trees that loom tall and heighten the darkness. In the gloom, she feels his eyes fall upon her again.

'You know, Anna, I must say, I never before noticed this, but you're a very attractive woman.'

She is considering her response when his hand slaps on to her bare thigh. She jumps, and looks down, and slaps his hand away. But the impact upon her leg is loud, too loud, and is accompanied by a mighty shudder throughout the whole car.

'Jesus Christ!' Eastman yells.

Suddenly she finds the car swerving, the wheel fighting her like something alive and angry. Her eyes are back on the black road and gloomy trees. Everything seems just A-Okay out there, but she knows something mammoth just happened.

'Oh, God, what was that?' she moans.

'An animal. You hit something.'

They take a curve and there, ahead, is a small lay-by. She pulls in with shaking hands. The car stalls, silence filling the world, but her fingers grip the steering wheel as if it's keeping her from floating away. Eastman roughly tosses aside his seatbelt and clambers from the car. The interior light stings her eyes.

Staring back the way they came, he slurs, 'Can't see anything. Maybe it was a dog.'

'God.'

'Maybe it limped off. Might have been a stray.'

'Should we go back and check?' she says, not certain she actually wants to. Not if the dog is alive but hurt.

He checks his watch. 'I'm not going back. No point. The next driver will shift it into the side of the road. Let's just get moving on.'

Now the thought of abandoning a hurt dog in the road appals her. But she knows he's more interested in meeting his date. She tries something that might appeal more: 'We could get in trouble, though, if we just drive off.'

He thumps into his seat and looks at her. 'We? I wasn't driving.'

'But… you touched me.'

He gives her a long look that she doesn't like. 'Just get out of the car. I'll go back and check.'

She gets out on weak legs and stumbles into the lay-by, and at no point casts her eyes back down the road, just in case. The cold wind chills a coating of sweat on her face. She finds a tree stump and half-sits, half-collapses on to it. As Eastman reverses and turns

the car, she sees the damage to the front, including a dent in the
bonnet. Breathing becomes hard as she realises the dent is high.

Too high to have been caused by a dog…

*

And breathing became hard as the memories bombarded her like
a rain of giant hail. Nick squeezed her hands tightly.

'And then he told me,' she said between gasps of breath. 'When
he was back. Two young people. I'd hit two people. Walking across
the road. He was shaking and traumatised, so I knew it was bad.
That's when he told me. I'd killed them.'

'I'm sorry you had to go through that, Anna. And to relive it.
But what has it got to do with kidnapping Josie?'

'He drove us back to his car. I couldn't face driving. He was
careful with what roads he took, making sure as few people as
possible saw us. He knew what he was doing. And then he called
the research centre to say he'd be attending the function after all,
but would be late. And he called for a taxi. But he even made us
walk into the garage to tell the cashier that he would be leaving
his car overnight. And then I would drive home, back the way I'd
come. That's what he said to do. If ever we had to answer questions
about our movements, we would say he broke down at the petrol
station and I came to help, and we were both there until his taxi
came and then he went to the function and I went home. And
the cashier would back us up.

'I couldn't face going back in the car, but he left me. I was
just left there, alone. So I had to. And I did. I was terrified, but I
managed to do it. I drove. I was a wreck, but I did it. I went along
with his plan and I just drove home.'

'There was blood in the engine bay. So you got home and you
cleaned the outside of the car?'

The hard breathing increased tempo, coming in short bursts.
'He told me to.'

'And then you told me a lie about a carjacking attempt, to cover your depression. And you virtually hid away from the world for a couple of days.'

'I'm so sorry about that. I couldn't face anyone. My family was way up north, so I would have time to adjust. But you were staying in my house by then and I knew I couldn't just pretend nothing was wrong. I had to have a reason why I was so messed up. Marc also made me come up with a story to explain my distress, because I couldn't hide it from you. Not you. I'm sorry.'

He touched her shoulder to calm her. 'And you needed a reason why you suddenly couldn't face being in a car. And still can't drive at night, even years later. You need silence, too, to concentrate.'

She nodded. 'It was also Marc's idea to scrap the car.'

Nick felt the old fear bubbling up. 'So the police wouldn't find it? To protect you? Because you were lovers.'

The final sentence wasn't a question, but a statement. It widened Anna's eyes. 'No, I… it wasn't like that. We never slept together. He always seemed dedicated to his wife. I read about those three affairs, those women the papers called the Witches of Eastman, but I never got an inkling that that sort of thing was going on. God, apart from that time in the car, I never saw him interested in other women. And that night was the only time he ever showed that he was attracted to me.'

'Then why did he help you cover the crime?'

'He did it all to protect himself, Nick. He said he had a lot to lose if people knew he was in the car when it hit those poor people. No worry for me, just himself. Just his image. He said he was going to change this country, do great things, and if I didn't help him to hide what had happened, I would be getting in the way of that. I would be ruining this country. He said he couldn't allow me to do that, ruin things.'

She dabbed her eyes. 'But he also mentioned you. You wouldn't wait for me to get out of prison, he said. I'd never have the family

I wanted. I would have to wait ten years or more to have a baby. That was what he said. I mean, I know that was just him trying to trick me, but he was right about going to prison. I would. I would have lost you. We wouldn't have had Josie. I hid it for us. It's why I ran yesterday. To sort this out and hope no one ever knew about… about that night.'

He understood, but still hadn't had the answer he wanted. Now he grabbed her face in his hands, but softly, just to force her to concentrate on him. 'But why kidnap Josie, Anna? What's in the safety box?'

*

Anna and Marc stand before the car, washed in its headlights like actors lit up on a stage. Her head is bowed, face in her hands. The head shakes. Marc steps out of frame. The sound of the rain materialises as the door is opened, and then the picture jerks slightly as Marc enters the vehicle.

The frame moves backwards, turns, the headlights illuminating Anna sitting upon a tree stump. Then it moves forward, still turning, and Anna slips out of frame. The car heads back the way it came.

Nothing to see but black road and hard rain striking the windscreen and white lines passing beneath the vehicle, like laser fire from a craft in deep space. Nothing to hear but the engine and low murmurs of grief from Marc…

And then, in the road, they appear. Not one but two shapes. Unmoving, lying together in the centre of the road, smashed by rain. Smashed in other ways.

Oh Jesus no – Marc hisses.

… but that was all she could bear to watch.

*

'Dashcam? It was recorded?'

'I never watched the whole video. I couldn't. And you know I never went back to work. I went out, to try, but I couldn't. Couldn't face it. I told Marc I was leaving. Leaving work and leaving London. He was okay with that, which I didn't expect. He said it would be a good new start for me, but I think he was glad that I wouldn't be around the people he knew, wouldn't let our secret out.

'But he had one final thing I had to do. A few days later, he contacted me. By then he'd heard that the police were looking for a blue 05 Punto. They knew the type of car from paint flecks. The police were tracing it. They wanted to analyse all cars of that type in London. Marc's wife, Iliana, he said she'd arranged for the car to be scrapped. Her family runs scrapyards. He said they would give me another car. Just the same. I didn't really understand until he explained. It was to fool the police. I was shocked that he'd told her, but he had, and she hadn't just stuck by his side, she'd actually thought up a plan to fool everyone.

'And I had to go through with it. Even if I'd sold the car, which I wanted to, the police would have found it. He said they'd know it was my car that… hit those poor hikers. I know it was covering up a crime, but I had no choice. Marc would ruin me. I would lose you, and we wouldn't have Josie. And I just couldn't go to prison, not for an accident.

'But Marc said he couldn't be tarnished by me, not driving drunk. But I hadn't been drinking, so I knew then, when he said that, that he wasn't going to take any blame. He was going to lie, if it came out. But he was the cause of it, Nick, because he tried to touch me. It distracted me. I knew if he told the police he knew nothing about it, but that I was drinking, I would go to prison for a long time. So I told him, if the police ever found out, I would tell them the truth.

'But he said there was no proof he was in the car. He went to a function and there were witnesses. And, he said, even if the police worked out that the accident happened before he attended the function, he could claim he was with his car in the petrol station. He was parked in a blind corner behind the car wash so no one would recognise him, and there was no camera there. My alibi was I was with him, helping him to try to fix the car, but he would say that I left early. It was my word against his, and his would carry more weight. He was the great Marc Eastman, MP. And if the police checked the cameras watching the entrance, they would see his car didn't leave the garage and mine did. And he would tell the police that when I came back, I was very upset and crying.

'So I told him. I told him about the dashcam. I'd thrown that thing in a drawer and tried to forget about it. I told him I had the video transferred to disk, and if ever he tried to lie, I would expose him. He'd got me the safety box and I was the only one who could access it. I said the disk would stay in there and no one would ever know about it as long as he didn't lie if the police found out. It was my protection. My Forcefield against him.

'And nothing came of it. The police checked the fake car and then forgot about me. There must have been no CCTV in that area that captured my registration or gave them anything. I was amazed. So I made the most of it. I moved on. I know I told you I wanted to change my name to get out of my father's shadow, because he was angry that I'd quit my job. But the truth is it was Eastman I didn't want to be associated with. I wanted to forget that period of my life. At first I kept watching him in the news and by searching the Internet, but before long whole days would go past without doing this. Soon I barely thought about him. I locked that whole terrible time away in my mind. And as the years passed, I forgot about the disk that still sat in the old safety box. And Eastman seemed to forget about me, because he never tried to make contact. Despite my name change and moving cities, a powerful man like him could have found me if he wanted. He probably locked it all away too and concentrated on climbing the greasy Westminster pole. It was a horrible thing to do, cover that crime and leave those families without answers, and I'm so sorry. But I got what I wanted, Nick. I got you. I got Josie.'

'Did he ask for the disk? Did you refuse?'

'I wouldn't give it up back then and now I have Josie in my life. So no way would I have handed it over. That disk is my proof that I wasn't drinking, that Marc was partly responsible because he distracted me. And he knew it. So, no, he didn't ask me for it. He must have decided to force me to give it up. I don't know how he recruited all these Ogres, but he did.

'I wish they'd taken me instead, but they couldn't. Nobody could accompany me into this bank, Nick, because a security guard has to take me up to the strongroom. But they couldn't just let me walk in alone, in case I raised the alarm. And I wouldn't be able to enter the bank if I was reported missing. I had to walk into this bank as if everything was normal. So they kidnapped Josie to force me.

'One of them told me their plan, Nick. It could have gone so much easier. They were supposed to leave us a note in Josie's bed. We were supposed to pretend to everyone that Josie was fine and wait for a call. It was to test us. They couldn't risk telling me what they wanted until they knew I wouldn't cave in and tell the police everything. Then we were supposed to drive to London, get the disk, get Josie back, and pretend nothing bad ever happened. No one would ever know she'd been taken.'

'But I ruined that plan by being awake.'

'You fought with them and they panicked that the police were going to come because of the noise. So they kidnapped you to confuse things. They wanted the police looking at you, not *me*, so they made out that you owed them something. And after you escaped from that lock-up garage and would have told your story, they called me at the hospital and demanded money, so the police would concentrate on that instead. Not on *me*. All of it was a smokescreen to stop the police looking for a connection to me and finding out about that hit-and-run. To make sure Marc's name never came up.'

'So, with police everywhere, they needed a new plan. They needed to get a secret message to you. One nobody else would understand, that you could easily lie about just in case something went wrong. Eastman knew you could read Braille.'

'He knows everything about me. We spent a lot of time together. So when I discovered a Braille message left in the phone box, that was when I knew Eastman was behind this. When they used the word "Forcefield". That was what I called the disk. My protection from him. I knew then that this was about the dashcam. About that long-ago night. When they wanted to meet in secret, I ran from the police. My plan was to hand the disk over and get Josie back. But I couldn't have the police involved, Nick. I didn't care about the disk any more. I just wanted to get it out of my life and get Josie back.'

He kissed her forehead and stood up. 'Then let's go get it.'

*

The concierge had to escort them upstairs, but he asked no questions. The quirky rich. And he left them alone once in the strongroom. The same card key that got her in the building unlocked an electronic lock on Box A.MID431. Amongst a few old pieces of useless paperwork she hadn't returned to Eastman, there it was. A CD in a plastic case, no label on disk or case.

Nick beat her to it.

'Why now, Anna? Years later? Why all of a sudden did Eastman decide he needed this disk? I understand that he's in a much bigger role now, with further to fall, but he's been Secretary of State for Education for six months. Why now?'

She shook her head. 'I've asked myself that, over and over. What could have prompted him? I follow the news, just in case there was ever some new interest in the hit-and-run case, but there's been nothing. No new witnesses or evidence, nothing that might have prompted the police to reopen the investigation. I just don't know. Can I have the disk?'

He didn't move. 'Whatever it is, it's important to Eastman. If he's worried about exposure, look at him now. Involved in kidnapping.'

She looked horrified. 'What are you saying?'

'I don't think they'll just let you walk away as if nothing has happened. So we're not just handing this over. I think we have to give it to the police.'

Her jaw fell. 'No, we can't.'

'If you hand yourself in, the sentence will be lighter, Anna.'

'But they've got Josie. They'll let Josie go. We can't risk it.'

'They must know we could get her back and then go to the police anyway. That's too risky for them. I don't think they'll let you go.'

'They won't kill her.' She shoved him in the chest, but he held his footing. 'They just want the disk, and we won't get Josie unless they do. Give it to me.'

She tried to snatch it, but was too slow. 'I didn't say Josie. I pray they don't want to hurt Josie, because she's an innocent child. She doesn't know anything. But you know enough to send Eastman down. It's you who's in danger, Anna. I think they'll kill you once they have this disk. Eastman has got too much to lose. His people will kill you so his secret stays safe. You ran away from home, didn't you? The police will think you fled the country or something to avoid prison.'

She said nothing.

'Anna, we give this to the police and we tell them everything. And we just have to hope Josie is let go. I hate the idea of antagonising these people, but we can't give them the disk. It's got to go to the police now. No more running and lying.'

He was taken aback when she immediately said, 'Okay. You're right.'

They composed themselves and walked downstairs, where Nick planned to use the phone in reception. The concierge smiled as they appeared, and asked no questions. And that was when it happened.

She put her fingers in his eyes, and while he was distracted the disk was snatched from his hand.

'Help me,' she yelled.

A trick, he realised. He grabbed her hand as she ran for the door, but someone then grabbed him. The big concierge, who clearly doubled as security given his bulk and strength and speed, twisted Nick's arm behind his back and swept out his legs. He hit the marble floor hard enough to lose his breath.

'Anna! No. Stop.'

But she didn't stop. She slapped the button to release the door and barged it open, and vanished.

Upon exiting, Anna stopped on the marble steps and took a breath to prepare herself for the next stage. She would walk the forty metres along the Strand, and then she would stop level with the side street where the car was parked. But instead of heading down, she would call out over the heads of pedestrians with no knowledge of the terror in her heart. She would order the Ogres to fetch her daughter. And they would have to do it. No choice. No way could they abduct her in plain sight of hundreds of people. And Josie would be brought—

'A disk?' Ball Cap said, appearing out of nowhere like a spirit and clamping his hand around her arm. No one saw, or they saw and didn't care. He took the disk from her fingers. 'Aw, I just have to know what's on this.'

'When I get my daughter. I want her right now.'

'Well, maybe we should stop standing around here waiting for Superman to rescue you, eh?'

He started to lead her across the road, his grip hard but useless because she actually got to the other side before him. Every step was one closer to Josie. He reached out to open the back door of his car, but her hand got there first. If he was planning to force her down on to the floor, no need. She assumed the position. His feet lay on her back. The car was on the move two seconds later.

'It's a disk,' he said. Dominic told him to not worry about it. 'But what's on it?' That would be worrying about it, and I told you not to. 'Must be the unreleased new *Star Wars* film for them to want it this bad.' Let's pretend it is. Just keep it safe.

The car turned this way and that, deep in winding streets, probably reversing the route they had taken to get here. Thirty seconds, maybe forty. Closer and closer to Josie. She could smell her scent on the pyjamas still.

'We didn't come this way,' Ball Cap said.

'It's fine.'

'You look puzzled, pal. Want me to drive?'

'It's fine. Just watch the countess.'

After another turn, the car made a sharp stop.

'Are we lost?' Ball Cap said.

'This'll do,' Dominic said.

'This'll do?'

'This is it, I meant.'

And right there she realised something was badly wrong. She struggled upright, on to the seat. Ball Cap was otherwise engaged and didn't resist when she got away from his feet. She saw that they were at the end of a narrow road, a row of white garages on the left and a blue townhouse on the right, all overshadowed by taller buildings. But she focussed on what lay ahead: a chain-link fence at the end of the road, beyond which the land tumbled away.

'So where's the kid?' Ball Cap said.

'Where's my daughter?'

'Don't know, don't care,' Dominic said. He turned in his seat and stared at her. One hand held a knife, but it was the other she couldn't get her eyes off. It fingered the necklace he had no business being within a thousand miles of. 'Sorry, but we can't let you go. You might tell the police after all.'

The shock numbed her. 'My daughter,' was all she could manage.

'Your kid's seen our faces. Ten years from now, some police hypnotist will get a decent photofit out of her and we'll all be doomed. Sorry. But I've gotta make sure she doesn't do that.'

'This wasn't the plan,' Ball Cap said. 'We got what we needed. If the kid's not here, just kick her out and let's be on our way. She can't tell the cops anything about us.'

Dominic shook his head. 'We'll steal another car. Get out, Alan. Shit, I used your real name. You want to risk it now, Mr Anderson? Ooops.'

'Jesus Christ, Dominic Watson-Bruce.'

Dominic looked pained for a second, but quickly seemed to decide it didn't matter if his name was out there. He also started to get out, then changed his mind about that, too. He grinned at her.

'Since this is the end, I have to know. What's this all about, countess? What's on the disk?'

He didn't know? That threw her mind into a tumble. 'Something else you don't know, then.'

'What's that supposed to mean?'

For a reason she didn't know and cared never to learn, his obliviousness to their connection suddenly spiked deep and painfully. 'You don't know who I am, do you?'

His eyes leaped away from her, to behind, and for a fraction of a second she put it down to shame, that maybe something had dawned on him because of her question. But all she got was that fragment of time, because in the very next she felt a terrible impact in her back. The car was shunted forward, hard, to a score of rending metal. The chain-link fence lost resistance at one post and opened like a door to let the vehicle through.

The front dipped, as if about to tumble over a cliff, but in the next moment the car was bumping slowly down a slight decline, carving through flowers. Stones the size of sleeping dogs marked the boundary between the small hill and the rear carpark of a Perry's car dealership. The car struck one, wobbled violently as the front end climbed atop, and stopped dead. She was thrown forward to crack her temple on the headrest of the driver's seat.

The next thing she knew, her door was yanked open. Dominic was there, grabbing her with his powerful arms, pulling her out. He must have lost the knife. The struggle caused the carefully balanced front end to list here and there like a great beast injured and staggering.

'You bastards,' she heard a familiar voice yell.

Nick. He must have escaped the concierge in time to see which car she got into.

Barely able to comprehend, she looked up the hill, which was a lawn decorated with red and blue and green and yellow flowers: a 'Britain in Bloom' logo inside a ring of turned earth. A little graft of nature in the centre of the concrete jungle. The car had sliced twin tracks right through it. Atop the ruined lawn she saw her father's car, smashed front end poking out over the cliff like a nosey animal. She had no idea where they were, but, despite the garden, it had to still be the centre of London.

And Nick was there, staggering out of the vehicle, his head wound leaking blood again.

As he started down the slanted lawn, she tried to break free of Dominic's grip and go to him. She got only a few feet before her head scrambled. Her brain cut contact with her legs and they shut off. Her head got another whack, this time by mown grass.

Looking up, she saw Dominic step forward, up the hill, getting between her and Nick, who was coming down like a runaway train. Dominic turned partly to his left and raised his right arm, curling it before his face, like someone trying to protect himself. But in his hanging left hand, hidden from Nick's view by his leg, was a short piece of metal that instantly elongated in length with a click.

Nick stumbled on.

'Where's my daughter?' he yelled.

A trick, she realised. She tried to shout, but it was too late.

Feigning cowering behind his raised right arm, Dominic suddenly turned and brought his left arm up and around, swinging the extendable baton at Nick's head. Full of forward momentum, he took the blow hard, almost on the same spot where he'd been struck the last time he'd met this man. His legs collapsed under him. She almost felt the earth vibrate under the hard impact of his body hitting the dirt. He tumbled past her and came to a stop in the ring of turned earth, face up.

'Déjà vu, asswipe,' Dominic said. He took four strides down the hill and bent over Nick.

'Nick!' she yelled.

Dominic grabbed Nick's shoulder and flipped him over easily. Then he knelt on her husband's back and put hands in his hair, full weight bearing down on locked arms. She actually saw Nick's face sink two inches into the soil.

A shadow fell over her. Ball Cap, standing nearby.

'It's over, don't you hear the sirens?'

Dominic ignored his colleague's shout. Nick was thrashing under powerful hands intent on forcing the life out of him, but no match for the skinnier, smaller man. She was too dazed from the crash to get up, to help him. But over the drumbeat of rushing blood in her head, she heard the sirens, loud and getting louder. She expected the two men to flee.

But Dominic remained right where he was, hard fingers locked on the back of Nick's head.

'You go kill her, I got this guy. Race you.'

*

'It's over, pal. Let's not add years to the sentence.'

Dominic ignored his partner. Knowing he didn't have time to end Nick by suffocation, he reached for his discarded baton. Even in daylight, Anna saw the air above the road at the top of the lawn pulse with blue light. The sirens seemed so close that another inch would put them in her head.

'Dom, c'mon, man, stop.'

Up the baton sailed, ready for the downward curve. Anna turned away. At the top of the lawn, bodies appeared at the cliff edge. Blue uniforms and high-vis jackets. Police. Lots. They crowded around the car, filing past, sailing over the edge and down, like a tide.

And that was when Ball Cap slid his arm around Dominic's neck. He fell back, peeling Dominic off Nick like a plaster from skin, and tearing away those lethal hands. Nick seemed to use the last of his energy to heave himself over on to his back, and lay coughing as he tried to suck in air.

'You'll thank me later, Dom,' Ball Cap said.

On his back, with Dominic's spine against his chest, he locked in the chokehold. Thrashing, Dominic's legs kicked fast and hard, and she watched them strike Nick's chest and face. He struggled even to raise his arms to defend himself. Quickly, she crawled to him and collapsed on top, and those heavy blows dug into her flesh instead.

Policemen shouting. Policemen everywhere, looming over, cutting off the light. Someone tugged at her and she rolled off Nick to lie beside him, and found herself staring up at a face she knew. It was Lucy Miller.

'They don't have my girl!' she screamed up at the woman.

Other police moved into her vision, surrounding her. She looked to one side and saw police prising Ball Cap off his unconscious partner's back. She screamed it again: '*They don't have my girl.*'

She lashed out, swiping aside two police officers and crawling between them. Someone grabbed her arm, but her free one lashed out again, this time towards Dominic, who was unconscious and being sat upright by two officers. Before anyone could stop her, she pulled her arm free and both hands clamped hard around his throat. Her fingernails raked skin as she was dragged backwards, away, and she clutched her fists hard to her chest.

She looked around. Nick was still awake but groggy as he returned her stare from just inches away. As Miller tried to soothe her and Bennet knelt by Nick to help him sit up, she heard her husband speak through lips coated in soil:

'There was a third option after all. That they would just kill Josie and I'd never see her again. That she was already dead.'

*

As Ball Cap was being led to a police car in handcuffs, he called out across the heads of a dozen police officers:

'I want to talk to you, Anna. Just you. Talk to me, I'll tell you what I know. Or the police can drag it out of me over the next month or so.'

She was being escorted, with Nick, to an ambulance, but she stopped. Miller said, *Not a good idea*, but her grip loosened. Anna tugged free, turned and ran. Policemen rushed towards her. Miller had slyly given her freedom for this, but couldn't pretend to treasure the rulebook any longer. When she was grabbed and it was over, Miller only gave it a second's thought:

'Let her go.'

Just moments later she was in the back seat of a police car with Ball Cap again, who now didn't have a cap. And had no control over her. Officers surrounded the car, ready in case he tried anything, even cuffed. She wouldn't look at him. But she asked him, *Please, help me.*

He wouldn't look at her, either. 'I don't know who's got the money and I don't know where your kid is, first of all. Sorry about that.'

She took a deep breath. But didn't move. She was willing to hear the rest.

'And I'm sorry about that.' He nodded at her shoulder, and she put a hand there. Her hand brushed her hair, catching something weighty and solid. Bubblegum. She hadn't even noticed. She didn't care.

He got that and said, 'My name is Alan Anderson. I'm in this with my woman, Elsie, and she's got your girl. Her and my partner's girlfriend. Her name is Louise. Someone decided a couple of girls should watch the kid. Me and Dom back there, we got you. And there's another guy involved, I think. But all I did was help snatch the kid, make some stupid phone calls, and then bring you here. It's all I know. Bring her to this bank and get what she brings out, go home, get paid, live happily ever after. That was my orders. The kid wasn't my business. What I'm saying is the kid side of it is all separate and I can't help you get to her. After the last of the ransom calls, we all had to get new burner phones and I ain't got my girl's number, so I can't call her for you or anything like that. Not allowed, probably in case the cops grab one of us. Which they just did. We're to stay hidden for today and tomorrow we meet up at a place where Dom says. I don't know where and his girl is running things the other end.'

Now, finally, he looked at her. 'But based on what my man there just tried to do, seems obvious they didn't plan to get her back to you or let you go. So I did what I could to help. I can't do any more. Didn't want you holding your breath while the cops put the thumbscrews on me. Dom probably knows more. Maybe he will have a change of heart and call his girl. I don't know. I hope so. I ain't got a say in that. All I can say is this: I'm sorry.'

'That doesn't mean anything to me. It doesn't get my daughter back.'

'I was working at a scrapyard in Fatfield with my girl and she offered me the kidnap job. I don't know who planned it, okay? I don't know who's calling the shots and I don't know what any of this is about. But there's a scrapyard in Northampton. Maybe your kid's there. She's not at the one in Fatfield. I don't know of any other places.'

'She's not there. The police checked.'

'I'm sorry. Look, I did this for the money, but no one was ever supposed to get hurt. We don't know anything about you, so none of this was personal. They offered us £25,000 if we could snatch your kid and get this Forcefield. Like I told you, the kidnap was never about the money, we just needed to pretend it was a basic cash ransom thing, to distract the police. But when you decided to pay it... well, why not, eh? That's what we thought. Why not? £50,000. Why not put a bit of extra work in and get a bigger payday? They said your dad was rich, so we thought he could easily afford to lose it. I never thought the kid would get hurt, and your dad could easily afford the ransom. So when you got her back, you yourself wouldn't even be down any cash.'

'And you thought I would be happy about that?'

He shrugged. 'If I was that smart I'd be... Look, I hope you get her back.'

She got out.

He said one last thing: 'Answer me one question. I need to know.'

She stopped with her hand on the door. If he wanted to know what was on the disk, what had caused all this, what his employers had wanted so badly that they would kidnap a child, then she was going to tell him, she realised. Murder, on video, which they wanted to make sure the world never saw. Hopefully, it would instil more regret in this man.

'What's your daughter's name?'

She slammed the door in his face.

CHAPTER SEVENTEEN

Only when she saw a sign for the M1 North on a gantry over the North Circular Road did Anna realise they were about to leave London. And stasis. Because that was how it had felt until now, in the back of DCI Lucy Miller's car. The slip road felt like a path into the rest of the day. Into a new life. One in which Josie played no role.

She couldn't ever forget Josie, and the little lady wasn't yet gone for ever, but she managed to put her aside long enough to focus on the immediate future. So she asked: 'What happens next?'

Nick's head had been on her shoulder, but now it jerked up. Miller, in the passenger seat, looked round at her. She was blinking rapidly, as if having dozed for a moment.

'You need to take me into custody, don't you? Put me in a cell. Because I'm a murderer.'

Nick squeezed her hand. Knowing the police had retrieved the disk from the kidnappers' car, although they hadn't yet viewed it, she had earlier started to tell her tale. DS Bennet had been willing to record her statement on the move, but Miller had warned her not to say a word. They would deal with it when they got home. And she shouldn't say anything without a solicitor present.

'The case belongs to the London boys and girls, dear. They'll want to question you, but I'll try to make sure they travel up here, instead of you having to go down to them. But this case has waited eight years and another day won't hurt anyone. I'll call those guys and gals tomorrow. You need some sleep.'

The detectives hadn't slept, either, she knew. Both looked ragged, Miller especially so. She knew they had been up all night, watching Nick's car, watching the bank. Even after she had approached Jefferson's, they had waited. The plan had been to make arrests once they knew where Josie was, but they had been forced to make a move when it became clear that Anna wasn't being taken to her daughter. They had allowed Nick to travel to London, already knowing exactly where he was going. Because her father had told them, although she had no clue how he'd known.

Miller continued: 'We'll run you by our station when we get back, Anna. Just to quickly process you. Apologies and all, but it's something we have to... But we'll get you bailed quickly, dear, and you can go home for the rest of the day. There's no reason we can't give you some good news about Josie before tomorrow.'

She didn't know the ins and outs of police procedure, but got the feeling Miller wanted to help her more than she wanted an arrest for the scorecards. But she didn't want help.

'Stop the car. I want out.'

'We can't. We have—'

'No, I'm not under arrest, am I? You didn't say you were arresting me. I want to get out.'

Miller stared at her. 'You're coming with us voluntarily. At the station, yes, we'll have to—'

Anna stared back. 'Don't treat me differently just because my daughter is missing. Stop being so damn nice to me. I killed two people—'

'Anna, you—'

'No, Nick, keep out of this. I don't want their sympathy or their help. I want what I deserve. I want to tell my story and then get the punishment I deserve. So I want them to do their damn jobs. Right now.'

Miller turned in her seat. Anna couldn't read anything in that expression, not relief or regret or anger or sorrow, when the detective said, 'Anna Carter, I'm arresting you on suspicion of...'

At four driver location markers on the M1, four things happened.

M1/A/11.9

Eleven point nine miles away from Charing Cross. The warmth of Nick's embrace made her sleepy, and she welcomed it. There would be a lot of sleep in the future. Oblivion allowed her to forget, although she didn't doubt this gruesome day would haunt her dreams. But there was something important to do. Something she'd forgotten about due to recent events, including telling her story to the detectives as the car cruised away from the capital. The fact of her forgetfulness caused a stab in her heart.

'I want to phone Jane. I didn't tell her. God, she has no idea.'

Bennet, driving, handed his phone over his shoulder.

She had to compose herself before making the call, and rightly so. As expected, Jane was very upset.

'Anna, where are you? Where have you been? We've been worried. You vanished, and Nick went off in Father's car. The police didn't know anything, or wouldn't tell us anything.'

'I'm sorry, Jane, really, but there was something I had to do. But it... I failed. I didn't get Josie. I was found by two of the kidnappers, but they don't know where she is. I lost Josie. I'm sorry.'

'God, don't apologise. I'm so sorry for you. What's happened?'

The explanation pushed Jane's distress into the stratosphere. The last portion of a long monologue was: *'The police are keeping the arrests secret, so it doesn't make the people who have Josie worried. But I don't know how long that can last until they find out, and then God knows what they'll do. I can't deal with this.'*

She heard her father in the background, then closer, and a noise as he ripped the phone from his blind daughter's hand.

'Anna? Where are you? Good Lord, what's going on? Are you there? Can you hear me?'

'I love you, Dad, even though I don't act like I do. And you love me, even though I've never heard it said from your lips. I can't explain now. We didn't get Josie. Jane will tell you. We don't know where she is—'

He tried to interrupt, but she didn't want a conversation like this on the phone. She interrupted right back. 'Look, please, Dad, I'll talk to you in a couple of hours. We're heading back. Don't call back. Please wait for me to return. Get money, Dad. I want as much as you can spare for me. A lot. As soon as you can.'

'Anna, it's out. Someone must have spoken. Everyone knows. All the neighbours know. There're people outside. Reporters have been calling. Somehow everyone knows Josie has been kidnapped.'

'Bye.' She hung up.

Everyone was looking at her.

Nick especially. 'Anna? What's going on? What's the money for? We can't expect the kidnappers to trust us again. What are you thinking of doing?'

She lay her head back, turned her face away. He didn't press it. She felt his hand stroke her arm, and then his head once more on her shoulder. Like everyone else, he would wait for her. She decided not to burden him just yet with the news that Josie's kidnap had become citywide, maybe even nationwide, gossip. And that the cadaver dogs would be coming out.

M1/A/76.8

Anna started to scrabble for the door, right out of the blue, after drifting off and jerking awake. Nick tried to grab her arms, and Bennet pulled into the hard shoulder.

'I don't want her body to be found,' she moaned, still fighting to exit the vehicle.

'Anna, no, don't say that,' Nick said.

'I don't want a funeral! And I can't always think she could be alive out there, growing up, when she might be dead.'

'Please, Anna, stop.'

But she forced herself out of his arms, and ran into the undergrowth, and climbed the bank, through the trees. Because she wore high heels that couldn't get a grip in the soil, Nick stayed right behind her, close enough to stop her doing something silly but willing to let her burn energy, which he prayed would calm her.

At the top, he reached out like a relay runner passing a baton, grabbed a wrist, dug in his more practical heels, and she hit a dead stop. Just in time. No way, even if she'd seen the land drop away sharply, could she have hauled up in time.

The jerk in her shoulder dropped her into a side-sit. She stared up at him, just feet from a dangerous drop.

'Let me go. I've got nothing left.'

He turned at a noise. Miller was halfway up the bank, Bennet's oversized form struggling behind. But she was stopped, having realised the danger was over. Then she was heading away, aware of a private moment.

'I've lost Josie, and I'll go to prison, and my sister will hate me. I have nothing. Why?'

He knew she didn't mean *why did she have nothing?*

'Why did I stop you? You were about to run off the edge. Why did you run?'

She tried to jerk her hand from his, but his grip was so tight that he was pulled down, on to his knees. 'You think you helped me?' she said. 'Helped me do what? Mourn my daughter, from prison?'

'You think that's the answer? Killing yourself?'

'My daughter is dead, so what do I have left?'

'She's not dead, Anna. So stop—'

'She is! I didn't say her name to them. Not once. They didn't know. I should have called her Josie and they would have seen her as… as…'

He knew what she was struggling to find the words to say. 'No, you can't think like that.'

'But it's true. I didn't use her name and now she's dead and I have nothing left.'

She started to struggle free again, but nothing alive could have broken his grip. 'So this is all about you? Anna is all that matters?'

He was almost as shocked as she with that line. Like a defibrillator, it kick-started some reaction inside her. The sniffling ended. The shaking stopped.

'You go over the edge, I get left alone,' he said. 'My daughter's missing. Now my wife wants to kill herself and leave me to suffer losing everything.'

Wide-eyed, she stared at him.

'You don't want me. Without Josie, you have nothing, you just said. So I've already lost you both. I'm jumping as well. I'm going first, though, because if I land on your body down there, I might survive, then I'll have no wife or daughter and be stuck in a wheelchair.'

He got up, as if about to actually take a leap over the sheer drop. She kept hold of his hand and yanked him back down. 'But then I get the wheelchair,' she said, forcing a smile of sorts, just to show him she was over her insane moment. At least for now.

'So what can we do? Leap together? Thing is, what if Josie comes back? Which I'm sure she will?'

She dropped her head into his chest hard enough to hurt. 'I'm sorry. What was I doing? That was stupid and insane. I'm so sorry.'

'It's OK. It's going to be OK.'

Anna had never wanted to believe anything more. But it was just silly hope.

*

M1/A/101.2

They approached roadworks and Bennet started to slow. Like everyone else, he increased speed almost immediately because there was no workforce and no sign warning of a reduced speed limit, so the average speed cameras would be turned off. The change in pace, in rhythm, pulled Anna out of a trance. It also stirred Miller, whose head was resting on the window.

'Don't let me sleep,' she told Bennet. She turned in her seat, saw that Anna was alert, and handed her an electronic tablet. The long night had taken more of a toll on Nick, who was asleep against Anna's shoulder.

Miller said, 'The first picture is of—'

'Dominic Watson-Bruce. Iliana Eastman's nephew. The bastard who kidnapped me.' She wanted to spit on his picture. 'I met him once. Way back when he was only about eleven. A kid on a bike. When I went to the scrapyard to do that evil thing.'

'Don't talk about that yet, dear,' Miller warned. 'You've said enough so far. Not here. Please.'

Anna ignored her. 'He nearly crashed his bike into me. I remember hoping my own child could grow up to be as polite and handsome.'

'Don't think about that, Anna. Please.'

'It was a mistake. If I hadn't stopped him crashing, maybe he would have paralysed himself or died. And none of this would have happened to Josie.' She rubbed her face.

Asleep still, Nick grumbled and tried to take back his hand. Only then did she realise she'd grabbed hold of it at some point and was squeezing tightly, nails dug in. She let go of his fingers. She tried to set her mind straight.

'Okay. I'm sorry. Continue. You were saying how lucky Iliana Eastman is to have a criminal in the family.'

'Apologies,' Miller said. 'It's worse than that.'

Watson-Bruce Salvage was a *very* family-run business – every single one of the nine registered employees there was someone's son or cousin or brother or girlfriend or boyfriend of. The Watson-Bruces were notorious in Northampton because just about every one of them going back fifty years had a criminal record. Except Iliana. Perhaps that was why Iliana, who had bigger plans for herself, decided to flee the nest and settle in London, where she broadcast her skills and personality in the power halls of Westminster and kept her history wrapped in shadows.

'Marc never mentioned his wife's family to me,' Anna said. 'I don't think I ever heard the name Watson-Bruce. Not until after… that night. It was only when DS Bennet mentioned that Dominic was from Northampton that I realised these people were involved. And I knew then I was going to go to prison.'

But the Watson-Bruces were also a fiercely loyal family, Miller told her. Angry at Iliana for abandoning them, or pleased that she struck out on her own and made a success, it didn't matter. Blood was thicker than water, and when one of the clan needed help, the family stepped up.

'And I mean the entire family, dear. Dominic Watson-Bruce has admitted recruiting his girlfriend, Louise Mackerson, into the mix – one of the two women we were told have Josie. But how was Dominic recruited? By his father, Robert Watson-Bruce, owner of Watson-Bruce Salvage and brother of Iliana Eastman. Iliana had called her brother for help. You told me he didn't recognise you, didn't know about the dashcam video, right? I reckon he wasn't told anything except the details of his tasks.'

'He'll know who I am soon. Maybe there will be regret.'

Miller didn't reply to that, but moved on to Anna's other abductor. Alan Anderson was, as he'd claimed, wanted by Northumbria Police for a series of arson attacks on vehicles. But empty ones. No murders to his name, this fool. Just ego and low morals.

When Northumbria Police pegged him as a suspect in the fire bombings, he fled his home town of Newcastle Upon Tyne and settled in Fatfield, and there met a girl called Elsie. She got him an off-the-books job at her mother's scrapyard. The mother was Rhona Watson-Bruce, sister of Iliana and Robert. Rhona was called by Robert with a tale of woe from Iliana, and then she had a sit-down with Elsie and Elsie's boyfriend.

But Rhona Watson-Bruce also had a son, Darren, twenty-one, who'd recently been issued a nuisance vehicle warning by police. For riding his *quad bike* on pavements.

A family affair indeed.

Miller flicked the screen to show side-by-side pictures of Robert and Rhona Watson-Bruce, mugshots from years ago. 'These two and Iliana are conveniently away in Spain on holiday. A neat alibi. But it won't help them, dear. We'll get these three at the airport when they return, or we'll get them over there if they don't. We've got the phones of the two men who took you and soon we might have some good information on Darren. We'll get them all, Anna. Including Eastman.'

Miller flicked again. New pictures, ripped from Facebook: two women who barely looked twenty. Louise Mackerson, a black girl with hair like springs and big eyes she could see the men falling for, was in a nightclub, pouting for the camera, drink in hand. Elsie Watson-Bruce, a skinny and petite girl with hair blonde and long, was in a bowling alley, laughing while struggling to hold a heavy bowling ball above her head. Both pictures had comedic tags, thus increasing Anna's struggle to imagine them as kidnappers of a child.

'Police up in Sunderland who raided the scrapyard found an address for both girls. No one home. They're searching for clues, so we might soon know all there is to know about this pair.'

Anna let the tablet slide on to the floor. 'All that matters is where they are.'

'I told you: I promise we'll find Josie.'

'And I told you not to make promises, remember?'

'I need the happy face, remember?'

'The money from my father,' Anna said without a pause. 'I want it to go to the families. Of those two poor people. It won't stop their pain. It's all I can do. And I want to talk to them. I want them to hear it from me, before it's in the news. It will look like false remorse because I was arrested. But I need them to know I really am sorry. They won't believe it, but I always have been. But even if they don't believe it, I need to say it to them.'

Miller nodded. 'For the moment, dear, let's just get home.'

'It's not home without Josie. Besides, I'm not going home. I'm going to prison for murder.'

M1/A/126.5

'A present?' the boy says. 'I nearly got smashed dead, now I've got presents?'

Smiling, she removes her lucky five-yen coin from a pocket. It's been everywhere with her since her mother passed it on, but she's not even sure why. Has it brought luck? She is alive, but right now that doesn't feel like a blessing. It's part of her old life, and it has to go. Her father will ask, but she will simply say she lost it.

The boy takes the offered coin and rubs a wet thumb across it, then puts it to his eye so he can stare at her through the hole in the middle. She manages a rare smile. He asks if it's a lucky coin and she nods, somewhat reluctantly. Japanese, she tells him. Grants luck-wishes. 'You should make sure it's the first thing you put in a new wallet.'

'Are you sure you don't need it?'

She sees the sun glint off the freshly cleaned coin, giving it a renewed sparkle. 'My mother gave it to me, but it ran out of power for me. Now, with a new owner, maybe it will be refreshed for you. Wish for luck and hopefully you will be successful in everything that you do.'

'Jumbo-giganto thanks. Maybe it will help me marry you,' the boy says. She manages another smile. He jumps on his bike and she watches him ride away, out of sight beyond a wall of battered old cars. She never wants to see him again but hopes he will have good luck and achieve greatness. Jumbo-giganto greatness…

She was cast out of her daydream by Bennet's voice, telling her to wake up. Nick was staring out his window. Miller was asleep against the window again. Miller, not Anna, was the one Bennet was trying to wake. Anna reached into her pocket.

'Is she ill?' she said. 'She seems worse than the rest of your team.'

Bennet looked away from the road only to check his watch. 'She got no break before this investigation. The rest of us got half an evening off, but she worked through. Fifty-two hours and counting.'

Miller had mentioned a break for the team between investigations, but not her own lack of one. As Bennet tried to shake his boss awake, Anna warned him to leave her alone.

'She can have an hour till we get back.'

It wasn't to be because Miller's phone rang and she jumped awake. She turned towards the back seat, wide-eyed as if fearful she'd missed a major development. 'No sleep, I said,' she told Bennet, then answered her phone.

As Miller listened to her call and Bennet watched the motorway, Anna buzzed down the window and stuck her arm out. The cold wind immediately bit into her hand and filled the car with noise, although nobody reacted except Miller, who stuck a finger in her free ear in order to hear her call. Anna was preparing to lob an item taken from her pocket, but something deep inside was giving pause.

When she looked at Miller again, the detective was watching her in the rear-view. But not because of her actions…

Bennet got the same funny feeling Anna did and leaned close to his boss, like an invitation to whisper in his ear. Which she did. In the next moment, Anna felt the car gain speed as it drifted right, across two lanes, into the fast one. Even Nick was drawn from the countryside gliding past his eyes.

Before either could ask, Miller turned to face them. She even knelt on her seat in order to reach out both hands, one for each of them. Still with her hand in the cold wind, Anna felt the buzz of something new and meteoric in the air and burst into tears, even before Miller had spoken a word.

'We know where Josie is,' she said. 'And she's safe and sound.'

Shocked, and disbelieving, Anna pulled her chilled hand into the car and against her chest. In tightened fingers was the necklace that she had wrenched from Dominic Watson-Bruce's throat.

The string was grimy and roughened with age, but the old five-yen coin seemed to suddenly have a renewed sparkle.

*

Trowell Services, fifteen miles south of them, but they had to do another mile away from Josie to reach the next junction. Bennet hit a button that put on a siren and there was a pulse of blue from an LED light bar above the rear-view mirror. Flashy drivers in the fast lane quickly jumped aside and everyone remembered the speed limit.

Despite the speed of over a hundred for the journey south, Nick and Anna were impatient. Nick thumped his fist constantly against his thigh; Anna had her fingers in the door release lever the whole way.

There was a BMW SUV in the forecourt of a petrol station by the slip road, and a Mercedes Vito van, and two police cars, and police tape encircling the Vito. Nobody but police around. They drove by, onwards to the Services building.

At least here there seemed to be no buzz, as if nobody knew who they were. It allowed them to walk, brisk but ignored, into the Services, where immediately Anna spotted two uniforms, also being ignored, standing outside an arcade area. She got there first, at a run. Nick was happy to let her.

'Josie!'

There she was in a little blue tracksuit with stripes down the sides, and her blonde ginger hair all a mess atop her head, and her special necklace still around her sweet, pale little throat. She was standing with a man at a large gaming console, blasting away at flying dinosaurs with a plastic rifle. Both turned at her shout.

'Mum!'

Bubbling under the surface: a terrible fear that they would deliver the wrong girl, and kill her by heart attack while they scratched their heads. But there was her little face, all hers, unmistakably hers. Josie dropped the gun and ran, and launched herself into her mother's arms from a whole metre away. Anna snapped her arms around her like a bear trap and Josie moaned at the pressure. She had to dig deep to let her go, as if fearful she could be snatched away again in a half-moment.

''S'posed to scratch over a towel, Mum.' Josie's fingers rubbed over the coarse and broken skin on Anna's neck. Then she put on her sheepish face. 'Soz for scribbling on the wall. I don't want to stay away at night again.'

Anna planted her lips on Josie's cheek so hard she moaned again, but they both laughed about it. And Josie had to wipe away wetness transferred from mother to daughter.

'You weren't being punished, Josie. Those people were…'

No lie would come, but there was no need because Josie was nodding. 'Good dream police.'

She didn't ask, not yet. She would be told the story later by—

'Dad!'

She turned to watch her girl – *her* girl – run to her father. Nick had stopped a few metres out, his face in his hands. He bent to his knees with one arm out to receive Josie, but the other hand trying to cover his whole face still. She knew he didn't want to be seen crying. When Josie thundered into his embrace, Nick disguised his emotion using the shoulder of the blue tracksuit.

Anna faced Miller and, through tears, gave her a big smile. 'That'll do,' Miller said.

Josie high-fived her father and ran back to her mother with a demand to challenge her on the video game. Miller noted that the girl didn't seem very upset by recent experiences.

Nick stood and watched with joy, and that was the moment both parents actually took note of the man with Josie for the first time. The man who had saved their little star. He wore jeans and a bomber jacket and didn't look like a policeman at all.

Nabi, the foul detective constable.

But he didn't act like a hero. He handed Anna the big plastic rifle without looking at her. It even looked like he ignored her words of thanks. And the direction of his walk suggested he was going to ignore Nick, too.

But Miller alone saw this, because the parents were blinded by relief and gratitude and a blend of many more emotions. Nick sidestepped with his hand out. Blocked, Nabi took that hand in his, but they didn't shake. The detective pulled Nick close, as if for a conspiratorial whisper.

'Watch your bloody kid in future, okay?'

And then he strode past, and out the door, as carefree about praise as a comic book superhero. Bennet followed. Nick found himself frozen with a confusing mix of anger and adulation. Then he forgot all about it and watched Josie trying to educate her mother on how to properly hold a rifle, but she kept interrupting to plant kisses on Josie's face.

Nick watched Miller step up, say hi to Josie.

'I'd like to know about these Good Dream Police,' he heard her say. 'Can you whisper to me while you shoot dinosaurs?'

*

Good Dream Police: people who randomly selected a good and happy child to take in their vehicle, because sleeping while constantly moving guaranteed a night of good dreams.

Anna had called her father and Jane, who were en route to pick them up, and that meant killing time. Anna wanted hers alone with Josie; Nick, though, chose to indulge a desire to see where his daughter had been held prisoner. Staring into the Mercedes Vito, he understood Josie's bizarre statement.

The cargo area was slick, no seats, and there was an added black Perspex partition to separate the cargo area and cab. There was a toybox, and toys strewn across the floor. A battery-operated small TV. A mattress and pillow and duvet with cartoon characters on the covers. Biscuit wrappers and crisp packets in a wire mesh bin, other snacks in a cardboard box. Sausage rolls. Bananas. Across the blacked-out back window was a large poster framed like a window and with a sea view. There were large stickers all over the walls and ceiling. Not quite the dank cellar Nick had imagined.

It was like a child's bedroom.

'They were constantly on the move? But where were they going?'

Miller explained. The Vito, which the female kidnappers must have swapped into at some point between the lock-up garage and the M1, had indeed gone south down the motorway, to the point twenty-five or so miles away on the A28 near Sutton – and Kirkby-in-Ashfield. Where the kidnappers made the 5 a.m. call to the house. East of the M1, because a slip road on the south run would poke east. They had simply pulled off and found a place to park.

The next call, to the hospital on a new mobile, had come a few hours later, but only eight miles south, in Nuthall – west of the M1. Not because the kidnappers had taken a slow journey on to the other side of the motorway, but because by then the van had travelled further south, turned around, and was heading north, which meant exiting to the left.

The final call from a fresh burner phone had originated again in Nuthall, but east of the M1 this time. Which was where you'd end up if you exited the motorway while travelling south. Not a zigzag. But:

'A loop?' Nick said. 'They didn't stop. They just drove up and down the M1 all night?'

DC Nabi had worked it out. He used the timeline of the phone calls to determine a loop between Sheffield and no further than Leicester, about seventy miles. Being on the motorway would allow them to travel anywhere they wanted quickly if they had to flee. They would know the police wouldn't expect to find them on the move and police cars don't often roam motorways. No chance of a random stop if they stuck to the speed limit. And the monotony of engine noise and vibration are said to simulate conditions in the womb, which is why young children so easily fall asleep in vehicles.

'So he just watched and waited? And without telling you?'

He was off the case, but apparently wasn't happy with that. Nabi's brother, when both boys were nine years old, went missing. He'd been with their father, but the father had gone into a pub and left his boy to play outside. Got drunk, forgot about him, came out hours later to find him gone. For good.

Nick figured that explained his attitude towards Anna and himself. 'But how did he know what van to look for?'

The roadworks they passed through about a hundred miles from London. Nabi got the cameras turned back on, but with no warning for drivers, everyone blew past at well over the fifty miles per hour limit. He got a list of triple area sightings, which meant the same vehicle being captured going south twice and north once, or vice versa. He got it up and running by midnight, and by the time Miller's car had been heading back to London, Nabi had his list. Two vehicles had made the relevant trips, and one of those was a biker who'd travelled from Nottingham to Cambridge, realised he'd forgotten his best man's suit, and gone back for it. The other: the Mercedes Vito. With a description and registration, he simply waited near Junction 26, the Nuthall turnoff, which the timeline made him pinpoint as about the halfway point, and gave chase when he saw it go past, heading south. He forced it into the Services, made the arrests.

'Quite ironic, you know. Apologies for the lie, but it wasn't my superintendent at all. Calling in the search dog to your house, I mean. All DC Nabi, that. Off his own back. He offered my superintendent the idea of moving you to a hotel, too. And then he about-faces and does this.'

Nick didn't care. He looked into the van again, but its cosmetic mask slipped. Just because Josie had been kept comfortable, it meant nothing. This was not a bedroom, but a prison cell. Had Nabi not found her, Josie's captors would soon have found out about the London arrests of their boyfriends and she might have been killed.

In response to a question about the captors, both already headed to the police station, Miller showed him a pair of photographs. Two women. One was Elsie Watson-Bruce, girlfriend of the man who'd had a change of heart. One of the hired help. But it was the other woman he focussed on. Louise Mackerson, the girlfriend of Dominic Watson-Bruce.

'I recognise her,' Nick said, shocked. 'She came to the house a few days ago. Pizza girl. She wanted to know about my sleeping habits and family and stuff, to see if I could benefit from an organic lifestyle. Jesus Christ, I even told DS Bennet about her.' He quickly explained his sarcastic answer to Bennet's query about people Nick had come across in recent weeks. 'She sounded so... genuine. But... all those questions... she wasn't seeing if an organic lifestyle would suit me in order to sell a damn product. She was milking me for information, wasn't she? And getting close to the house. Were they watching us all that time?'

'Probably, my friend. They were very good. Some don't know how criminally adept they are until they try it.'

If Nick had somehow known, when he opened the door to this girl who had tried to engage him in chat, that she was planning to steal Josie... He slapped the side of the van, which sent a gong-like sound rushing away.

'All this, and for what? It had better be to avoid something catastrophic. I hope that bastard Eastman did this to prevent another Middle Eastern war.'

'Nothing so respectable, I fear,' Miller said. 'Last week a newspaper exposed three affairs Eastman had over the last fifteen years. Each of those women was contacted and agreed to tell their story, probably for a fee. The three Witches of Eastman. Suppose there was a fourth Witch, as yet unknown? Someone who might sell her story soon.'

Nick said he didn't understand.

'None of those Witches lived in Greenford. Eastman told your Anna that the lady he was meeting lived near All Hallows Church in Greenford. That's barely a few hundred metres from where those hikers were killed.'

Nick still didn't understand.

'Just my opinion, mind. Witch number four comes forward to say that Eastman planned to forgo an important function at Hammersmith Medicines Research to meet her. Not a great piece of detective work to find that date, 5th September 2011. Same time, nearby, two hikers are killed by an 05 plate blue Fiat Punto. Such as was owned by Eastman's caseworker, a lady known for ferrying him around when he wants to remain inconspicuous.'

'Someone would connect the dots. The police would find Anna, find out about the scrapped car, everything. And she would have no choice but to expose the disk to back up her version of the story. So this bastard kidnapped my daughter so there would be no proof he was even there when Anna killed those hikers. Why not try to get this woman to say nothing?'

'Just my theory, like I said. No evidence. I've already set the wheels of his arrest turning, so perhaps we'll know before long.'

Nick barely heard. Inside, he was rebuking himself for a horrible thought: if Eastman had instead chosen to send his goons to kill the woman who might expose their affair, none of this would have happened.

Josie was first out of Middleton's Range Rover, running for the door with Anna close behind, as if unwilling to let her get more than a few feet out of reach, even here. Middleton helped Jane into the house, but Nick took a moment to walk to the end of the driveway and peer down the road. DCI Lucy Miller's car had parked about fifty metres away. He noted that it had only a driver, no passenger. And it was Bennet who got out. He started approaching.

Nobody on the street seemed to care, which was a world away from what he'd heard was happening at his own home. The plan was to hide out here at Anna's father's house until the gawkers and reporters had cleared away, but he had a rising feeling that they would never be returning to that house, at least as a complete family.

'Where's your boss? I think Anna would prefer her to take her in. No offence.'

'I'll be taking it from here. DCI Miller has tasks to do.'

'That's it?' Nick said. 'She's done her job and so long? Without even a goodbye? Just another day at the office for you guys, right?'

'No, Nick, no. Far from it. Personal cases, like this one, they're the hardest. We're not supposed to get emotionally attached. You got to her. All three of you got to her. You amputate that limb before the infection spreads, so to speak. I'll deal with it from here.'

Nick thought he understood. 'Because you've got that heart of ice, right?'

Bennet returned Nick's grin. 'You guys have an hour. I'll wait out here.'

Nick stuck out his hand. 'This is my way of apologising for being an arse while you were trying to do your job. Thank you, Detective Sergeant Bennet. Maybe you'll rise to inspector for this.'

Bennet shook the hand. 'I'm due to go downhill, not up. Long story I won't bore you with. Get back to your family, Nick Carter.'

Nick turned to go, still thinking about the hour Bennet had agreed to give them. Anna had been promised police bail, which would mean freedom later today, but what if that went wrong? Their family might be whole for only an hour, and then exploded for ever.

Jane was making tea in the kitchen and Middleton was at the top of the stairs, outside the bathroom, beyond which Nick could hear the shower and Josie and Anna talking. Anna had been eager to get Josie washed, and not just because she'd gone overnight without bathing. She wanted all trace of the kidnappers removed, like their smell, their skin cells, their sweat. Their whole aura.

Middleton put out his hand. Nick took it and they shook. But then the younger man moved past and grabbed Josie's tracksuit from the floor. He entered another bathroom just down the hall, grabbed a tealight candle and a box of matches from the windowsill, and tossed the tracksuit into the bath.

It was aflame when Middleton appeared in the doorway. He said nothing and both men watched the outfit burn, sending black smoke up to stain the ceiling. Nick finally turned the shower on it.

'Sorry if I ruined the bath. And for leaving your Jaguar in London.'

Middleton put his hand on Nick's shoulder. 'I'll get Anna the best solicitor in this country, Nick. So long ago… she shouldn't have to go to prison. If that evidence shows that bastard Marc Eastman was at fault for Anna not watching the road, then – Nick, where are you going?'

But Nick ignored him and a second later his feet were thumping down the stairs.

*

'I want to see the video Anna gave you.'

Bennet's heart was still beating from the shock of Nick jumping into the car. Focussed on his phone, he hadn't spotted the approach. 'The disk? It's evidence, Nick. Sealed. And it's not a good idea to watch it.'

'This is the DCI's car, and I watched her put it in the boot. So open the bag. I want to see what this Eastman guy is trying to hide.'

'Look, Nick, you should know that none of the people we've arrested have mentioned Eastman. They're saying they don't know anything about his involvement. It's his wife's family and she might have set this up behind his back to protect him. He might know nothing of the kidnap.'

'No way, Bennet. He touched my wife in that car that night. It was partly his fault the hit-and-run happened. He went running to his wife afterwards and they're neck deep in this together. He's terrified of that dashcam because the audio will burn him. And that means it can help my wife. I want to see it. It's a disk and there's a laptop in this car. Nobody will know.'

Bennet, Mr Red Tape, didn't look sold and Nick felt anger rising. But he chose another tact. He leaned forward, and he touched the detective's arm, and he begged.

*

While Anna dried Josie off in the pink bedroom Middleton had allowed his granddaughter to design, they talked about things she wanted to get for Josie, things they were going to do together, and what kind of bouncy castle she wanted, because her grandfather had promised to buy her the biggest he could find. But Josie delighted in telling Mum that she wanted pints and pints of milk. Unaware of Josie's allergy, the kidnappers had given her milk, just as Nick had feared, but there had been no illness and Josie was overjoyed to find that she was 'normal' now. The joy on her little lady's face put a mixed bag of emotion in Anna, because this was a revelation that wouldn't have come about had Josie not been kidnapped. A village of good in a world of bad.

A couple of times, Josie seemed about to broach the subject of something one of her captors had said or done and Anna changed the subject. She now knew the girls who'd taken Josie had been sweet, no worse than babysitters, but still she had no desire to let her daughter talk about them as if they were good people. Because they were not. She hoped they would rot in a cell for years.

And that brought her around to what she really wanted to talk about. She'd cycled through ways of starting this conversation and had settled on:

'You know how you have your Calm Corner?'

She did. At school, the Calm Corner was where a naughty child got sent in order to wind down.

'Well, Mummy did something naughty, and she has to go to the Calm Corner.'

'At school?'

'No, that's for children. This Calm Corner is for adults. It's a place where all the naughty adults get sent. Mummy will have to go there soon.'

'Today?'

'Not today.' She'd already been told she'd probably get police bail, so would have a number of weeks of freedom. But there would be a custodial sentence for sure, despite any praising testimony in court from DCI Lucy Miller.

'What did you do?'

'I did something a long time ago and I didn't admit to it. And some people have been hurting for a long time because of it. I can't tell you what it is, but you'll learn about it as you get older.'

'We have to go on for ten minutes. Is it ten minutes?'

She wiped her wet eyes, in part to delay having to tell Josie that, no, it wasn't going to be ten minutes. That she wasn't going to see her mother for a long time, except for when she visited her at the adult Calm Corner.

But she didn't get chance. The pink door with its unicorn poster burst open. Nick stood there with wide eyes and ragged breath. Wordlessly, he grabbed her arm and dragged her out of the room.

'Surprise for your mother, Josie, back in a mo.'

'Nick? What's going on? Let me go.' A wild thought appeared: someone higher up than Miller had insisted that she had to be locked up right now. But she cut that idea down immediately because there was no way Nick would be part of that.

But he didn't let her go. He marched her into the neighbouring room, where Jane had exercise equipment. When he slammed the door, she noticed he had a laptop under his arm.

'Nick, what is this? We've left Josie alone. Tell me.'

His heart went out to her. Even here, with Josie in her own bedroom, surrounded by family, Anna was fearful to be away from her daughter. He opened the laptop, put it on the floor, and forced her gently to her knees. He knelt beside her. That was when the penny dropped, and her eyes widened.

'No, what are you doing? I don't want to watch it. No.'

'I know it'll be hard, but you have to.'

'No, no, no. Why are you doing this?'

She tried to stand, but he dragged her back down, and put his arm around her, locking her in place. It was a somewhat rough grip, but the lips that touched her cheek were so soft.

'To give you peace.'

*

Anna and Marc stand before the car, washed in its headlights like actors lit up on a stage. Her head is bowed, face in her hands. The head shakes. Marc steps out of frame. The sound of the rain materialises as the door is opened, and then the picture jerks slightly as Marc enters the vehicle.

The frame moves backwards, stops, moves forward at a turn, slipping past Anna. It curves in the black road as the car makes a turn and heads back the way it came. Nothing to see but black road and hard rain striking the windscreen and white lines passing beneath the vehicle, like laser fire from a craft in deep space. Nothing to hear but the engine and low murmurs of grief from Marc.

And then, in the road, they appear. Two shapes, unmoving, lying together in the centre of the road, smashed by rain.

'*Oh Jesus no,*' Marc hisses.

The headlights light them up and the car stops just a few metres away. Not a wandering cow at all, then. A bearded guy and a girl, both decked out in soggy denim and wearing rucksacks. The male sits in the road and the girl lies across his lap, her head in his hands. There's blood on her face and on his hands and leaking from somewhere under his bushy beard. Both turn their eyes towards the car. Not dead at all, then.

'*Thank God, yes,*' Marc wheezes.

The door opens and the sound of the pelting rain is back. Marc appears in the headlights, blocking one. He moves towards the two injured people, but the male swipes a hand.

'*Get the hell away. Call an ambulance.*'

He clearly knows this isn't a driver stopping to help.

'I'm sorry. We didn't see you.'

The male is jabbing a finger.

'I know you, I bloody know you. You're that politician. You think you're above the law. Get an ambulance. You're going down for this, you damn lunatic. Look at her. She's hurt. You're going down for this. Burn in Hell. Now get an ambulance.'

As he's screaming, Marc backs away. The picture wobbles as he gets in the car, and the sound of the rain and the shouting ceases as the door shuts.

The injured couple slip to one side as the car pulls forward and curves past them. It drives on, and then it slows. Throughout, Marc is moaning, cursing. Things like *can't blame me* and *just an accident* and *can't do this to me*. The car stops. There's an animal roar from the politician.

The car moves on, but it turns in the road. Heading back. Left side, almost touching the edge so that he can drive past the causalities.

'Can't do this to me,' Marc moans. The right-hand headlight illuminates them.

'Just a stupid accident.'

Closer now. The male tries to turn his head to see.

'Ruin me, you bastards,' Marc screams. Even over the engine, there's the clear sound of sobbing.

Just metres away now and the couple are about to whizz by on the right, out of the spotlight washing over them, out of frame, out of sight.

'You're not going to do this to me, to this country,' Marc screams.

Both headlights suddenly spear the injured hikers as the Punto veers slightly to the right. The hikers jump immediately into centre frame. And over the sobbing there's a roar from the engine as he stamps the accelerator.

EPILOGUE

At about the time Anna, many miles away, was staring through iron bars and watching Nick walk away from her, Josie leaned forward to kiss a gravestone as Middleton got to his feet and brushed off his knees.

'Times flies,' Josie said.

'And it'll fly until next week,' her grandfather said. He held out his hand and she took it.

'One more thing for Grandy,' she said, pulling her hand free. From a pocket she extracted a little item, which she laid in the urn of fresh flowers. Middleton saw that it was an 'Employee of the Week' badge.

'Did your dad give you that?'

'Yes. He said you gave it him for being brill at his new job. And he gave it me for being brill. So I want to give it Grandy for being brill.'

He nodded. 'Daddy sure is brilliant. And I'll get you a badge for Mummy, because she's brilliant, too.'

She cast her eyes downwards. 'I wish Mummy was here.'

'I know. But this is normally our Sunday together, isn't it? Our Sunday with Grandma. And Mummy told you she had to go away. You remember?'

Josie nodded. 'Because of the bad thing she done. She has to stone.'

He ruffled her hair, which shone like battery wire in the sun. '*Atone*, darling. She has to *atone*. Like sitting in your Calm Corner.

But she said she'd phone you this afternoon, didn't she? Come on, it's time to go and get your dinner. Your auntie's doing her special roasties again. How can we miss those?'

They turned from the grave and, hand in hand, headed along the path. Ahead, two big men waited by a car. Josie said, 'Them men, Grandpo. They protect us, don't they? Because there might be people who don't like what Mummy done?'

'They're there so people don't come and try to ask us questions, sugar. Some people in this world aren't nice.'

'Like those people who taked me away.'

He stroked her hair, but didn't answer. But he was glad of her smile and what it said about the heart of the mind that put it on her face.

'But we don't need them big men because I have super-luck and I'll give you and Mummy and Daddy and Auntie Janie all a luck-wish each. Did I show you this what Mummy gived to me?'

'You did, you did,' Middleton said as his little granddaughter lifted the new pendant on her special necklace and shook it at him. 'But you don't need to do anything for us, sweetie. We already got all our wishes granted.'

Many miles south, Anna called Nick's name through the iron bars, her heart full of dread. He stopped and turned. But he didn't ask what was wrong, as she expected. She was ready to tell him she was scared, that she couldn't do this. But instead of asking, he held out his hand.

So, she slipped alongside the iron fence, through the open gate. He waited until she took his hand and then together they walked the flagstone path, still wet from rain an hour earlier. He stayed by her side until they reached their destination, at which point he stopped and told her she had to do this alone. He had to forcibly peel her hand out of his and give her a gentle push to get her moving. The tears were already dripping off her chin.

The grave was marked only by a wrought iron ornate cross no higher than her knees and a stone slab flush with the mown grass. The slab bore debossed lettering filled with rainwater, so the inscribed words seemed to shimmer:

Jon Adams
24/12/87 – 5/9/2011
Our Treasured Son
Taken on a Journey, Away for Ever, but Always Here.

'Taken on a journey,' she moaned.

Nick approached and knelt by her on the wet grass. He looked at the marker, read the words, and knew Anna was wondering what Jon Adams's parents had actually meant. Death takes us on a journey, but Jon Adams was on a journey when he was taken. Nick squeezed her hand. In her other hand was a rose she'd brought. One of four.

'How can they forgive this?' she whispered.

'But they did, Anna. That's why we're here.'

She shook her head. 'Trick,' she said, barely audible. 'Trick.'

He understood. 'It's not a trick, Anna. The parents wouldn't be doing this today. This boy's dad wouldn't have stood up in that court and said those things. You didn't kill him—'

'But I—'

'And before you say you covered it up, don't. You were terrified and confused. Look up, Anna, and you'll see clouds, not the ceiling of a prison cell. Look at the clouds and you'll see that you were forgiven. It can't stop what you feel inside, but that also comes with time.'

She didn't answer, instead choosing to scrape rainwater from the lettering on the grave marker. Then she laid the rose. One of four.

He rubbed her back, full of pity. It was early into a long, hard day. He told her they'd be back with Josie by nightfall, because that was what he was using to get through this. And it was a thousand times harder for Anna.

'Poor Josie,' Anna said.

He knew exactly what she meant. They had been living in Anna's father's house since the story broke, to avoid negative attention, but they hadn't wanted to upset Josie's routines, so she still attended the same school. Most of the kids there didn't really have a clue what was going on, but they knew Josie's family was being talked about and she had suffered some bullying. They had had to talk to her about why, but it didn't really penetrate deep and her young age meant she had no idea that her mother's past actions would cast a shadow over the rest of her life.

A constant source of terrible tension for Anna, but Nick focussed only on the present. As long as Josie continued to laugh and enjoy childhood, they could deal with the future as it unfolded. Rightly so, most of the media and public attention was on Marc Eastman and his wife and her clan, and the story would erode to nothing over the years, leaving just the storms inside the heads of a select few. A big starting point of that erosion had been the words of Jon Adams's father in the courtroom at Anna's sentencing hearing as he read from a prepared statement.

'I'm sorry…' Anna began, reading aloud from her own prepared 'statement'. As he'd promised, Nick backed away so Anna could do this part alone. He watched her, but he imagined Josie in her place, adult and knowing everything, and compelled to pay a lifelong debt passed from mother to daughter like a hereditary disease. And when it was done, they clasped hands and headed out of the cemetery, and into stage two of this long, hard day, where Anna would plant a second rose. One of four.

But the remaining two weren't for the dead.

*

'In the years since our beloved son was snatched away, I did the rainbow of emotions. Initially I occupied one end, praying that I could get my hands on the person who killed Jon and Joanne. I spent long nights imagining tortures, I don't mind admitting that to the court. But the passage of days, many, many days, brought a growing calm. I accepted Jon was gone, and then I started to move on. By the time I heard that the police had made arrests, I bore no ill will, just a desire for justice and closure. After the upcoming trials of those involved, primarily the former Secretary of State for Education, Marc Eastman, for murder, and his wife Iliana, for obstruction of justice, this story can close. Of course, those defendants have separate trials for kidnapping.

'But that is for another day. Today we are to sentence Anna Carter for her role, and Your Honour has allowed me to speak with a chance to influence the sentence he proposes. She has been charged with obstruction of justice, concealment of a crime, leaving the scene of an accident. But not murder. She did not murder my son or his girlfriend Joanne. Truly, I do not now concern myself with her actions in delaying justice for eight years. She did not kill my son and I bear her no ill will. She made this judicial process easier by admitting guilt, she has been defended by a number of police officers in South Yorkshire, she has given heartfelt apologies, and the country has seen video evidence and heard testimony proving that she suffered, too, in a terrible connected crime of the kidnapping of her young daughter. She was tricked and cajoled by the man who did kill my son, and eight years later dragged by that same man and his wife into a second nightmare. But she did obstruct justice and she has been found guilty of that. But what should the next step be?

'I see nothing dark inside her that needs rehabilitating, and without a desire to rehabilitate, a prison sentence can be only to punish. I believe she has served her punishment, to lie under the weight of another's terrible lie for eight years, and to have had her daughter's life put at risk. I do not want to see another family ruined. I do not want to be part of tearing her from her family, her little girl, who was very nearly lost for ever. Mrs Carter's story will not close following this hearing, unlike mine, for she must endure the trial of the Eastmans for kidnapping. Her suffering continues. Don't punish another for one's actions.

'It is your decision ultimately, Your Honour, and you are somewhat bound by sentencing guidelines, but you sought my opinion and it is the will of myself, my wife and the parents of Joanne Padley that little Josie Carter's mother is not taken away from her. To the joy of some and no doubt anger of others, primarily those with little grasp of the entirety of this story, I say now sentence her to the six years she was offered in return for compliance – but suspend, Your Honour. Suspend. Send her home to her family. Otherwise, you will be sentencing us all.'

A LETTER FROM JAKE

Hi all,

I want to say a huge thank you for choosing to read *The Family Lie.* If you did enjoy it, and want to keep up-to-date with all my latest releases, just sign up at the following link. Your email address will never be shared and you can unsubscribe at any time.

www.bookouture.com/jake-cross

You chose to buy this book, which means a lot. But most important is that you're satisfied with it. I hope no parts bored you, confused you except where necessary, or made you skip pages. No novel is to everyone's taste, so to those who enjoyed this one: thank you. To those who didn't: I'll get you next time.

My intention with this story was to stay with the characters at all times, because I felt that skipping a few hours here and there might reset the pace or erode tension. Because of that, I found this novel surprisingly comfortable to write; the constant attachment to poor Anna and Nick, riding right along with them, meant little need for notes or flicking through pages to remember a name or date or some other detail. At the end, I was actually disappointed that there was no more story to tell. I might have to be cruel and snatch little Josie away as a teenager, just to be selfish.

Since I'm no John Grisham, I have the time to read every review this book sparks. If you have the time, please leave one at Amazon or Goodreads, or on your own blog, website or social media page.

If the review is bad, I suggest taking the time to word it correctly. A couple of years should do it.

Thanks,
Jake

f jakecrossauthor

🐦 jakecrossauthor

ACKNOWLEDGEMENTS

Thanks to everyone at Bookouture for sheer brilliance: the authors, for advice, for the jokes and the gossip, and for reminders that I'm not the only one who finds lows as well as highs when constructing stories; Kim Nash and Noelle Holton, the gurus and now authors themselves, for helping to get this story out of my head and into others'; and Celine Kelly for word surgery. A special shout, though, to Christina Demosthenous, in part for all those things mentioned above, as well as patience. Lots of patience. Cheers.

Printed in the USA
CPSIA information can be obtained
at www.ICGtesting.com
LVHW040915070124
768343LV00007B/287

9 781786 814418